DAMNED IF SHE DOES

Kathleen Kelley Reardon

ISBN: 978-1-945917-51-6

Printed in the United States of America

Cover Design by Chris Noblet
Cover Photo courtesy of Grant Abramson

"Making other books jealous since 2004"

Big Table Publishing Company
Boston, MA and San Francisco, CA
www.bigtablepublishing.com

To women everywhere…

CHAPTER ONE

Shamus Doherty itched to board the New York City bound train, but his construction clients insisted on seeing him that morning. Wealthy far beyond his own modest dreams, they were accustomed to having their every wish accommodated. Shamus sat in the massive living room as Harrison Woodbine III, phone held at chest level, dressed down a hedge fund manager.

Not far away, Harrison's wife fumed over a spot in their china white carpet. She was a tall, slender woman with alabaster skin and shoulder length dark hair. Shamus thought she would be attractive if she managed to smile. Probably she would change the carpet within a year, as was known in the local trade to be her practice. That didn't seem to be the point, though. Someone was going to catch hell and Judith Woodbine was intent on practicing her diatribe.

Shamus' company had built and remodeled many houses for families like the Woodbines. Indeed, such projects were the bread and butter of his business. To his mind, however, multi-millionaire blow-ins to Ridgefield, Connecticut over the last two decades had done more harm than good to the once remote enclave of farmers, tradespeople and middleclass families. As he occasionally did, Shamus briefly pondered whether such thoughts were borne of jealousy and a sort of local elitism on his part. Once again, he decided not to decide. At least the vintage facades of Main Street had held firm against the ever-rising tide of affluence.

Harrison raised the index finger of his right hand, signaling that he would shortly end the phone call. Shamus glanced at his watch. If this kept up, he'd miss the next train to the city and arrive late to the Midtown academic conference session his sister, Meghan Doherty, would be chairing. But his crew needed this project. Unlike him, they had families to feed. Shamus' sole domestic responsibility was Boots, a golden retriever puppy named after its favorite item of destruction.

Judith adjusted a vase on a table nearby. The aroma of local wildflowers evoked thoughts of springtime and long walks in the woods Shamus would soon take with Boots. He smiled at the notion that this year his companion would be trained to heel, stay, and sit. He'd never trained a dog before, but how hard could it be?

When at last the telephone call ended, Harrison sat down in a chair across from Shamus. "If you want something done right, you have to do it yourself," he observed.

Shamus nodded politely, anxious to move on. But Harrison looked less than satisfied, so Shamus obliged further. "That's what they say, and they're usually right."

Mollified, Harrison cleared his throat as if he were about to begin a prepared speech. "We selected you to build our extension because your work is well regarded. You're the only contractor we'd hire without an architect on site. Your crew is punctual, which Judith insists upon, quiet rather than blasting radios all day, cleanly as a rule, and precise."

Shamus got stuck on "cleanly as a rule." *What the hell did that mean? When weren't we cleanly?*

"You've given us a price we can accept, and you've agreed to complete the work on the date stipulated."

Judith joined them. She was looking sternly at her husband, brow furrowed. "Tell him we're serious about the completion date, Harrison."

It occurred to Shamus that she could easily tell him herself. She turned sharply as if having heard his thought. Her eyes drilled into his. Shamus pasted on a smile.

"I'm sure Shamus will take note of the penalties detailed in the contract for tardy completion," Harrison said, looking directly at Shamus before smiling warmly at his wife.

Reasonably appeased, but unwilling to reciprocate in kind, Judith moved away to resume obsessing over the carpet spot.

Shamus allowed his jaw to relax. After giving a few more instructions, Harrison's phone rang. He took the call.

Shamus rose, waved to the Harrisons and slipped out the front door. As he drove to the Branchville station, he was feeling satisfied. His crew tended to worry that he might fail to coddle potential clients. They knew he occasionally had difficulty reining in his gruff side. Earlier in his career, he had challenged customers on minor points and tended to say whatever came to mind. With practice, he'd become more skilled at such interactions. It was part of being a professional. The "cleanly as a rule" comment had gotten to him, but he'd contained his annoyance. Surely, that was progress. His crew would be pleased.

He barely made the 11 o'clock train. As he took a seat, the other passengers were texting, talking on phones, listening to music or fiddling with one app or another. Shamus had little use for phone apps except for the flashlight, which he found handy for peering into small spaces. It was practical, and he liked practical. He'd entered the 21st Century only at Meg's request, swapping a flip phone for a new smart phone so his two-year-old nephew Johnny could video chat from Los Angeles and catch a glimpse of Boots chasing about.

Being an uncle had brought Shamus far greater pleasure than he could have anticipated. Before Johnny's birth, he'd been essentially estranged from Meg for more than a decade. She had called regularly during that time. Shamus had listened and spoken a few words, but had held fast to a grudge against his father that he'd let infect his relationship with his sister and his mother. Now, however, that was all history. The world was no longer a place where he went about his business and denied any need for family. Whenever he flew to L.A. or Meg visited him in Connecticut, they picked up right where they'd left off.

They were closer than most adult siblings now, despite what Meg described as his tendency to take on the big brother role with unmitigated zeal. He had to admit that she was right about that. Just because she was three years younger and a single mother didn't mean she needed his protection. He'd learned to tone it down, not wanting to risk alienating her. Knowing that Meg and Johnny were there for him, as he was for them, had enriched his life. It had given him a reason to do and to be better. In a real sense, he owed her.

His mind turned to the fun they'd all have in two years or so, when he'd finish refurbishing the small house that had become his personal project—his escape and creative outlet, a nondescript bungalow slowly being transformed into a jewel. Cape Cod gray shingles, a wrap-around white porch, and a new bay window in the living room were giving it a second life. He pictured Johnny and Boots running out the back door to a tree swing. Meg and Shamus would follow, lemonades in hand, to sit on the porch and soak up the sun. For some time, he had anticipated that Denise would be there as well, but that relationship now seemed on hold.

His thoughts were interrupted by a snap, and the unmistakable scent of pink bubble gum. He checked over his shoulder and saw a girl of about sixteen, gazing out the window, chewing intently, blowing, snapping and popping bubbles. He hoped she'd notice his gaze, cringe with apology, and chew more quietly. No such luck. She removed an elastic band from her long auburn hair, flipped it up and back, replaced the elastic, and pulled two halves of the ponytail. He turned back around and tried to distract himself.

If Meg were on the train, Shamus thought, she would advise him that one day he'd be a teenager's father and then he would understand. He smiled and told himself there were indeed worse things in the world than popping bubblegum on a train. Another loud snap and he ceased to consider what those might be.

CHAPTER TWO
Two Hours Earlier

If anyone in the capacity filled conference hall made a loud sound, the young professor seated on the dais along with four silver haired eminences wouldn't have heard it. His mind was elsewhere. Everything was on the line for Mitchell Avery. A rising star who had accepted a seat on the panel of a career, this thin, tremulous man of 25 years clearly wished to be anywhere else but there.

Stanley Evans, professor of economics and management at Cornell University, took his seat on the dais. Evans had just delivered a 20-minute diatribe objecting to the presence of Avery on such a prestigious panel.

A distinguished looking professor sitting beside Avery nudged the tremulous young man's arm. He then tapped two fingers on a yellow legal pad that lay on the table between them. Avery read the note. He checked the professor's expression and slowly nodded his understanding.

At the back of the room, Meg Doherty looked at her program. It indicated that Avery was scheduled to speak next. Yet, he was now leaning back in his chair as if his presentation had been postponed.

"We have had a change of speaker order," the panel chair announced. "We don't do this often, but when Professor Timothy Baron, Chambers Chair in Network Science at the University of Chicago, makes such a request, we honor it."

"Most of you are familiar with Professor Baron's work on social and knowledge networks for which he has won our field's highest awards. He is a Phi Beta Kappa, Phi Kappa Phi, Rhodes and Fulbright Scholar, former editor of two of our leading journals and past president of this association. As you know, he is a prolific author and eminent researcher. It is my distinct privilege to invite him to the podium."

Professor Baron pressed his hands together and bowed to the chairman. Silver haired, casual of dress, and needing no assurance of his stature, Baron took the podium, raised the microphone with his large, manicured hands to a height that suited his imposing frame, and began.

"I decided to speak ahead of my appointed time in order to address Professor Evans' comments while they are still fresh in all our minds. Although, I suspect their gratuitous barbarity will be etched there for some time to come."

Amusement rumbled throughout the audience as Baron continued, "Young scholars like Professor Avery are a credit to our field. Their work, though admittedly flawed as all work must be so early in a career, promises great things to come. I actually shuddered when Professor Evans referred to Avery's writing as 'stilted and lacking vision.' I remember many years ago when the work of a young Dr. Evans could be described in just that way. Indeed, I remember when he regularly made more of a spectacle of himself than he did moments ago—as difficult as that may be to imagine."

Evans slapped his notebook shut and started to rise.

"Sit right there, Stan. You've dished out far worse than that over the years."

Reluctantly, still peeved, Evans complied.

"I recall when as a young professor you publicly maligned the work of my mentor," Baron continued. "And at times you tore into my own research, providing me with many of the gray hairs I sport today."

Staring down at the ivory linen tablecloth, his hands smoothing imaginary wrinkles, Evans allowed a slight smile.

"My research team and I study how people form connections and collaborations, as well as the consequences of such choices. Let's look, for example, at what has just occurred on this panel. Professor Evans callously dismissed a young scholar. That likely precludes future interactions between them. It's easy to see what a loss that could be to our field. Our primary goal as scholars is to share what we know, so that those who come after us may benefit.

"I'll leave you with this: Isaac Newton observed that he stood on the shoulders of giants. If we arbitrarily shred the contributions of young scholars, we risk dropping the weighty baton passed to us by the best and brightest of our predecessors. So, I leave you with this thought today: Surely, we can do better."

The audience expressed its robust approval. Evans looked irritably at the clock on the back wall. Beneath it, Meg Doherty was applauding. His eyes met hers, stern and resentful. Meg ceased clapping. Her hands dropped to her sides. She stared at Evans with reciprocated rancor and left the room.

CHAPTER THREE
Three Hours Later

Meg glanced at her watch as she moved through a wide corridor. Instead of the ominous situation that awaited her, she tried to focus on positive aspects of her life. She smiled at the thought that she would video chat with Johnny later in the day.

For a year after Johnny's birth, she'd declined to attend any conference more than two hours from home, no matter how important to her career advancement. Even now, given half a chance she'd leave the hotel and fly home. She envisioned Johnny, eyes alight, running toward her with outstretched arms, the two of them encircling in pure joy. She sighed and reluctantly nudged the image from her mind.

Unfortunately, a vision of Stan Evans' hateful continence took its place, and she shuddered. How could she stomach sharing the same dais with him? Yet, in a few minutes time she'd be doing just that.

"You stupid idiot!" she muttered to herself. Why hadn't she refused the invitation to chair the session? Why hadn't she done so weeks later when she'd seen the schedule of participants?

If Shamus had arrived early as they'd planned, at least she could have talked to him when entering the session room. The distraction would have helped. But he was a no-show and hadn't answered her calls or her texts.

Stan would already be in the session room, rehearsing how he would annihilate his fellow presenters. The session was not scheduled to begin for another twenty minutes, but as chair of the panel, she felt it necessary to arrive before the other panelists. No one else would be there. They'd know better than to interrupt Stan's pre-session contemplation. It was well known that he would verbally skewer anyone who did so. She detoured to the women's room, buying time.

Eventually, she found herself in a shallow alcove that framed the door to the session room. She placed her briefcase on the floor, straightened the cuffs of her blouse and smoothed her skirt. There was no turning back now. As she reached down for her briefcase the door burst open, slamming her into the wall. She fell to her hands and knees as the figure of a man shot past her.

Recapturing her breath, she struggled to her feet. The hallway was empty. She pulled the door open, noting someone seated at the dais.

"Jesus Christ, did you see what just..."

She fell silent. Stan Evans was propped in a chair, eyes on the ceiling. A sleek, silver letter opener protruded from his throat; blood seeped red and recent down his face. His lips were swollen tight around what appeared to be a rolled-up magazine. Horrified, she edged up the steps of the dais, impelled by the remote possibility that he was still alive or that she was part of a sick joke. A large piece of bloodied paper jutted out from Evans' torn, white oxford shirt. In large letters it read "REJECTED!"

She froze. A terrible crackle then a gurgling sound emanated from Evans' throat. She peered into his wide, bloodshot eyes: fixed, angry, and blaming her.

CHAPTER FOUR

Police were everywhere when Shamus entered the conference hotel at the corner of Avenue of the Americas and 56th Street. It was a field of dark blue punctuated by police cars parked at irregular angles.

"Are you staying here?" a burly, young police officer gruffly demanded in a thick Bronx accent.

"My sister is."

"This is a crime scene. No one is allowed in unless staying here and I have that list right here."

As the officer flourished the already dog-eared paper, Shamus glanced at his nametag—Officer Long. There was nothing long about this guy. He was wide in the shoulders like a running back, arms crossed, eyes intense. Arguing with him would be useless.

"Is everyone okay?" Shamus asked.

"No, sir. This is a murder scene. We understand your dilemma but contacting your sister by phone might put your mind at ease." The suggestion had been offered as if memorized from a police training manual. A dash of empathy with a dollop of finality.

Shamus exited the hotel lobby and took out his phone. There'd been three missed calls and two texts from Meg. He dialed her number. No answer. "Shit."

A television crew removing equipment from a van rushed up the steps past Shamus. A young guy, likely an intern or new hire, grabbed a few items and slammed the van doors. The remote lock beeped as the agitated man rushed past Shamus to catch up with the crew.

Leaning against the van were two black deck chairs with the station name and letters on the backrest. Shamus glanced about furtively, then grabbed the chairs and positioned himself behind another film crew moving unabated by police through the lobby to a room reserved for the press. Shamus placed the chairs against the wall, located a bar, and sat where he could view the lobby. Grabbing a newspaper on a nearby table, he opened it and peered over the top. His sister was being ushered by two police officers into a room behind the reception desk. One of the officers spoke with her. She nodded solemnly. Thirty-two, slender with sandy blonde hair and blue-eyes, his usually resilient sister appeared vulnerable.

When all the police officers in the lobby were preoccupied, Shamus slipped into the room. Her strained eyes met his. She threw her arms around his neck and held on tight.

"What's going on?" Shamus asked.

"I found the body! I knew him!"

"What body? Who?" Shamus gently cupped both of her arms and looked into her eyes. "You're shaking like a leaf."

"It was horrible. I just…ran. I couldn't think straight."

"Jesus, Meg. That's not like you. Running was the worst thing you could have done!"

"I know," she said, reaching a shaking hand to cover her eyes as her knees buckled.

"Hey. Easy." He steadied her. "You need to sit." Shamus helped her to a chair, just as a middle-aged man with a commanding presence approached them. "Who's the big shot in the Saks Fifth Avenue get-up coming our way?"

Meg looked up. "That's Detective Jeffries. He and his partner, Detective Krawski, have been grilling me."

"Who are you?" Jeffries asked gruffly.

16

"Shamus Doherty. I'm Dr. Doherty's brother."

Jeffries smirked, amused it seemed by Shamus' insertion of the title *doctor*. "I need to see an ID."

Shamus took out his wallet and produced his driver's license.

Jeffries nodded and handed it back. "How'd you get past my officers?"

"I guess they didn't see me."

"That's not Officer Long's version."

Shamus shrugged.

"Tell you what," Jeffries said gesturing for Shamus to walk a bit further from Meg. "You can stay with Miss—I mean *Doctor* Doherty." He smiled slightly at Meg. "You're related, and she's clearly had a shock. But no more sneaking around. Where I put you, you stay. Kapiche?"

"Got it," Shamus said.

"As she tells it, your sister came upon a murdered colleague. She didn't scream or call for help. She fled. So, you can see why we are holding her here."

"Does she need a lawyer?"

"Not my call," Jeffries replied. "For now, she's our only witness—likely not to the crime itself but much that occurred after it. That includes a man apparently running from the crime scene. He could be someone she knows, someone she's protecting."

"You don't know my sister."

"She doesn't look like a murderer or an accomplice, but who knows?"

"She wouldn't hurt anyone."

"Neither would my cat, but don't try bathing her."

"She didn't do this. And if she knew who ran from the room, she'd have said so."

"In any case, we're done here for now. She can go to her hotel room. She'll stay there until she hears from me."

Jeffries began to turn away, but Shamus hadn't finished. "I get the bad cop thing. Kudos. It's working. My sister is a wreck. But let me save you some time, detective. You're barking up the wrong tree."

Jeffries' eyes tightened. "You know," he said as if the thought had just occurred to him, "most of the time I'm right about people when I first meet them. Hopefully, for your sake, this isn't one of them."

The elevator door opened. Shamus and Meg walked silently along the corridor. The oriental style carpet was resplendent with lavender, yellow and pink flowers. Dark leaves bent gracefully like rows of ballerinas along burgundy lined borders. The walls were a pale blue lit by replicas of New York gas lamps. Any other time, Shamus would be memorizing the colors and decor for some future client.

In the room, Meg collapsed onto one of the two queen beds. Shamus sat on the other, watching his sister gaze at the ceiling.

"Who could do such a thing?" Meg asked.

"Tell me what happened."

Taking a deep breath, she reported the events: the man who burst through the door, discovering Evan's body, the blood, the letter opener, the rolled-up magazine, the note. "It was awful!"

"Why did you run?"

Meg placed her hands over her eyes.

"Meg?" he persisted.

"I froze. There was blood everywhere."

"But..."

"Shamus," she blurted, "it's done. I can't change it."

"Okay. Okay. Well, do you have any idea why the word 'rejected' was written on his shirt?"

"He was the senior editor of one of our leading journals. He brutally reviewed and rejected most paper submissions."

"Sounds like a jackass."

"If young professors publish in that journal, they're nearly guaranteed tenure. Stan had a lot of power. He bludgeoned people with it. To make matters worse, two years ago without seeking anyone's opinion, he turned the journal into a business magazine complete with slick advertising. Senior professors were livid."

"More enemies?"

Meg nodded. "Not that Stan cared. Besides, he landed on his feet. Publishing in the journal stayed the holy grail only with a wider audience. The slick, easy-to-read format meant that CEOs could understand what they were reading. University presidents and business school deans love that kind of exposure. One article accepted by Stan and suddenly you were like a rock star, even though research purists labeled you a sell-out."

"Where in all this is a reason for murder?"

Meg shook her head. "Nowhere. Along with what I just told you, though, Stan was known in academia for the way he tore people apart publicly on conference panels. He targeted them, ruined their careers, and left a lot of misery in his wake. He flaunted his financial success at conferences and on Cornell's campus. He drove a flashy car and gave young co-eds rides to God knows where."

"A real creep," Shamus said.

"Yep," Meg replied.

"One more thing. Last question, I promise."

She turned to look at him, her eyes still red.

"You said a man ran past you. Knocked you down."

"I only saw his legs, maybe his torso. They're sending a sketch artist tomorrow, but it'll be a waste of time."

Shamus sat in the chair by the window, pulled the curtain sheer aside and scanned the midtown skyline as Meg tried to rest. His mind was buzzing like an electric drill, wondering who could have killed a professor, mean or not, and why Meg had run. Suddenly he stood.

Meg sat up. "What's wrong?"

"Jeffries should have put a cop at your door."

"What? Why?"

"The runner may have recognized you." Shamus picked up the room phone, called reception, and asked if Jeffries was still in the lobby.

"Yes, he is, sir," said the woman at the desk. "Hold on."

"Don't get him angry," Meg entreated.

Shamus held up his finger to shush her. He paced. When Jeffries came on, he said, "This is Shamus Doherty. We need an officer guarding my sister. The runner might have…"

He listened to Jeffries, hung up and then walked over to the hotel room door. A sturdy-looking female, Hispanic officer, likely in her late twenties, was standing at parade rest against the far wall. Shamus opened the door.

She straightened. "Going somewhere, Mr. Doherty?" Her burnt sienna eyes were intent on his. No one would be getting past her. He read her nametag—Tamayo.

"No, officer. Thanks."

She nodded.

Shamus shut the door, turned to Meg and repeated what Jeffries told him: "One of New York's finest is out there. Her name is Officer Tamayo. She doesn't take crap from anybody, according to Jeffries. Has a black belt in karate and can outshoot and outrun most guys on the force. She'll be a detective within a year. The youngest ever."

"That's reassuring," Meg said, lying down again.

Shamus walked back to the window and looked out. Two large blackbirds were basking in the sun on an adjacent window ledge. One was slouched, wings spread, head tipped like an inebriated cruise passenger. The other, noticing Shamus, lifted a wing to capture some warming rays in seeming mock contradiction to the onlooker's anxiety.

He'd have to tell his clients that he'd be delayed in the city for a few days, and get one of his neighbors to take care of Boots. Judith would be livid, and Harrison agitated. Nevertheless, leaving Meg was not an option. Derek, his foreman, would fill in. He would hate doing it, especially having to up his game in terms of wardrobe. He and Judith would be like oil and water. Smartest builder Shamus had ever met, Derek was not social. He abhorred talking to strangers and especially clients who considered themselves superior.

There was no choice. Officer Tamayo wasn't seated outside the room simply to protect a post-murder witness. Before hanging up, Jeffries mentioned that he'd interviewed people who'd seen Meg run. She hadn't sought help, despite ample opportunities. She hadn't gone to the front desk or called security. Jeffries had assigned her a new status. "No choice," he'd told Shamus. Meg was now "a person of interest."

CHAPTER FIVE

A meeting was called for all conference attendees. The elevator Shamus and Meg took became overcrowded in just one stop. Shamus worked his way to a back corner while Meg began chatting with a tall, good-looking, thirtyish man who'd been on the elevator before them. He sympathetically touched her cheek.

The elevator stopped at the mezzanine level. Shamus waited for everyone to exit.

"I thought I'd lost you," Meg said when he rejoined her. "This is Wesley Farnum. Wesley, this is my brother, Shamus."

"I'm sure Meg is glad to have you here," Wesley said as they shook hands.

"She is a trooper," Wesley continued, "but I'd be worried about her if you weren't here." To Meg he said, "I would have to leave my parents' home to stay here and keep an eye on you."

"How are your parents?" Meg asked.

"Dad is as demanding as ever, and Mom is even more crotchety."

"It's good of you to stay with them."

"There was no way to justify getting a hotel room with them living in the city. Mom would have made my life miserable."

While they chatted, Shamus scanned the crowd, wishing he'd engaged in a few more masculine ablutions before leaving the hotel room. Few of the male academics measured up to Wesley's coiffed and sartorial standards, but there wasn't a tweed or hint of stereotypical dishevelment in sight. The academic business conference style bar was higher than he'd expected.

"I see one of my old professors over there," Wesley said. "I'll catch you later. Nice to meet you, Shamus."

"He certainly isn't torn up about Stan Evans' murder." Shamus said, watching Wesley energetically shake hands with several people. "What's the deal with him?"

"It's a long story."

Shamus' eyebrows lifted inquisitively.

"He may not get tenure. He blames close-minded editors like Stan."

"Still," Shamus said. "He could tone it down a bit."

They both looked at Wesley who was laughing, clapping a colleague on the back.

"That's Wesley," Meg said. "Highs and lows."

Detective Jeffries walked into the hotel security office. He flashed his ID to a uniformed man in his forties already looking irritated, and asked to see the officer in charge.

"He's not here."

"Where is he?"

"Out with the flu."

"Who are you?"

"I'm the guy you want if you're in this room."

"I mean your name."

"Ralph."

"Well, Ralph, I need the security video for the room where the murder took place."

"Can't do it."

Jeffries glared. "What the hell does that mean?"

"Goldman Sachs holds meetings there. They're paranoid big shots. They thought we might steal their secrets. We had to turn off the cameras."

"You guys caved to them?"

"Let's just say the hotel could have been sued. Case closed."

"Goldman Sachs wasn't having a meeting in that room when the murder took place," Jeffries asserted. "The cameras must have been on."

"Nope. Other Wall Street big shots meet in that room. They don't want cameras either. Big hassle keeping track of who's in there. So, cameras are always off."

Jeffries threw up his hands. "What about the hall leading to the room?"

"No camera there."

"Where's the closest camera that was on around the time of the murder?"

Ralph went over to his computer and pulled up a chart. He spoke inaudibly with a security officer seated in front of screens displaying various locations inside the hotel.

He returned to Jeffries. "There was a camera on in the stairwell across from the room. Fred says he already viewed it, though. Nobody there."

"Jesus Christ." Jeffries removed his card from his jacket pocket and handed it to Ralph. "Send me everything you have from that day."

"Yes sir," Ralph replied, tossing the card onto a pile of papers. "You have a good day, detective."

Jeffries studied Ralph, shot him a brief watch-yourself look, and strode out the door.

CHAPTER SIX

As they entered the huge meeting room, Meg was instantly surrounded by colleagues eager to show their support. Others kept their distance, glancing at her and whispering among themselves. Shamus dispersed a few of them with a derisive look, and then took a seat. A thin, gangly young man stepped past Shamus and sank into the next chair. He placed his hands over his eyes and rocked back and forth, muttering to himself words Shamus couldn't make out—other than an occasional, insistent "No!"

"Are you okay?" Shamus asked.

The man's dark brown hair was uncombed. His light greenish eyes floated like two dinghies adrift in a red-dappled sea. He exhaled a ragged sob as he wiped tears from his eyes with a handkerchief well beyond its use-by date. "He was my adviser and mentor."

Shamus reached into his jacket pocket and passed him a fresh handkerchief.

"Thanks. You're Meg Doherty's brother?"

"I am. How did you know that?"

"I saw you with her earlier. I'm Rod Cranville."

"You obviously thought a lot of Stan Evans?"

"He insisted on excellence."

"That must have been challenging."

"Worth every minute," Rod replied shakily.

Meg arrived and sat in the aisle seat Shamus had held for her. She regarded Rod sympathetically.

"Stan was his mentor," Shamus whispered.

Meg reached past Shamus and squeezed Rod's arm. "I'm so sorry."

Rod attempted a grateful smile and then sunk back into his misery, letting his head droop.

"May I have your attention?" came a familiar, deep voice from the front of the room. Detective Jeffries was wearing a dark, dapper suit and a red striped tie tacked against a perfectly laundered white shirt. He fiddled with a podium microphone as officers closed the doors.

"I am Detectives Arthur Jeffries. Beside me is Detective Mike Krawski. As you all know by now, Professor Stanley Evans has been murdered. We need to learn as much as possible to ensure that all of you are safe.

"If you are not seated right now," Jeffries continued, "perhaps wandering or standing against the walls, please find a chair and sit. Our officers are putting letter placards at the ends of all the rows. A clipboard will be passed to you. Print your name, row letter and seat number counting from left to right. Include your address, place of work, where you are staying, and how we can reach you. If you want to be in a different seat for the next hour, then you should move now. We will be taking photos of every section. Do not leave until we authorize it. Even after this meeting has been adjourned, we ask that none of you leave the city. We cannot force you to stay, but we strongly encourage you to do so. If that poses a hardship, please inform Detective Krawski and he will discuss options."

Groans and protest mumblings followed.

"You have three minutes to change your seats," Detective Krawski said.

Meg stood, edged her way around Shamus and sat in an empty seat next to Rod. She patted him on the back.

A woman in her late twenties sat in the now-empty aisle seat next to Shamus. She nodded and addressed the three of them. "Hi, I'm Emma Richards, soon-to-be assistant professor at Duke."

She had a mesmerizing smile, nearly turquoise eyes, and shoulder length chestnut hair.

Meg reached to shake her hand. "I'm Meg Doherty."

"I know your work," Emma said. "It was part of my dissertation."

"Shamus Doherty," he said reaching to shake her hand. "Brother."

"Weren't you supposed to present on Stan's panel?" Meg asked.

Emma placed her hand on her heart. "Yes. Thank God I never went into that room."

Meg nodded with a thin smile.

"Oh, my God! I'm sorry," Emma gasped. "You were there. It must have been awful!"

"It was," Shamus interjected to spare Meg further comment.

Meg squeezed Shamus' arm. "Congratulations on receiving the national dissertation award," she said to Emma. "Your adviser, Madison, must be very proud."

"She's over the moon. I don't know what I would have done without her. It's her award as much as mine."

"That's gracious of you, Emma, but I'm sure she'd disagree," Meg said.

Rod moaned, and Meg resumed patting his back.

Emma looked at Rod, puzzled.

"Professor Evans was Rod's adviser," Shamus explained.

"Oh, I'm so sorry," Emma whispered.

"So, advisors get some of the glory for outstanding dissertations?" Shamus asked.

"Madison owns me for some time. Anyone who works with her knows that. My work reflects on her and so I suppose it's natural for her to hold on for a while."

Rod slowly rose from his chair as if he might simply float off. He edged by Shamus and Emma and walked unsteadily to an officer who exited the room with him.

"On my way to the panel," Emma said to Shamus and Meg, "just thinking about what Professor Evans would say about my paper had me in knots." She glanced around for eavesdroppers. Seeing none, she continued. "Last night a group of us were taking bets on who he would shred. We couldn't remember the last time he'd said something positive about a grad student's paper or anyone's work for that matter."

Rod appeared at the end of the row. "They were shutting him up once and for all," he muttered as he returned to his seat.

Jeffries tapped the microphone. "Ladies and gentlemen, could I have your attention again please? First, thank you for your cooperation. We have gathered most of your names and information. Some of you will be asked questions by the officers standing to my left: Tim Morrison, Bill Hopkins, Jose Martinez, Francine Tamayo, Elise Roberts and Kevin O'Neil. We are simply following procedure, gathering information and working as quickly as possible to get all of you back to your conference activities."

"Our conference activities?" A red-faced, nearly bald man with a short, white-gray beard stood abruptly. "I'm Larry Kepler, University of Arizona. Aren't you shutting down this conference?"

"We don't advise that," Jeffries said evenly. "Certainly, precautions need to be taken, but the conference can and should go on."

Grumbling ensued. Professor Baron gestured to Jeffries that he'd like to say something. Jeffries invited him to the podium.

"It is understandable that some of you wish to leave," Baron said. "What happened to Stan Evans has all of us on edge. On the other hand, many of you have spent thousands of precious dollars to be here. Your submitted work was competitively judged. You now get to share that work with your colleagues. For many of you, doing so will lead to coveted publications in our journals.

"We should be alert, but let's not allow this tragedy to force us into an exodus. Conferences like ours are usually held in cities where crime occurs. Yet, each year millions of people manage to safely arrive at them and return home.

"The people of New York City did not stop living and working here after the 9/11 attacks. Bostonians didn't cancel marathons after the bombing and Parisians have refused to be cowered by attacks on their freedom. Those incidents involved many deaths."

He looked down at the front row for a moment, smiling warmly at two people, giving the audience a chance to digest his wisdom.

"I intend to stay. In all my years of attending conferences, there has never been so much as an assault, let alone a murder."

Shamus looked at Meg. Her mouth was open, eyes wide and focused across the room to a door just closing. "What is it?"

She didn't answer.

Jeffries had not missed Meg's expression. He walked to the door and opened it. After a few moments outside, he returned to the room.

"Was there someone there?" Shamus whispered to Meg.

"Probably just my mind playing tricks," she said turning her attention robotically to Baron.

"We need to get through this," Baron was saying, "and do whatever we can to assure it never happens again."

Baron looked at Meg. "We should also be here for those who saw Stan's body, who are no doubt shaken to their core, and for whom this horrific event will only become bearable with support from all of us."

Shamus smiled at Baron, then looked at Meg, expecting to see an expression of warm appreciation.

It wasn't there. Lurking in her eyes, locked on Baron, was something akin to dread.

"We will end this meeting with a few words to the wise," Jeffries said. "When you walk out these doors, you will see journalists in droves.

My officers will try to clear paths. Be polite, but please refrain from offering opinions about the victim, his history, the circumstances and anything that was said in this room. I urge you to decline interview requests. We need your assistance in solving this crime. You don't help us by being part of a media feeding frenzy."

As everyone filed out, Jeffries approached Meg. "What spooked you?"

"I thought someone was there—a man. He seemed to be glaring at me. It gave me the creeps."

Jeffries turned to Shamus. "I need to talk with your sister alone."

Shamus exited to find the corridor flooded with television camera crews and reporters holding phones and microphones.

Emma was standing among the reporters. He regarded her disapprovingly. She noticed, but turned away, smiling sweetly at a woman holding a microphone and pointing at a camera.

At the flick of a bright light, the camera moving closer, tears rolled down Emma's cheeks. She dabbed at her eyes with a tissue. The anchorwoman placed a hand gently on Emma's shoulder, comforting the suddenly grieving, young professor.

Meg welcomed time alone in her hotel room while Shamus went out for something to eat. She tried to rest, but it was no use; her mind raced from one unsettling thought to another. Had she seen a man in the doorway? If so, how had he escaped so quickly? And what of Tim Baron, voice sympathetic, eyes accusatory. She tossed and turned trying to force all such thoughts from her mind. But like a diligent spider, the worst of her memories edged through.

CHAPTER SEVEN
Six Years Ago

Meg grew tense as Professor Stan Evans approached her. She'd just finished a presentation. All the grad students knew he only spoke to young scholars when he was going to criticize their work.

"Could I speak with you for a moment alone?" Evans said softly.

She nodded, managing a smile as she descended the dais steps to join him near the wall, her knees weak. The *alone* threw her a bit, because usually he preferred to have an audience for his heartless diatribes, but perhaps he had something particularly mean to say to her.

"Yes, Professor Evans?"

"Call me Stan, please. You're nearly a professor yourself."

"About five more months."

"It will fly by."

"Yes," Meg replied.

"Let me get right to it," Stan said. "I was impressed with your presentation."

She started to respond, but he raised his right hand, gesturing for her to remain silent.

"I wonder if you'd like to co-author a paper for publication?"

"I'm, uh, I'm sorry…what did you say?"

"Perhaps my timing is off," he said.

"No! I mean, yes, I'd like that very much."

"Good. Let's begin working on it tonight, while ideas are fresh in both our minds. In fact, we can start now."

"Right now?" Meg said, eyes wide.

"No time like the present. I mean if that works for you."

"I'll just get my things," Meg said. She returned to the dais, gathered up her notes and briefcase, and followed him out of the session room.

"I never stay at the conference hotels," Stan said. "I can't stomach the incessant lobby chatter, and the rooms are invariably sterile. I have a suite nearby."

Looking back, of course, it was easy to see how she'd walked into it; how she'd been so stupid to think that all he wanted to do was work. But out they went, into a cold rain pounding the pavement as they dodged between hotel porticoes and restaurant awnings, his arm chivalrously around her shoulders. When the rain intensified, he pulled her into the covered doorway of a small Italian bistro. It smelled wonderful. She was about to suggest that they work there.

"Let's run now," Stan shouted over the torrential rain.

She nodded. Water dripped from the hood of her coat and bounced off the tip of her nose. They laughed.

He pointed. "Just a block from here."

"Okay!"

They braced for the onslaught and ran. A few minutes later, he ushered her through the glass doors of a large corporate lobby. The security guard nodded.

"I do a lot of consulting for this law firm," Stan said as they entered an elevator. "The suite is gratis. I think you'll like it."

She did. A black marble fireplace had already been set alight. A hint of men's cologne blended with the comforting scent of burning wood. The carpet was a lush, pristine ivory—as if he'd been the first guest. The floor to ceiling windows overlooked the Chicago skyline and Lake Michigan.

He helped her shrug out of her wet coat, and then removed his tailored Paul Stuart jacket, which he folded and laid across a chair. Straightening the collar of his blue checked shirt, he next tugged the sleeves and touched each gold and blue star sapphire cufflink as if to draw attention to them.

They worked for an hour, while she took notes. As Stan poured his third scotch, Meg was distracted by the bejeweled skyscrapers, clear now that the rain had ceased. Her stomach growled. Fortunately, she'd stuck to water despite Stan's repeated offers of wine.

"We've worked long enough," Stan said, taking her notepad. He walked through a set of French doors into the bedroom and tossed the notepad on the bed. Rejoining her, he picked up his glass and gestured for her to take a seat on the sofa.

"Chardonnay?" he asked.

She hesitated. "Okay, yes. Thanks."

He stepped over to a small bar, poured the wine, and handed it to her. He sat beside her. She nudged over a bit. "You're a brilliant young woman. A rising star in our field. A few years from now, you'll be tenured at a major university on your way to becoming editor of a prestigious journal and president of this organization."

She sipped. "That's quite a crystal ball you have!"

"I can pick the winners."

"Thank you." She smiled. "It's an honor to work with you."

Stan raised his crystal tumbler. "Let's toast a guaranteed publication, given that I'm the journal editor."

Meg began to lift her wine glass and stopped. "Shouldn't we submit to another journal? That way no one will question the objectivity of the review process."

He placed his drink on the coffee table, as if she'd disappointed him.

"I just think another journal would be best," Meg said.

"You're very young."

It wasn't the first time a senior male professor had twisted a reasonable suggestion into evidence of youthful, feminine silliness. Inside, she bristled, but then a part of her that she liked least allowed the insult to pass.

Stan retrieved his glass and smiled as if the last few minutes had never happened. "All such decisions are far off, don't you think?"

"I suppose so," Meg said, leaning forward to place her glass on the table. She sensed his increased nearness even before she felt the coolness of his hand on the back of her neck. She jerked away. Her eyes met his, defensive.

"Meghan, I find you attractive." He slowly wrapped a wave of her hair around the fingers of his left hand. He let it fall back. "There's no reason why we can't enjoy each other's company even if we're working together."

"You're very attractive, Stan. You're brilliant. I'm more than flattered. But it's late. We came here to outline the paper. I don't want us to regret this."

"I won't regret anything we do here, Meghan."

The fingers of his left hand began to undo the top button of her blouse. She watched, frozen, unsure of her next move.

"There's no need to pretend, Meg. We both know why you're really here."

She pulled back.

"Oh, come on," he spat. "Let's not play games." He gripped her wrists.

She struggled to get free. "Stan, please, I don't want..."

He pulled her to him. She pushed back. "I said stop! Stop it, Stan!"

"Don't be ridiculous!" His forehead was taut, eyebrows angled downward. "You're a smart girl, Meghan. There are doors opening for you tonight." His face was an inch from hers. "Grow up! You want this publication. You wanted *this* to happen or you wouldn't be here. So, stop playing games."

He pushed her down on the sofa. Before she could struggle free, he was on top of her. His right hand, still wet from his glass, was sliding up her inner thigh.

"I said *stop!*" She kneed him in the groin. With a yelp, he fell back, scraping his forehead on the edge of the glass coffee table before he hit the floor, their drinks drenching his face.

Meg grabbed her coat and briefcase. "Keep your fucking article!" she shouted and ran out.

"Your career is over," she heard him yell.

She ran to the stairwell, pulled open the heavy door, and raced down floor after floor, her heart pounding.

When she got to the lobby, she slipped into the restroom to wash her hands, her face, her neck—any skin that he had touched. She was shaking and fighting back tears. Staring in disgust at her reflection in the bathroom mirror, she admonished herself. *How could you have trusted him? How could you have gone to his suite alone?*

She made herself turn away, riddled with self-loathing. As she reached for a paper towel, the door flew open, and before she could move his hands were around her neck, squeezing. She yanked on his arms and kicked him in the shin as hard as she could.

"Bitch!" he snarled as he knocked her to the floor. He grabbed her again.

"Let me go!"

He pulled her by her hair toward the door. She struggled to break free as he reached behind him, and she heard the unmistakable clack of the door locking.

CHAPTER EIGHT

A high-pitched phone ring awakened Shamus from a deep sleep. Fumbling for the receiver, he knocked over a glass of water he'd set out the night before.

"Shamus here," he said, managing to get the receiver to his ear.

"Good," came the familiar voice. It was Jeffries. "I'm inviting you to breakfast."

Shamus wasn't a morning person. Anyone on his crew was fully aware of this. No calls before 8:30 a.m. Instructions for the early morning were gotten the night before. He glanced at the clock beside the phone. It read 8:05. He sighed. "I'll be there in about fifteen minutes."

"Perfect," Jeffries replied. "I'm in a booth near the entrance of the lobby café."

Shamus hung up. He rubbed his eyes and then noticed Meg's empty bed. Apparently, she'd arisen at some ungodly hour. He shook his head.

After tossing water on his face and donning the clothes he'd worn the day before, he took an elevator to the lobby. As he slipped into the booth seat, Jeffries signaled a waitress to bring coffee. The rich aroma of pancakes and maple syrup being devoured by two people seated nearby captured Shamus' attention.

"Order some," Jeffries said. "It's on me."

"I'm surprised you're not a wreck by now," Shamus said.

"How's that?"

"I assume you've been guzzling coffee for hours."

"I'm an NYPD decaf detective," Jeffries said.

"Is that allowed?"

"We have a decaf don't ask, don't tell policy. You, however, look like you need the real thing."

Shamus picked up a small stainless steel pitcher, and carefully allowed three droplets of cream to fall into his coffee. Then came three-quarters of a packet of sugar. He examined the spoon, turned it over, back again, wiped it with a napkin, dipped it into his coffee and stirred. He raised the cup, blew slightly across the surface, eyed it one more time, and took a sip.

"Not poison?" Jeffries kidded.

"It's pretty good, actually."

The waitress stopped by the table holding up the decaf decanter. Jeffries covered his cup. She nodded and smiled at Shamus, who said, "All set, thanks."

"Let me know when you'd like more," she said.

"Will do."

"Women like you," Jeffries said as soon as she was out of earshot.

"Me?"

"What a waste. You're probably the oblivious type when it comes to women. Wavy hair, baby blues, and boyish charm, but subtlety is lost on you. Am I right?"

"Are you trying to soften me up before you get your other personality back?"

"This is the real me. The other guy is just an act."

"R-i-g-h-t," Shamus said. "Okay, let's get to it. Why me as a breakfast companion? Surely there are some actual suspects roaming the hotel."

"I saw your sister earlier."

"Was she one of your breakfast companions?"

"That would have been my choice, but she was rushing somewhere. She seems to have gotten past whoever spooked her yesterday."

"Are you following up on that?"

"As we speak, Detective Krawski is doing that and what he does best. He's a whiz at victimology. He's reconstructing the last 24 hours of Stan Evans' life. Anyone who was with Evans or even had a brief conversation with him in person, by phone or on social media will be interviewed. We'll start with those people. By the end of the day, we'll know who didn't like Evans and why."

"Several hundred people at this conference despised the guy. That ought to keep Detective Krawski busy for some time."

"There is only one person of interest at the moment. That's my specialty."

"Murderers always rush past people, tears streaming down their cheeks, looking terrified," Shamus scoffed.

"She and Evans had a history."

"I doubt it."

"Not a romantic one," Jeffries said.

"What kind?"

"Ask her."

"You're the detective."

Jeffries nodded. "You're her brother. That's why we're talking. She might be more forthcoming with you. It could save her some interrogation time at the station, maybe even some lock-up time."

"Is that a threat?"

Jeffries smirked. "I don't threaten. This is an opportunity to help your sister return her life to normal. Take it or leave it."

"She's shaken up right now."

"You pick the time to ask her. Just remember one thing."

"What's that?"

Jeffries stood and tossed some dollars on the table. "Hatred is a motive."

"A woman Meg's size couldn't have killed Evans."

"Not alone," Jeffries said, tapping the knuckles of his right hand on the table. "I'm not talking about alone."

CHAPTER NINE

When Shamus returned to the hotel room, he sent Meg a text asking her to call him. Thirty minutes later, she had not replied. He was about to text her again when the door opened, and she appeared.

"You're up," she said.

"Where the hell have you been?"

"Officer Tamayo was with me. Why? What's up?"

"I had breakfast with Jeffries."

"And?"

"Yesterday you found a man dead. You do remember that. Right?"

Meg frowned. "What did Jeffries say to get you like this?"

"Meg, you found the body! You ran! You're suspected of being involved in the murder! And yet, you're flouncing about the conference as if it all happened to someone else. It's not normal. It makes Detective Jeffries more than suspicious."

"I wasn't 'flouncing'!" She put her purse on the bed. "Would you rather I stay locked up in this room, dwelling on what I saw?"

"You know I'm not saying that."

"What are you saying?"

"You need to convince the detectives that you're trying to help."

"I've agreed to meet with the sketch artist even though I know it won't do any good. I answered all of Jeffries' questions."

"Not enough to please Jeffries. He thinks you're holding back. Supposedly, you and Stan had a history."

She stared at him. "What does he mean? What kind of history?"

"Hatred."

"Him for me or vice versa?"

"You for him."

Meg was silent for a moment, looking as if she might tell Shamus something. Instead, she turned away. "Jeffries just needs someone to blame. He's using you to squeeze me, but I've told him everything I remember."

Meg went into the bathroom and slammed the door.

"I'll tell Jeffries that. We'll see how he takes it." When she didn't respond, he said, "When are you coming out of there?"

There was no answer. He sat on the edge of his bed, breathed deeply, and looked up at the ceiling. Meg was running the bath water. He flopped back on the bed and closed his eyes. His thoughts turned to Johnny. *If Meg winds up in prison, who'll take care of him?*

Police Interview: Larry Kepler

I should have known if I spoke up at that police meeting you guys would have me in here. The tall tree catches the wind. I just have one thing to say. If you hear the same thing a few times from different people at a conference like this, you take notice. The scuttlebutt is that Meg Doherty and Stan Evans weren't what you'd call simpatico. I don't know why. It was before my time. But I'd be glad to do some inside snooping around for you. I have a detective's nose if you know what I mean.

Meg met with a sketch artist, which was as pointless as she knew it would be. She hadn't seen the runner's face.

To appease Shamus, she arranged to talk with Jeffries again. It had been difficult for them to find a room where journalists weren't swarming like panicked bees at summer's end, but eventually they sat across from each other at a small meeting room table.

"So," he started. "Have you had anymore thoughts about the man who ran from the room? Maybe what he was wearing or something else?"

"He was wearing jeans and runners," Meg said.

"Hair color?"

Meg shrugged. "I don't know."

Jeffries squinted as he studied her. "What about why you ran?"

"It was the wrong thing to do. I wasn't thinking."

"Your mind was a blank?"

"No," Meg replied, stifling annoyance. "I was in shock."

"I see."

"You don't believe me. It's obvious."

"How is it that a smart woman like yourself just up and bolts when she finds a colleague dead? You don't strike me as the delicate type. There's steel in your eyes. I'm told that you can be tough as nails when challenged on an academic panel. You're no shrinking violet afraid of her own shadow. Not you."

She closed her eyes briefly and sighed. "The truth is that I'd never seen the body of someone murdered, let alone someone I knew. It was awful. I felt sick."

Jeffries stood, rounded his chair, gripped the back of it with both hands and looked directly into Meg's eyes. "If you were going to be sick, why didn't you run into a restroom?"

"I don't know. All I know is that I didn't kill Stan."

"That's getting harder and harder to believe."

Jeffries sat again. "Why were you the only one there, other than the man you can't remember?"

"Everyone knows not to arrive early when Stan is on a panel. He becomes irate. He owns the room. I was panel chair—an exception."

"Why then do you suppose a man was there?"

"He could have been the murderer who knew Stan would be alone, or a first year graduate student who hadn't yet heard about Stan's rule."

Jeffries sat for a few moments, fingertips of both hands together, looking at the table.

"You're single," Jeffries said.

Meg's brow furrowed. "Yes."

"You have a young child."

"Yes."

"I'm not judging," Jeffries said.

"You already know these things about me."

"I do. But I'm wondering why a smart, attractive woman like you is single."

Meg frowned.

"Maybe that was sexist," Jeffries said. "Let me ask this, though. Who will take care of your little boy if you go to jail?"

Meg moved sharply to leave.

Jeffries grabbed her arm above the elbow and pulled her back. "Okay. It's a cop thing. We try to get under the skin."

"Leave my son out of this."

"It's just that you have so much to lose. He has so much to lose."

"All the more reason for me not to have killed Stan."

He looked at her as if trying to read her mind.

"Are we finished?" Meg asked just before a camera flash startled her.

"Get lost!" Jeffries shouted at two journalists who quickly accommodated.

"They're everywhere," Meg mumbled.

"I think we've done enough for today," Jeffries said. "Maybe we have pushed you too hard. Why don't you and your brother go out to a restaurant tonight. Don't go far. Maybe time away from here and fresh air will help your memory. Detective Tamayo will tag along."

Meg closed her eyes for a moment. One minute he was vile, the next paternal. Surely, she thought, it's all strategy—all fake.

She nodded. "Okay."

"Good," Jeffries said. He stood, looking down at her for a few moments. "I'm not the enemy."

"I know," Meg said. She looked up at him resignedly. "I know."

Shamus and Meg walked along Fifth Avenue, looking for a place to eat. It was a clear, crisp New York City evening. Tantalizing smells of pretzels, hotdogs, gyros, and toasted chestnuts vied for attention. The atmosphere was full of possibility and promise.

They paused beside a large window. Inside, a man of about thirty had taken to one knee. The woman seated in front of him dropped her napkin and reached with both hands to cover her mouth. Her Romeo was holding an open, black velvet box. A diamond ring shimmered. The world seemed to slow as passersby, waiters, and diners paused to participate. The woman gazed lovingly into her prospective husband's hopeful eyes. Tears rolled down her flushed cheeks. A few more suspenseful seconds and she excitedly nodded. Boisterous clapping ensued as the couple leaned toward each other and kissed.

"That was lovely," Meg said as they began to walk again.

"Bet that doesn't happen often in Los Angeles," Shamus taunted.

"Here we go again," she said, rolling her eyes playfully. "Los Angeles is your idea of a vast wasteland of indifference and disregard, right?"

"I never said that. Not exactly. It's just that New York City is unique. There's a sense of being somewhere extraordinary. On a night like this, you can nearly feel a heartbeat."

Meg looked at him.

"What?"

"Just when I think you're hopelessly out of touch, Shamus Doherty, a bit of poetry tumbles from your lips."

"Is that so?" Shamus chuckled. "Can't say anyone has ever said that to me before."

"Maybe you just haven't been listening."

A small French restaurant was Shamus' choice. He'd been there many times. Its savory onion soup, succulent steak haché au poivre with mouth-watering fries followed by a chocolate mousse or crème brûlée, drew him in over and over.

Meg smoothed her hands along the top of a red-and-white checked tablecloth. An arresting aroma of steaming béarnaise sauce drifted past.

Shamus ordered a bottle of pinot noir and warm bread. "Wait 'til you taste the dipping sauce," he said.

The first bite made her eyes pop. "My God!"

"Told you."

"Where do they get this olive oil?"

"There's olive oil and then there's great olive oil," Shamus said, eager to expound on one of his favorite topics.

"Extra virgin for sure," Meg said confidently. "You can tell by the deep olive scent."

"That's not enough. How the fruit was grown, harvested, milled into oil, under what thermal conditions, and manner of transport are just as important." He dipped a piece of bread, placed it in his mouth, and moaned with delight. "Perfect."

"Speaking of perfect," Meg said after another delectable bite, "when did you last speak with Denise?"

He glanced away for a moment as if to buy time. "I guess the subject had to come up."

"You love her."

"And how do you know this, little sister?"

"I'm not blind. Your unrelenting defensiveness gives it away."

"It's over between us."

"Don't be stupid," Meg persisted.

"She's dating someone else. Case closed."

"That's the only thing stopping you?"

"Let's not do this," he said impatiently.

"Fine, fine," Meg said, looking away, studying photos on the walls.

The waitress returned, and Shamus ordered his usual.

"I'll have that, too," Meg said.

Shamus helped himself to another piece of bread. "Sorry Meg. I didn't mean to snap."

"I know. It's just that I've never seen you happier than when you were with her in California."

"I tried to make it work."

"You must have done something right. She wanted to come to this conference to see you."

"No, she didn't," Shamus dismissed.

"She did. But you hemmed and hawed about it like you do. So, she's not coming."

Shamus rolled his eyes. "What should I have done, Meg?"

"Forget it," Meg said. "You're right. Let's talk about something else."

"No. What was I supposed to do to avoid losing her?"

"You could have moved to California. People build and remodel houses there too."

"Or she could have moved here. This isn't the 1940s, Meg. I don't have to do all the chasing."

"A little wouldn't hurt. Ask her to move here."

"She won't."

"She will."

Shamus sighed. "Let me ask you a couple of questions now."

"Fine," Meg relented.

"They're about the murder. I'll keep it brief."

"But..."

"Really brief."

Meg sighed.

"Did Detective Jeffries or Detective Krawski talk with you about where you were before you found the body?"

"Yes. I was in my hotel room preparing to chair the panel. Just before I entered the session room, I was in a nearby restroom."

"Did anyone see you in either place?"

"No one I remember. Most people were finishing lunch before the afternoon sessions. Detective Krawski is looking into who might have passed by me."

Their food arrived.

"It smells wonderful," Meg said.

"Wait 'til you taste it!"

Meg looked at Shamus in silence for a few moments. "Let's not talk about Stan's murder right now. This is a charming place and tonight is all about getting away from what's going on."

"Okay. Fair enough. How about sharing those fries?"

She teasingly covered them. The conversation turned to Johnny: words he'd learned to say, how much he enjoyed preschool, when Shamus could visit him in Los Angeles, and how much he'd one day enjoy Boots and the Ridgefield bungalow.

As they walked back to the hotel, he wanted to pump her for more information. He noticed her contentedly taking in the buzz of the city and thought better of it. He'd never been good at talking to women about anything serious anyway—not his mother, not his sister, not any of them "You're a diamond in the rough," Denise had said affectionately not long after they'd met. It was a kind of get-out-of-jail-free card for the communicationally compromised. Apparently, this imperfection had ceased to be adorable to Denise, as had been the case with other women before her. Sister or not, no use pushing his luck with Meg any further tonight.

CHAPTER TEN

Morning coffee in hand, Meg found an alcove away from the hustle-bustle of conference goers, sank into a soft leather chair and leaned her head back.

She mentally kicked herself for having made it so difficult for Shamus to help her. But what was she supposed to say? *"I went to Stan's suite one night to work on a paper and he raped me. No, I didn't report it. Yes, that was stupid and selfish."*

She'd read articles on the prevalence of victim self-blame and yet here she was doing just that. She covered her face with her hands, berating herself for trusting Stan and for years of distrusting her brother.

She and Shamus were hardly speaking when Stan had attacked her, Meg reminded herself. There'd been no well-developed, positive relationship to soften the blow of such a revelation.

Now he'd likely say all the right things, at least to the best of his ability. He might even take her into his arms, hold her head against his shoulder as she grieved—this time not alone. *But what of his eyes? Would she see disappointment in them? Would he wonder why she hadn't been braver?* She couldn't bear that.

She'd once believed that Stan's death would cause her self-loathing to crumble like a false witness before a perceptive judge. But that had not happened. It stood tall, mocked her intellect, and maintained long-term residence in the recesses of her mind. *And why was that? Whose fault was it?* She'd come close to death as a teenager when a canoe had capsized spewing her and several friends into the sea. They'd all nearly drowned. She didn't get into a boat for years. Eventually, though, she put the horror behind her. Rape was different. She'd been assaulted, demeaned and left for dead by another human being—someone she'd trusted.

When not at conferences, her mind sometimes settled for weeks. But one problem continued no matter her progress. Whenever a male senior colleague who'd known Stan held her eyes for longer than a moment, she wondered how much he knew. She felt naked, humiliated and horrified.

She'd tried forgiveness, to be one of those amazing people who pray for their perpetrators' souls. She'd asked herself with each passing year if she was yet capable of such generosity of spirit. Could she forgive Stan not only for what he'd done to her but for her subsequent inability to be truly close to a man, to make love without seeing flashes of his vile face inches from hers? Each time the answer had been the same: the bar was much too high.

Police Interview: Emma Richards

"I saw the way Shamus looked at me when I was talking to that reporter. What right does he have to judge me? I knew Detective Jeffries didn't want us talking to the press, but there's no law against it. This is a free country. I was in front of a camera before I could even think straight. Besides, I'm not the one who found a colleague murdered, and ran."

Derek had risen to the occasion. He and Shamus talked each morning. Harrison had been displeased with Shamus' absence, of course. No doubt there'd been a couple's row when he'd told Judith. Still, things had worked out. Derek had even found a few hours to put some work into Shamus' bungalow. New, solid white doors had been installed along with light, wide-width Canadian oak floors. Derek had offered to text photos, but Shamus wanted to see all of it first hand—to touch and smell each addition to his small but charming work of art.

He decided to upgrade Meg's hotel room to a suite, so he texted her to say she could get a new key at the reception desk. He ended the text with a smiley face emoji, then went up to check out the two-bedroom suite. Decorated in a subtle beige and peach, it smelled of clean, crisp linen superior in quality to that of the room they'd vacated. He opened the curtains, cracked open a window, and took a seat on the sectional sofa.

The door opened. "Oh it's really nice," Meg said, looking around.

"Since we have no idea how long we'll be here, I thought we could use more room," said Shamus, proud of himself.

Officer Tamayo stepped loudly into the suite, carrying a folding chair, which she placed by the door. Shooting Shamus an annoyed look, she went right to work, checking the bedrooms and both bathrooms.

"I'll be just outside the door," she said when she was satisfied it was safe. "Any more changes in venue get run by me first." She exited with a huff.

Meg put her briefcase and card key on the coffee table. She smiled. "I don't think she's pleased."

"That's just her cop face. She likes me. Kind of thinks I'm cute. I have that effect on women."

Meg chuckled. "Not that woman. She wants your head on a platter."

"Nah," Shamus chuckled.

Meg dropped onto the sofa and put her feet up on the coffee table. "This room can't be cheap."

"Nothing is cheap," Shamus replied. "We're in New York City. But, it's on me."

"We'll see," Meg said. She stretched. "God, I'm beat. There's a reporter who keeps trying to corner me. She's relentless. I've shaken others, but not her. I told her I don't have anything to say, but she won't take 'no' for an answer."

"What's her name?"

"Penelope something. She's with the *New York Times*."

"You definitely don't want to talk to her! Jeffries would have a conniption."

"She's like a dog with a bone. She keeps asking me how well I knew Stan. I just walk away. A few hours later, there she is again."

Shamus said nothing. He wasn't about to go down the Stan history road again so soon.

"Okay. Listen," Meg said. "I'm sorry about last night. I owe you more openness."

"You're under a lot of pressure."

She smiled gratefully. "Yes, but I've been refusing to talk about Stan. Jeffries is right. Stan and I had a falling out."

Shamus sat forward, ready to listen.

"When I was a newly-minted professor, he verbally shredded one of my papers at a conference session like he'd done to so many others. But I didn't turn the other cheek. Instead, I used my ten-minute rebuttal time to demolish a paper he'd just published. Believe me, he had it coming."

Impressed, Shamus let out a low whistle.

"A few weeks before that conference," Meg continued, "I analyzed the same data he'd used in the published article. My results were totally different. I repeated the analysis over and over. I never planned to mention it. But, when he started dismantling my future, I did some remodeling of his."

Shamus' head lowered. He pinched the bridge of his nose. "Wait. So, before you analyzed his data you knew there was something amiss with it?"

"I had my suspicions."

"Doesn't a top journal publication go through a lot of reviews and editing?"

"Usually," Meg said. "But Stan was both author of the paper and editor of the journal."

"You assumed he'd given himself a pass?"

"That's right," she said. "The re-analysis of his data was an insurance policy just in case he tried to destroy me on the panel. You heard what Emma said about people expecting that from him. And that's exactly what he tried to do."

"So, did Stan land on his feet that day?"

"He rebutted my position, smirking the whole time. So, I went for the jugular. All studies have weaknesses, but I'd found the fatal flaw — the analysis he'd failed to run. By the time I finished, anyone in the audience with a reasonable level of statistical expertise knew I was right. I saw it on their faces. He was apoplectic."

"Why didn't you just let him look like a jerk for vengefully attacking a young person's work?"

"Not in this field. You stand your ground. It's the culture—destroy or be destroyed."

"This is what academics do with their time? Go after each other?"

"Not usually. But we have our share of imperious researchers. Everyone in that audience expected Stan to rip the new girl to shreds. Standing your ground shows them you can take the heat and go the distance. By the end of the session, there was no doubt that Meg Doherty knew her stuff and wasn't about to take attacks sitting down."

"Whew! Where'd you put my sweet sister?"

"The point is that if anyone was going to murder somebody, Stan would have murdered me, not the other way around. If you'd seen his hateful expression, you'd agree."

"And you think that's the history Jeffries mentioned to me?"

"What else could it be?" Meg grabbed a magazine and shuffled through it.

Shamus stood and walked pensively to the window. "I wonder how many people's careers Stan Evans damaged?"

"Quite a few."

"It would be interesting to know more about his journal. Like who submitted papers and got rejected? Who was livid about it? Maybe Stan received some threatening emails. If so, that would take some of the heat off of you."

Meg looked up from the magazine, eyebrows raised. She snatched her card key and made a beeline for the door.

"Where are you going?" Shamus asked.

"To find Blake Packard."

"Who?"

"He was Stan's associate editor and right-hand man," Meg said as she opened the door. "He'll know who was carrying a grudge."

"Jeffries must have talked to him by now."

"Blake isn't a talker," Meg said.

"Then he won't tell you anything either."

"I know what buttons to push. I'm not an outsider like Jeffries."

"Meet me back here in two hours," Shamus called as she stepped out the door. "And for God's sake, don't lose Tamayo."

CHAPTER ELEVEN

Shamus was at his computer dealing with project issues raised by Derek back in Ridgefield when he heard a knock at the door. He peered through the security eye. The dark hair, coffee skin and sparkling brown eyes were unmistakable. "Holy shit!" he said, opening the door.

Rashid Singh, adjunct professor at Meg's university, her dear friend and confidant, smiled broadly.

Shamus gripped his hand and pulled him into the room. "You are a sight for sore eyes."

"And you as well," Rashid beamed.

"I missed that accent and smile," Shamus said as he took Rashid's jacket and tattered briefcase.

"Careful—that is my good luck briefcase," Rashid said. "I tried a new one, but my case competition teams began to lose."

"No point messing with the briefcase gods," Shamus said, placing it and the jacket on a chair.

"They're rather entitled, the gods and goddesses," Rashid said as they both took seats. "Surely you've read *Ulysses*. James Joyce was smitten by the gods."

"The little I remember of *Ulysses* has more to do with repugnant toilet habits than gods," Shamus said, chuckling.

"Oh, yes!" Rashid exclaimed. "You mean the bulbous Leopold Bloom whose appetite included the inner organs of beasts and fowl. His life was a cascade of offensive odors. One of my favorite Joyce lines is from Leopold's toilet where he was 'seated calm above his own rising smell.'"

"English class, age fourteen!" Shamus pointed at Rashid. "I remember."

"Ah, to be fourteen again," said Rashid. "To once again find all manner of defecation hysterically funny."

"I've missed you, and times like this," Shamus laughed.

"And I you. Unfortunately, I cannot stay long. My students have a case competition tomorrow morning at New York University. I must return soon to calm their nerves. They were glad to see the back of me for a few hours, though kind enough to not say so. I must do all I can to prepare and assure them. After the competition, I will have more time."

"You're sticking around in the city?"

"I am."

"That's great news."

"If we win the competition, I will be floating on air. If we do not, I will be a less desirable companion."

"That's hard to imagine."

"It is a sure thing, believe me."

"How's Nida?"

Rashid's cheerful expression darkened.

"What's the matter?" Shamus asked. "Is she ill?"

"We are separated."

"That can't be! You're so close."

"I cannot yet talk about it."

Shamus nodded sympathetically. "You know I'm here for you. Does Meg know?"

"No one at Pacific Coast knows, and I prefer to keep it that way."

"But you and Meg are good friends. You're like another brother to her."

"This news would sadden her greatly. She loves Nida. It is best to wait. Besides, she is going through a very tough time right now."

"You heard?"

"Yes. I'm worried about her."

"She's keeping busy, maybe too busy."

"It is her way. We all cope differently. But to have found someone you know brutally murdered is not something most of us ever endure."

Shamus fell silent. It was true. He'd been so busy trying to protect his sister, to find answers, that he'd missed the most important fact. He'd never walked in her shoes, never experienced the horror.

"I'll be staying at this hotel for a few days," Rashid said. "Stop by my poster session if you have time. It will be in the Grand Ballroom in two days. I will have a small section with posters of my teams over the years along with coaching tips. You'll find it in the program. It's not prestigious like a research panel session, but it will give me the opportunity to put out some feelers for a job."

Shamus' eyes widened. "You're leaving Pacific Coast University?"

"If Nida and I divorce, I must leave our home. That will be expensive. Being desired by another university is the only way for a professor, especially a non-research, adjunct professor like myself to get a raise and promotion. You must be valued somewhere other than your own university."

"That's bizarre. They don't know what they have without outside confirmation?"

"The game must be played. A pawn does not make the rules."

"You're no pawn," Shamus said. "Far from it."

Rashid smiled appreciatively as he retrieved his briefcase and jacket. After he'd departed, Shamus thought back to the first time he'd met Nida. He'd liked her right away, appreciated her quick wit and striking beauty. She did not shirk from argument, much to Rashid's admiration. She said what was on her mind even to university presidents and deans.

Rashid would sit back smiling, always assured that she would win the argument and often their respect as well.

Such love was rare. They were the couple Shamus thought of when considering if he would ever marry. If Rashid and Nida could not stay together, he wondered, what hope was there for anyone?

Police Interview: Tim Baron

"Stan was a callous man. Death was a high price for him to pay, but he will not be missed. Being brilliant wasn't enough for him. He had to make others feel small. I took him down a few pegs the other day. He didn't dare take me on. He was a coward who sought to destroy young scholars for sheer sport. Only one of them ever made him pay in public for his arrogance. He never took her on again."

CHAPTER TWELVE

Shamus had waited in the suite for three hours. Meg had not returned. He was imagining the worst. *If the runner was the murderer, wouldn't he try to shut her up?* The image permeated Shamus' thoughts like the stench of next-day garlic. He couldn't wait any longer.

He came out of the elevator on the mezzanine level where most of the sessions were taking place and noticed "Primary Event" on a poster beside a closed conference room door. Beneath it was printed: "PLEASE TURN OFF ALL PHONES BEFORE ENTERING." He quietly slipped in beside several people in the standing-room-only audience.

Speaking from the podium was a man in his early fifties, impeccably dressed in a dark, pinstripe suit, light pink shirt and subtly hued silk tie. His platinum hair offered a striking contrast to his tanned skin and sparkling blue eyes. Whether he hailed from a warm climate or had acquired his tan from a salon was difficult to determine. The whole package would have been over the top for most professors, but this man exuded comfort and charisma.

Shamus peered over the shoulder of one of the audience members reading the panel program. The speaker was the associate editor Meg had been chasing down—Blake Packard, professor at the University of Cincinnati.

Looking up again, Shamus caught sight of Meg sitting midway back in an aisle seat. His relief was instantly followed by annoyance. He wanted to walk over, sit beside her, and ask loudly, *What the hell happened to being back in two hours?"*

Instead, he took satisfaction in the guilty expression that crossed her face when she saw him. Stealthily, she reached into her briefcase, retrieved her phone, and tapped into it. Shamus' phone beeped. People turned around to glare while he fumbled in his jacket pocket, located the source of his social infraction, and read the message from Meg: "Sorry!"

He turned off the phone. Madison Wills, as he noted on her nametag, was standing to his left. She was tall, lithe and lovely. He smiled apologetically and shrugged. She smiled back, then shot a mind-your-own-business look at someone who was still regarding Shamus with a disapproving frown.

"No doubt a member of the phone police," she whispered to Shamus.

She fixed her onyx-colored eyes on his before returning her attention to the speaker.

Shamus tried to focus on Packard's presentation, but it was no use. The statistics were over his head. Besides, he was smiling to himself, revisiting Madison's comment and the warmth of her smile.

Blake Packard completed his presentation. All but one of his fellow panelists were clapping enthusiastically. The single dissenter appeared bored.

The chairman stepped to the podium. He called for questions. Madison's hand shot up.

"Yes, Madison?"

"My question is for Professor Chuck Crane."

The heretofore bored professor became alert and smiled guardedly at Madison. "This should be good," he said.

The audience seemed to sense that the two shared a history of cut and thrust. They were riveted.

"You know that I respect your work," Madison said.

"I do," replied Chuck gamely."

"But…"

Chuck smirked. "Here it comes."

Madison waited for a moment as the light laughter of audience members settled, then said, "You appear to have taken some liberties in your conclusions."

"Oh? And how so?"

"You stated that your older research subjects tended toward criticism. I wonder about that. One person's criticism is another's constructive suggestion." She paused to let the audience absorb her observation. "Do you see what I mean, Chuck?"

"I do, Madison. It's an excellent observation."

She half nodded as if waiting for a catch.

"We attached a positive or negative weight to each response based on coder feedback, and we found that the older subjects' questions were significantly more negative. We took that to mean critical."

Chuck's eyes rounded with pleasure at his apparent victory.

"I see. And I assume, with an abundance of caution, the trained coders were of the approximate age of the older subjects we're discussing."

Chuck hesitated. "That would be right," he said. But it was too late. Shamus had noticed Chuck's lack of conviction, so surely others had too. "We could discuss the research further over a glass of Chablis," Chuck hastened to add with a smile.

"I'm a chardonnay person, Chuck."

"Indeed," Chuck replied with a wink. "And only the best."

Madison paused, her eyes smiling, before offering a nod. The game was over.

The audience erupted into laughter and applause. The panel moderator called for more questions. Madison took the opportunity to slip out of the room and into the hallway.

Shamus was right behind her.

Sensing his presence, she turned to face him. "Hi, again."

"I'm Shamus Doherty."

"Meg Doherty's brother?" she asked.

"Yes."

"It's good of you to be here for her."

"She lives 3,000 miles away. We don't see much of each other in person."

"I'm one of five girls. No brothers. I would have liked a brother, especially one thoughtful enough to be here for me."

"So, tell me who won the little back-and-forth in there?" Shamus asked.

"Actually, I believe I did."

"I thought that might be the case."

"People will wonder if his research conclusions were justified. His answers could have been better."

"Does winning matter?"

"Yes. It may seem a silly game, but you should read Thomas Kuhn's *The Structure of Scientific Revolutions*. It justifies critiquing each other's work for the advancement of science."

"I'll put it on my wish list."

She laughed. "I'm sure you will." They looked at each other for an awkward moment, then she said, "I have to prepare for a presentation. Otherwise, I'd suggest we have coffee."

"Another time?" Shamus offered.

She smiled broadly before turning slowly and walking away. "Call me," she said without looking back, waving the fingers of her right hand over her head.

"Count on it," Shamus whispered to himself. He watched her turn a corner and smiled.

Police Interview: Wesley Farnum

"Yes, I'm Meg's friend. I've known her for years. She found Evan's body, but she couldn't murder anyone, let alone in that way. She arrived at the session before the panelists because she was the chairperson. Otherwise, she wouldn't have been there. She knew about Stan's precious pre-panel prep time, and how vicious he could be with people who violated it. I give her credit for taking her role as chair seriously by arriving early to protect other panelists from his predictable vitriol."

CHAPTER THIRTEEN

Officer Tamayo accompanied Meg to the lobby bar entrance. Blake was sitting in a dark booth at the back. He seemed agitated, peering around nervously, his brow moist with sweat. Meg nodded to Tamayo and the officer signaled that she'd be observing from the bar entrance.

"You look really stressed, Blake" Meg said as she sat across from him.

"I hate this."

"What?"

"All the cloak and dagger. The gossip is unreal. For Christ's sake, a man was murdered."

"I know it has to be particularly hard on you," Meg offered. "You worked with Stan for so many years."

"Let's just get this over with."

"I'd like to order a drink first," Meg said.

"I already asked for two Cokes. Let's just get on with it. You want to know who was angry at Stan, right? Who had an active feud going with him? I understand perfectly. If the police considered me a suspect, I'd want to know who hated Stan so I could point them in another direction. But this is the thing, I never divulge professional information like that."

"Of course you don't," she attempted to soothe him. "But don't you think this is a good time to make an exception?"

63

Blake shook his head. "Just because people are upset about having their papers rejected by a damned journal doesn't make them murderers."

"Absolutely. You're right."

Blake frowned. "I warned him."

"What about?"

"Editors can't go around ruining other people's careers and not expect repercussions."

"What did he say?"

"He brushed it off. You know how he is…was. It was his journal and he wasn't going to publish drivel. That's what he said. If some assholes wanted to fight about it, he'd be happy to accommodate them. Those were his words"

A waiter brought the drinks. Blake sat in silence until he was gone, then took an index card from his shirt pocket and placed it on the table.

"Look at it," he instructed. "You're on the journal board or I wouldn't be showing you this. There are names of three people who argued vehemently with Stan after he rejected their research. Read the names, then I'm going to destroy that list. Want to know why? Because not one of them is a murderer."

Meg picked up the card and studied it. "Sharing this isn't easy for you. I appreciate it."

"You wouldn't have let up anyway," Blake snapped. He took the card from her. "There's a name missing. Somebody who despised him. I was going to write it down, but I changed my mind. You know who it is."

"What do you mean?"

"Come on, Meg. Don't be coy with me."

"I'm not being coy."

"Do I have to spell it out for you? You were right to keep what he did under wraps. Hell, Meg, in your shoes I'd have done the same. After all, Stan always won until finally he didn't."

"What are you talking about?"

Blake responded with a dismissive wave. "Anyway, whatever happened years ago doesn't matter now. The rage that took Stan Evans was raw. The killer was suffering fresh wounds. As I see it, that pretty much leaves you out."

Meg studied Blake's expression. So there it was. He knew. No sympathy in his eyes, only a snickering sense of triumph. The room started to close in around her. She felt short of breath and stood. "You'll have to excuse me for a few minutes."

"Suit yourself," Blake said indifferently. "But hurry back. I'm not sticking around for long."

Meg caught Tamayo's eye, and gestured toward the women's room. The officer nodded and headed that way. Meg went inside, opened the cold tap all the way, and splashed her face.

Tamayo studied her. "Did this guy threaten you or something?"

"No. I just suddenly felt sick."

"Cut it short," Tamayo said. "He gives me the creeps."

When Meg returned to the booth and slid into her seat, Blake was staring into the distance.

"Sorry it took so long." The booth seemed darker than before. She noticed that the lamp had been switched off and was swinging slightly, back and forth. "Blake?"

He didn't answer.

Meg leaned forward. "Blake, what's the matter?" She touched his shoulder. His head drooped. She pulled back, nearly falling off the bench. It couldn't be. Her eyes drew downward. A knife was protruding from the center of his chest. Jutting from his breast pocket was a bloodstained piece of paper. It read "#2."

"No" she gasped looking upward at Tamayo. "God, no!"

"Check everyone in the bar and lobby," Jeffries ordered Officer Long. "If anyone acts even slightly suspicious, hold him or her in the seating section near the door. Put Davis there to watch. Make sure no one is armed."

"What's this about?" Shamus demanded as he was escorted by two officers over to Jeffries.

Jeffries held up his right hand, signaling for Shamus to wait, and went up to Officer Tamayo. "Where were you when this happened?"

"Outside the restroom waiting for Meg Doherty, Sir. When she rejoined the deceased, I was back at the door watching them."

"You didn't see anyone?"

"No, Sir."

"Your assignment, Tamayo, was to keep your goddamn eyes open!"

Tamayo, military straight, glared into his eyes. "I did my job, Sir."

Jeffries stepped toward her ominously. "You're supposed to be better than this."

"What the hell is going on?" Shamus interrupted.

Jeffries' eyes stayed locked on Tamayo's. "Go help Officer Long," he told her.

"That's not my job, Sir. He's junior to me."

"It's your goddamn job now," Jeffries shouted. "It might be for the rest of your short career if you don't get your sorry cop ass over there right now."

Tamayo left in a huff.

Shamus watched her. He turned back to Jeffries. "She's a great cop. You know that. What's the problem?"

"Your sister is the problem. She met with some professor named Blake Packard."

"So?"

"He's dead. Murdered."

Shamus stiffened. He pushed past Jeffries. "Where is she?"

Meg was seated to the right of the bar entrance at a small table with two police officers, both hands covering her face. At the opposite end of the bar, multiple police officers were gathered beneath bright lights shining on the pallid, blood splattered face of lifeless Blake Packard.

Shamus sat beside her and then gently moved her hands away from her face. She looked at him, red-eyed and dazed.

"Don't look over at Blake," Shamus said. "Just look at me."

"If only I hadn't left him!"

"You couldn't have prevented it, Meg."

She lowered her head as he took her hands in his.

"Did he tell you anything?" Shamus whispered.

Without looking up, Meg nodded.

After a few more minutes of comforting Meg, Shamus looked at Jeffries. He was signaling for Shamus to let the officers continue questioning her. Shamus reassured Meg that he'd be nearby and walked over to Jeffries.

"She needs protection. The murderer may have suspected that she and Packard were getting close."

"What does that mean?"

Shamus looked over at Meg.

"Listen, Doherty. This mess is now what we in the NYPD call a 'pain-in-the-ass' case because Blake Packard doesn't live in New York state. We're now obligated to work with cops from Cincinnati. We don't like doing that and they don't like it much either. I'm in no mood for games."

"Blake Packard was Stan Evans' co-editor," Shamus said. "He knew who was angry with Evans for rejecting their work — professors carrying grudges."

"And your sister has the names of these people?"

"Probably."

"This can go one of two ways. You get those names for us or she goes to the precinct where we get them anyway."

"And if I get you those names, Tamayo will be sitting outside our suite fifteen minutes after I take Meg there, right?" Shamus bargained.

"Officer Tamayo is otherwise occupied."

Shamus noticed a growing group of journalists being corralled by police.

"If she isn't there, I talk to the press."

Jeffries' jaw tightened. "About what?"

"Your attitude, mistakes, questionable temperament, inexcusable delays, pinning murder on a woman who is a victim—whatever they want to hear."

"You're fuckin' with the wrong guy."

"You've made that clear. It goes both ways."

Shamus turned toward the throng of journalists now bandying microphones, positioning cameras, and tapping into smart phones. "They're itching for a story. This is the second murder on your watch."

Twenty minutes later, Shamus and Meg arrived at the suite. Tamayo was sitting erect in her folding chair outside the door—fuming. Shamus watched her for a moment as he let Meg into the room. The officer's eyes were set as if boring a hole in the wall across from her. She turned to him. A faint flicker of light skipped across her eyes. She nodded appreciatively and turned back to focus on the wall.

CHAPTER FOURTEEN

Despite Shamus' arrangement with Jeffries, he and Meg were on route to the precinct. Someone above Jeffries had pulled rank.

"You'll be in the waiting room," Jeffries told Shamus as he parked the car. Cops were milling about, some taking breaks, others heading for cars. It was like being in a movie. "Nowhere else. Understand?"

Shamus glanced at his sister who was gazing out the car window in what looked like disbelief. Surely, Shamus thought, she was thinking, as he was, that no one in their family had ever been taken to a police station for questioning—let alone regarding murder.

"You didn't answer my question," Jeffries said sharply.

"I understand," Shamus shot back.

Jeffries' brow furrowed. He looked at Krawski who was sitting face forward in the passenger seat, smirking. "What?" Jeffries spat defensively.

"You're in a bad mood. The boss overruled you. Bet that burns."

"Shut up," Jeffries snapped.

Krawski chuckled. "Yep. It burns alright."

People came and went in the makeshift waiting room. Shamus was getting stiff sitting in a chair that had seen a lot of traffic over the years. The black cushion was shot, legs askew. All the chairs were like that. He rocked from one side to another. It took everything he had not to pick up the chair and slam it into a wall.

Competing odors of fast foot abraded his nostrils. Nothing an open window couldn't fix, but there were no windows, only yellowish tile half way up walls that hadn't seen a new coat of paint in what Shamus estimated to be several decades. He walked over to a soda machine just outside the room and studied the various sugared options. He heard Jeffries voice. Peering down a hallway where they'd taken Meg, Shamus saw a tall, dark-haired, wiry woman dressed in a gray suit. Her hands were on her hips, jaw jutted forward, eyes latched on Jeffries. Shamus pulled back quickly.

"Two murders," she said. "What am I supposed to tell Olson?"

"Tell him we're working on it, for Christ's sake. If that son-of-a-bitch thinks he can do better, let him try."

"Don't get cute with me, detective. I can take you and Krawski off this case tonight. There's one scalp missing from Olson's wall, one he's wanted most of his career. I don't have to tell you whose scalp that is. And this time I'm not running interference."

"That thin-skinned asshole has been holding onto a grudge since the early nineties."

"He's my boss. He wants answers. If you need more detectives, just say the word."

"Give us another twenty-four hours. Then we'll see."

"Have you read any of the *New York Times* articles?" the woman snarled. "We don't look good."

"I don't read that crap."

"We have two murdered professors. They didn't go out on the town wearing expensive watches, get drunk and wander down a dark alley. They were murdered in their midtown hotel. You have twenty-four hours to put someone behind bars or you and Krawski are off the case. Got me?"

"Right."

"And I don't care if Doherty in there looks like Cinderella and knits scarves for the homeless. She's a suspect."

"We don't have enough on her yet."

"She doesn't leave here until she's told her story ten times. Any inconsistencies and you lock her up or I'll do it for you." The woman held Jeffries eyes until he managed a miniscule nod. She crossed into an office.

Jeffries kicked an empty coffee cup just as Shamus stepped into the hallway.

"My sister wants a lawyer. Now!"

Snow fell heavily as Shamus walked along Fifth Avenue toward Central Park. The night was a benevolent contrast to the claustrophobic atmosphere of the police station. Shamus had located a Manhattan-based lawyer, who'd come out for the interrogation. On arrival, she promised to call Shamus when it was over, making it clear that no one wanted him hanging around.

He stopped in front of the Plaza Hotel. His parents had taken him and Meg there on pre-Christmas sojourns to see the decorations and to enjoy a brunch memorable for the steaming hot chocolate poured by fastidious waiters from gleaming silver, long-stemmed pots. He and Meg had looked forward to the annual pilgrimage almost as much as Christmas morning. It was a tradition of indulgence, a harbinger of more pleasures to come, costly for his parents, but one of exquisite happiness until things had gone sour between him and his father.

A little girl dressed in a red coat and matching wool hat raced past Shamus and up the steps. Shamus smiled. He and Meg had done the same years ago. He used to let Meg reach the top first. She always boasted "I beat him!" during brunch, on the horse-drawn carriage rides through snowy Central Park, and bouncing on the train seats as they headed home. He remembered his mother's soft smile—tender, and proud of his sibling generosity.

Crossing the street beside the hotel brought him into Central Park. A few minutes later, he was at the skating rink. He wiped snow from a bench and sat watching skaters glide and spin as his mind wrestled with how his sister had been nearly present for two murders. He'd have to shop around for a top-notch lawyer. The one he'd found would do for tonight. She seemed sharp enough in the few minutes they'd had to talk. But things were going from bad to worse, and Meg needed a shark.

Shamus purchased a hot chocolate, held it tight to warm his hands, and breathed in the rich, sweet distraction. He watched a woman twirl on one skate in the center of the rink and then began to make his way back to the hotel. Continuing along the park, cross-country skiers were taking to the roads now nearly clear of traffic. Another hour and the city would be pedestrians only, dodging the occasional determined plow. He looked up to find where John Lennon had lived and tragically died. Snow caressed the park trees, bordered and bejeweled the stone bridges, here and there spinning in mini tornadoes, as if this was perhaps its final show before bequeathing the stage to the colors of spring.

He shivered. The temperature was dropping. Reality was creeping back. His phone pinged: Meg texting that she'd meet him at the hotel. *Couldn't stay there another minute,* she wrote. *Okay,* he texted back. *See you there.* He'd planned to talk with the lawyer, but that would have to wait.

Reaching the edge of the park, he looked back one more time to watch children rolling in the snow beneath street lamps, young adults making snow angels, throwing snowballs and playing Frisbee. *Someday,* he thought, *on a night like this, maybe, just maybe, I'll bring someone special here.*

As Shamus approached the hotel lobby, he noticed Wesley talking to an elderly woman wearing an exquisite mink coat and matching hat. She was admonishing Wesley for something Shamus could not yet make out. He considered crossing the street to avoid eavesdropping on their altercation. It was too late. Wesley had seen him. He turned back to the woman and whispered something. She looked with deprecation at Shamus. He stooped to brush snow from his shoes, pretending not to have seen her expression.

"Shamus," Wesley called with a broad smile.

Shamus looked up. "Hey, Wesley."

"This is my mother, Evelyn."

"A pleasure to meet you," Shamus said as he drew near.

She nodded indifferently. There would be no handshake.

"We were just waiting for Mother's car," Wesley said.

"I hope you don't have far to go," Shamus said. "It's a beautiful night, but not for driving."

"Pay attention, Wesley!" she said, ignoring Shamus' pleasantries.

"I should go in," Shamus said, "Meg will wonder where I've gone. Nice to meet you Evelyn."

She was waving insistently to a black limo approaching the hotel.

Wesley shrugged. "Mother is very focused."

Shamus smiled. "It's a gift."

"That's one way of looking at it," Wesley said as he opened the limo door.

"Wesley!" his mother shouted. "Close the door before I freeze to death."

Police Interview: Chuck Crane

Two of us are dead and you guys don't know anything yet? Why am I here? A lot of people hated Stan. Blake is another story. Whoever killed Stan probably didn't want Blake to become editor. Stan was mean, vicious even. But Blake was no saint. And he sure didn't stay associate editor all those years by disagreeing with Stan. That's all I can tell you. Anything else happens, I'm out of here no matter what your people say.

Meg was sitting in the corner of the hotel lobby anxiously waiting for Shamus. Jeffries had been unrelenting in his questioning. Over and over she'd told him what she remembered. Finally, Detective Krawski had taken Jeffries aside. She'd heard him emphatically say, "No more!" Jeffries had initially resisted, but then let her leave.

She was looking around the lobby for Shamus when a woman of about fifty approached. Her hair was dark and coiffed to perfection. Makeup had been applied liberally, but could not hide the puffiness of the woman's eyes. She'd been crying.

"I'm Blake Packard's wife, Blythe."

"Oh, I'm so very sorry," Meg said standing.

The woman looked as if she might collapse. Meg reached for her, but the woman pulled away.

"Let's sit," Meg said.

Blythe hesitated before sitting. "You were the last person to see Blake alive."

"Yes, I was," Meg replied.

"How was he?" Blythe asked.

"A bit shaken by Stan's death, of course," Meg said.

Blythe closed her eyes and turned away.

"Is there anything I can do?" Meg asked.

"I came here to get Blake's things, and to meet you."

Meg looked into Blythe's eyes with sympathy. "I wish there was something I could say or tell you, but…"

"You were also there right after Stan was murdered," Blythe interrupted.

Meg nodded in reluctant admission.

"I imagine the police find that odd."

"I was the chair of the panel, so I arrived earlier than the others."

"And why were you alone with Blake just before he was murdered?"

"We were discussing journal-related business."

Blythe smirked. "Is that what you call it?"

"I don't mean to be rude," Meg said, "but are you angry at me?"

"I'm simply exploring the obvious. You were around when both Stan and Blake died. Not that I'm surprised. No doubt they found you very attractive."

"What?" Meg asked incredulously.

"Stan and Blake worked together on the journal for years," Blythe continued. "There is little they didn't know about each other and so, in turn, I about you."

"I don't know what you're getting at," Meg said. "But I'm sure you don't know me as well as you think."

"Is that so?" Blythe scoffed.

"No doubt you're upset, but…"

"Look at you," Blythe interrupted again. "You probably think most men are taken with your intellect. That they can just put aside the fact that you're young and attractive. You blink your pretty eyes, they respond like men, and then pay the price."

"Given your loss, I am trying to be understanding," Meg said, "but I suggest we delay this conversation to another time."

"I just wanted to get a look at you." Blythe stood. "I have to go. There's a lot to do." She picked up her coat and draped it over her arm. "You could have prevented this."

"Blake's death?" Meg asked stunned.

"Both deaths," Blythe shot back before turning abruptly and stiffly walking away.

Meg felt both angry and sick. *Blake told his wife. What else could she have meant? But why the hatred? Is Blythe one of those women who buy into men being innocent of harassment and even rape—who are convinced that the woman did something to make it happen?* "Patriarchal Stockholm Syndrome," she'd heard it called—women encultured to distrust and disparage their own sex. Was that what she'd just witnessed?

"You look exhausted," Shamus said, startling her by his sudden appearance. "Who was that? She didn't look happy." He sat.

"Blake's wife. She blames me."

"For what?

"I'm not sure. It was probably grief talking, but she thinks I might have killed her husband. Stan too."

"Put it out of your mind," Shamus said with a dismissive wave.

"That won't be easy. You should have seen the hatred in her eyes. Just one more thing to make me feel horrible."

"People are on edge, Meg. Her husband just died. And maybe, in any case, she isn't a nice person."

Meg shook her head. "It was weird."

"Let's put her out of our minds. She doesn't deserve the space. How did things go with Jeffries? Was the lawyer helpful?"

"Yes. Thank you for finding her."

"Did you give Jeffries the names?"

Meg nodded.

"Mind if I ask for them?"

When Meg didn't answer, Shamus placed a hand on hers. "I can't help if I'm flailing in the dark."

"Okay. Just don't go looking for any of them."

Shamus said nothing.

Meg waited, then sighed. "One of them is a senior professor. His name is Bill Carroll. Bill can't take criticism. He's extremely thin-skinned. I once wrote a very gentle review of a paper he wrote. He ignored my positive comments and memorized the minor suggestions. He has hated me ever since and takes every opportunity to discredit my work. Given his temper, I'm not the least bit surprised that he wrote angry emails to Stan."

"This guy presents at these conferences?"

Meg nodded.

"He's here?"

"Yes," Meg said. "But you need to stay away from him."

"Right."

"I mean it. He and his wife, Ruth, are what we call a power couple. Wrong one of them and you've wronged both. The price is high."

"You fear people like that?" Shamus asked, looking surprised.

"Why volunteer to be a target of their rage?"

"Who else was on the list?"

"Madison Wills."

"She didn't do it," Shamus shot back a little too quickly.

Meg's eyes widened.

"What?" Shamus asked.

"I saw you scoot out of the session with her after she and Chuck did their usual judo."

"Scoot?"

"Anyway, Madison and Stan had a major email confrontation. Blake thought it was serious enough to put her on his list."

"Still, she isn't a murderer."

"She's a user and a narcissist, Shamus."

"That's harsh."

"You've known her for five minutes," Meg snapped.

"Why are you getting so wrapped around about her?"

"Just remember that I warned you. Be smarter than most guys who fall under her spell."

Shamus chuckled. "So, she's a witch now?"

"You may think it's funny now," Meg said standing to leave.

"Hey," Shamus said. "Here's one less thing to worry about. I'll be careful."

Meg's annoyance melted. She smiled warmly at him. "The shoe is on the other foot. Look who's protecting whom. I kind of like it this way now and then."

"Just don't get used to it," Shamus said, returning the smile. "There's only one big brother here and it isn't you."

Shamus took a seat at a session where Bill Carroll would be presenting. The people seated around him and those standing against the back wall looked strained. Shamus figured most had gotten little sleep wondering if the bolt locks on their hotel doors were impregnable. He took a seat in the last row and removed the speaker list from his pocket. Bill Carroll would present second, after Madison.

Aaron Saffron, session chair and associate professor from the University of Connecticut, was heartily shaking hands with the panel members. Shamus watched as Madison stood to warmly greet him. Saffron moved on to welcome the man Shamus assumed to be Bill Carroll. He looked pompous. His shirt was wrinkled and his jacket threadbare as if he didn't need to impress anyone. He granted Saffron a begrudging nod without reaching to shake hands.

"What an ass," Shamus muttered.

A woman seated beside him stifled a laugh.

"Sorry," Shamus said.

"Not on my account," she replied. "I might have chosen something even more colorful."

She was small, understated, except her eyes, which lit up when she smiled.

"You know him well?" Shamus asked.

"Unfortunately, he was one of my professors."

"Lucky you."

"You don't know the half of it. He's a cad of the first order."

"In what way?"

She waved a hand. "It's too painful to get into. I've put it behind me. I'm only here to support Aaron."

Shamus offered his hand. "I'm Shamus Doherty."

"I know," she said as she took his hand. "Word travels fast here. I'm Belinda Mayfield, assistant professor at Westminster University in Utah."

They turned their attention back to the podium. Madison, scanning the audience, nodded at Shamus. He nodded back.

Saffron cleared his throat. "This panel promises to enlighten us regarding the paths our field will be taking in the next five to ten years. We'll hear about exemplary leadership research conducted by the speakers. I'm sure they'll refer to some of your research" He smiled. "If you don't hear your name, please direct your complaints to someone other than me."

He waited for gentle laughter to subside, and then continued. "Since short bios are in your program, I will only say a few words about each speaker. Professor Madison Wills comes to us from the University of Maryland, where her work was recently commended with a faculty research excellence award. As editor of a top journal, winner of numerous top paper and book awards, chair of two divisions and member of our association board, she has had a strong hand in generating the respect our discipline enjoys today. Her topic is, 'Political Culture and Leadership.' I give you Professor Madison Wills."

Madison rose from her chair to appreciative applause. As she headed to the podium, Shamus noticed Chuck sitting two rows in front of him whispering something derogatory to the amused man beside him.

"Thank you, Aaron," Madison said. "A few of us on this panel enjoy advanced insights into directions our field might take. As editors, we receive manuscript submissions many months before actual publication. We get to peek into the future, so to speak, while most of you wait for the lengthy review process to take its course."

"Another murder or two should speed things up," someone called out from behind Shamus.

He turned around. An unkempt man in his thirties had fixed his eyes on Madison. His nametag read "Bret" in handwritten, large letters. Shamus couldn't make out his last name or university. A woman seated beside him rose abruptly from her chair, regarded him with disdain, and strode angrily to the back of the room.

"I share your frustration at the length of time it takes from submission of a paper to acceptance or rejection," Madison went on without looking at the heckler. "It affects us all."

"Some more than others," Bret called.

"The publication process is imperfect," Madison continued. "That's for sure."

The other panelists were sitting erect. Bill Carroll cast a threatening glare at Bret. He seemed to know him, to be signaling with his eyes for him to be quiet.

Chuck suddenly rose from his seat. He grabbed Bret's lapel, pulled him close and said, "Leave!"

"You're just like every other hypocrite in this room," Bret growled. "I'm surprised any of you are still alive."

Chuck spun Bret around and shoved him toward the door. Two policemen rushed into the room. Shamus noticed Tamayo standing in the back, with one hand on her phone, the other hovering above her Taser.

Chuck pushed Bret toward the officers. Before they could grab him, Bret turned and pointed at Madison as if his hand were a gun. The officers yanked him back. Bret pulled an arm free and held up three fingers and then pointed again at Madison. The largest officer wrapped his arms around Bret and forcibly removed him from the room.

Madison's face was ashen, her mouth slightly open. She was shaking. Saffron switched off the microphone and whispered to Madison in a solicitous manner. She nodded and breathed deeply. She managed a short smile before switching the microphone on. Saffron placed a reassuring hand on her back and then returned to his seat.

"Shit!" Belinda whispered. "What was that about?"

"A third murder," Shamus said. "He was threatening her."

"My God. I hope not."

Madison spoke for ten minutes and returned to her seat. Bill Carroll walked to the podium and slowly arranged his note cards.

"This is his way of building suspense," Belinda whispered to Shamus. "He does it every time."

Carroll looked up. He nodded to a woman in the front row, who Shamus assumed to be his wife, Ruth. His black hair was graying above his ears and thinning on top. About 5' 11" tall, he was solid like a former rugby player.

"I will not be speaking about leadership in fields like ours because, frankly, it does not exist," Carroll began. "Academic leadership is an oxymoron. Elections to office in associations like this one are mere shams. Popularity contests. Editorships and board placements are no better. We punish true scholarship. Instead of leaders, we have socially adept networkers who compensate for their poor research by maneuvering themselves into positions of undeserved power. Our field has been hijacked, like so many others, by weak minds who reward mediocrity."

The remainder of Carroll's presentation was focused on two professors whose work he admired. One was deceased, and the other had long since retired.

"The work of these two eminent scholars is stellar, yet they never held office in this association nor editorship of a journal. They refused to condone mediocre work emblematic of so much of what we publish and advance to prominence today."

Madison, eyes closed. She shook her head with disgust. Saffron consulted his watch, then scribbled *1 minute* on a yellow notepad and held it up where Carroll could see it.

Carroll continued talking. A minute later, Saffron held up the same pad on which he'd written *0 minutes!*

Carroll didn't even pause. Saffron, growing increasingly agitated, held up the yellow pad again. This time in large letters he'd printed the word *STOP!!!*

"I won't belabor the issue further," Carroll said.

"Praise be to God," Belinda sighed.

"The truth is often difficult to digest, and so it is rarely spoken," Carroll concluded haughtily, and turned to take his seat.

"Truth," Belinda scoffed. "I'd like to stand up here right now and show him what truth feels like."

"Do most of the full professors talk like that?" Shamus asked. "I mean, you know, snooty, like they're above it all?"

"No," Belinda said. "Some of the older ones do because that's how they were trained. Even they sprinkle their talks with humor. Bill is not that old. 'Snooty,' as you say, is how he compensates for having nothing of value to say."

"How did he get so far? He's tenured at least."

Belinda chuckled under her breath. "There are ways, believe me."

Saffron walked to the podium wiping perspiration from his forehead. Belinda held up her right thumb. Saffron noticed and smiled.

"Aaron is a sweetheart," she whispered to Shamus. "He did well. Most chairs just let the windbag go on forever. Fortunately, there are more of Aaron's type in our field than there are bloviating idiots like Bill Carroll. His type draws more attention, like Stan Evans did, but it's yeoman work by people like Aaron, and your sister, whose egos aren't on a rampage that hold this association together."

"I'll tell her you said that."

"Please do," Belinda beamed.

Saffron introduced the next speaker, a nervous graduate student who finished her presentation quickly to gratifying applause. Carroll didn't clap at all. Doodling on his pad, he made no effort to hide his boredom.

Shamus worked his way toward the front of the room where people were waiting to speak to the presenters. He wanted to check on Madison. She noticed him, smiled reassuringly and pointed to the door. Shamus signaled that he'd meet her outside the room.

Once there, he thought about Madison's name being on Blake's list. What he'd just witnessed confirmed for him that Madison was a target, not a murderer. About to take a seat, he caught sight of Bill Carroll and headed over to him.

"Excuse me, Bill," Shamus said.

Carroll turned around.

"I'm Shamus Doherty." He extended his hand.

Carroll accommodated him reluctantly.

"My sister is…"

"I know who she is," Carroll grunted.

"I'm sure you do."

"What do you want?" Carroll asked.

"Just wanted to look into the eyes of the guy who keeps hassling my sister."

"Can't she fight her own battles?" Carroll said, scornfully.

"Oh, she can do that. I'm just trying to spare you some pain."

Carroll chuckled imperiously before turning away.

"You're on the list," Shamus said. "Did you know that?"

Carroll turned back. "What list?"

"Detective Jeffries' list of possible murderers. Puts you in a bit of a pickle. Not so high and mighty."

"Did your sister put me there?"

"Blake did. Seems you had a vitriolic email dispute with Stan."

"I'm no murderer," Carroll spat. "I wasn't the one there when it happened."

"Where were you?"

"Get lost," Carroll said, about to step away.

"Just remember what I said about Meg. And this is how I sound when I'm in a good mood."

"I'm so scared," Carroll mocked.

Shamus removed a piece of lint from the professor's lapel and flicked it to the floor. "Stay that way. For your own good."

He locked once more on Carroll's eyes, turned and walked away.

CHAPTER FIFTEEN

Madison was in the corridor finishing up talking with two people when Shamus approached her.

"Nice presentation," he said.

"Thank you. I saw you arguing with Bill just now."

"I shared some things we don't have in common."

"It looked like you were going to slug him."

"Not this time."

"I'm about to get some lunch. Want to join me?"

Shamus hesitated, feeling a twinge of disloyalty to Meg.

"You have other plans?"

"No. Sorry. Yes, let's do that."

They were about to get onto an elevator when a short young woman with curly, disheveled, black hair cut in front of Shamus, nearly tripping him. She had striking violet eyes and a determined look. She was clutching a notepad in one hand and a plastic hotel pen in the other. Dressed in worn jeans, a wrinkled white cotton blouse, and barely tied runners, she didn't appear to be a professor.

"Penelope Ames with the *New York Times*," she announced, tapping the pen on the pad repeatedly. She licked the tip and tried to scribble. No luck. As Shamus and Madison watched in puzzlement, she retrieved another plastic pen from her jeans pocket. She looked up at Shamus. "I have a couple of questions."

Shamus stepped away from the elevator. Madison joined him. "I don't have anything to say. Furthermore, I wish you'd leave Meg Doherty alone. She's been through a lot."

"Nope. She's in the middle of this," Penelope said abruptly. "There's no way I can just give her a pass."

"You could give her more time."

"Can't do it," she snapped, tapping the pen on the pad again to no avail. "Two people were killed. Your sister was nearby both times."

The pen, with a hard tap, splattered ink across her blouse, her chin and lips. She tore the damaged page from the pad, crumbled it, stuffed it into her jeans pocket and looked up undeterred.

"She wasn't nearby when Stan Evans was murdered," Shamus said. "When Blake Packard was killed, she was in the restroom."

Penelope pulled a pencil out of her pocket and jotted down a few words.

"We're on our way somewhere," Madison interjected. "This will have to wait."

Penelope eyed Madison's nametag and jotted on her pad.

"That's enough," Shamus said. "We have nothing to say." He put his hand gently on Madison's back and they turned to face the elevator. He pushed the call button.

"Thanks for nothing," Penelope said. "I'll catch you both later."

"Don't count on it," Shamus said without looking back. The elevator doors opened. He and Madison entered, joining three male conference guests.

"Oh, hey! Just one more question," Penelope called. She blocked the closing elevator door with her knee. It shook, rattled and buzzed in protest.

"Push that open button, will you?" Penelope said to one of the men before suddenly cringing in pain. "Hold this for me, will you?" She shakily held out her pad and pencil to Shamus.

Annoyed, he took them from her.

She formed a fist with her right hand, and then covered it with her left. "Arthritis attack," she grimaced and bent forward.

Shamus started to reach out to her.

Suddenly her right middle finger popped up through the spread fingers of her left hand. She pushed it down. It popped up again. She looked straight into Shamus' eyes.

"There!" she said, taking her pen and pad from Shamus. "You all have a nice day."

As the elevator doors closed, Shamus looked at Madison, brow creased with confusion.

"Did she just give me the finger?"

Madison looked down, hand angled over her eyes, but Shamus could see her smile. The other passengers were turning away, stifling laughter.

"She did," Shamus said still flummoxed. "That little..."

He glanced at Madison who was biting her upper lip to suppress the laugh evident in her eyes. He looked away, then shook his head and smiled.

They arrived at Chipotle. Following Madison's lead, Shamus selected a natural cranberry drink rather than the Diet Coke he craved. They sat at a small table away from the door where snow-covered customers were ushering in the cold.

"Hope this place is good enough," Shamus said.

"I'd rather go to my favorite upscale restaurant, L'Escale, but this will do since no one is paying the bill for us.

"It's close to the hotel at least," he said.

Madison unwrapped her burrito. "How is Meg?"

"She's doing okay."

"Good."

"What about you? That guy police dragged out of your session was creepy."

"It was unnerving. Chuck told me that he's a graduate student with a chip on his shoulder about journal rejections. A heavy drinker too."

"Rejections from you?"

"And others."

He watched as she used a plastic knife and fork to neatly open her burrito, and considered his etiquette options. Convinced that the cranberry drink was sufficient dining pretense for one day, he picked up his burrito and took a sizable bite. Half the contents fell out the back end.

"You must be hungry," Madison said, amused.

Shamus grabbed a napkin to stop the burrito from falling out of his mouth as well. "Sorry."

"You have something on your mind," she said pointing her plastic fork at him. "Spit it out."

"I think you should know that Blake mentioned your name to Meg before he was killed. Supposedly, you're one of a few people who had a very strained relationship with Stan."

"So?"

"Jeffries knows. I imagine he thinks that could implicate you."

"That's just great," Madison said, tossing her fork down.

"Better you should know."

"Stan didn't like women, especially smart ones. His record for not publishing women's research was appalling. I let him know what I thought about that."

"Has Jeffries contacted you yet? You'll want to tell him about that."

"He told me he wanted to talk to me." She poked at the burrito. "Now I know why."

"Madison, listen…"

"I despised Stan," she interrupted.

"It might be better to lead with sympathy for a dead man when you talk to Jeffries."

She shook her head. "I didn't kill him or Blake. I've published a lot. I'm a full professor for Christ sake. Murder isn't my way of dealing with the assholes of this world."

"I doubt anyone thinks you murdered either of them."

"Who else did Blake mention?" Madison asked.

"Wesley and Bill Carroll."

"Wesley?" she laughed. "That's absurd."

"And Bill Carroll?"

"Not a chance. He's a loudmouth coward. He writes irate letters to every editor."

"So, you have nothing to worry about," Shamus said. "The list is worthless."

Madison nodded distractedly. She sipped on her juice and entered her own world.

CHAPTER SIXTEEN

When Shamus and Madison walked into the hotel, Jeffries was waiting in the lobby. He shot Shamus a don't-join-us look, and guided Madison to two opposing, stiff-backed leather chairs with chrome arm rests. There would be no small talk.

Shamus saw Meg and Rashid at a table in the lobby bar. He made his way over. "Congratulations must be in order, Rashid, from the look on your faces."

"It was a wonderful case competition with a perfect outcome," Rashid beamed. "I have not stopped smiling since the announcement that we won. The students are off enjoying New York City. They invited me, but they don't need their coach hovering."

"I'm sure they wouldn't mind," Meg said.

"They have seen enough of me the last few months. Now is their chance to put all that practice and worry behind them and have some fun."

Rashid reached under the table and retrieved a large silver bowl. It read, "Pacific Coast University" followed by "NYU Case Competition Champions."

"We will put the names of the students here," Rashid said pointing at the center front of the trophy.

"And the name of the coach," Shamus added.

"We shall see," Rashid replied humbly.

Shamus looked at Meg.

"No worries. I'll definitely make sure they include Rashid's name."

As Rashid placed the trophy under the table, Shamus peered over to where Madison and Jeffries were engaged in intense conversation. He noticed Penelope near the reception desk, pen and pad in hand, talking to a group of young men and women sporting conference nametags. Her eyes lifted and coolly held his for a moment.

"She does not like you very much," Rashid goaded.

"She's a force to be reckoned with, I'll tell you that."

"She is actually quite tiny," Rashid replied.

"Like dynamite," Shamus said. "Trust me."

Penelope stepped off by herself, hailed a waiter and handed him a note. He followed her instructions and placed it in front of Shamus.

He read it, frowned and placed it in his coat pocket.

"Perhaps she does like you," Rashid taunted.

"As much as cats like dogs," Shamus said, glancing again at Penelope.

"It happens sometimes," Rashid said.

"Not to this dog," Shamus replied. "And definitely not with that cat."

Meg had excused herself and headed to the room. She decided that work might be a useful distraction. It had to be better than dwelling on things she couldn't change. She sat at a small desk, opened her computer and tried to focus on her writing.

It was too much to ask. Blythe's oblique accusations were replaying in her mind. She felt emotionally torn between sympathy for the grieving woman and resentment at the way she'd talked. *How much did Blythe really know? More importantly, who would she tell?*

Tears rolled down her cheeks. Disgusted with herself, she dried her eyes and opened her briefcase. Inside, neatly-folded, was a sheer, white silk scarf perched on the top of her files. She lifted it slowly. *How had it gotten there? Had someone thought it was hers and slipped it into her briefcase?* Light brown stains threaded through the soft, transparent material. The edges were frayed.

It slipped through her fingers as her hands reached to cover her mouth. It was hers, the stains her blood. She could again feel the cold tiles of the restroom wall against her back, Stan's body crushing hers, yanking the scarf from her neck and dropping it to the floor.

The freight elevator lumbered its way downward as if reluctant to descend so far with a hotel guest. Penelope's note asked that he meet her in the hotel basement laundry. As the door opened, Shamus felt a blast of heat. Rows of massive dryers groaned inharmoniously. Behemoth washing machines sloshed their complaints, some banging restlessly as if in futile efforts to escape.

He'd expected more people rushing about. Instead, only two white-clad women were busily removing sheets from dryers. He slipped undetected around a row of machines and reached the back of the room. Penelope poked her head out from a large, floor-level cabinet. She scanned the room while gesturing for him to hurry.

"Get in," she whispered pulling on his sleeve.

Shamus fell forward into the cabinet. "What the hell?"

She covered his mouth, eyes wide as she listened for something. She placed her index finger over her lips and released her other hand from his mouth.

"Jesus! What are we doing here," he whispered as he brushed lint from his clothes. He scrutinized their surroundings. Penelope had created a miniature office with computer, phone, small lamp and candied snacks. She poked her head out again and looked several times to her right as if she knew that someone might soon be coming from that direction.

"We only have a few minutes," Penelope whispered.

"I want to apologize…," Shamus began.

"Never mind that," she said. "We don't have much time."

"For what?"

"Making a deal. I'm an investigative journalist. Before I print anything useful to protecting your sister, I can let you know. I also have an NYPD connection. I'm willing to help you manage Jeffries, to let you know what he's about to do so you're not blindsided. Who hates him, who he owes, stuff like that. He has to find this killer. He's getting pressure from all sides. If he can't, he'll have to pin it on somebody. Right now, your sister is the most likely candidate."

"What do you want in return?"

"Keep your ears and eyes open. Tell me what you learn. You're on the inside. I'm not. Your sister won't even talk to me."

"Let me think about…"

She suddenly crunched down, covering his mouth again. She opened the cabinet door a crack. Shamus could see a middle-aged man wheeling a laundry cart. He stopped a few feet from them, retrieved clean sheets from one of the shelves and placed them in the cart. He moved as if on automatic pilot.

Penelope's eyes were shifting back and forth. The man moved a few feet further away. He opened a dryer door, rustled the contents, and slammed it shut. The machine started up again with a roar. The process was repeated at another machine.

It reminded Shamus of hiding behind a huge grocery store refrigerator when he was 8-years-old. He and a friend had taken a candy bar on a bet. The terror had been intense—his first brush with the law.

Footsteps stopped beside the cabinet. A man cleared his throat. Penelope was still as a statue.

"The manager will be through here in about ten minutes," the man said nonchalantly, as if talking to himself.

Penelope opened her eyes. She smiled. "Thanks, Jeff," she said softly.

"Jeff?" Shamus whispered.

"I couldn't be sure it was him."

"Are you a regular here?" Shamus asked.

"He found me last night and I played the investigative journalist card. I think he likes being part of the intrigue. He's a nice guy."

Penelope opened the cabinet door and surveyed the large room.

"So, let me get this straight," Shamus said. "*New York Times'* journalists skulk around hotel laundry rooms?"

"This journalist does," Penelope replied as she gingerly stepped out of the cabinet.

Shamus climbed out, brushing laundry detritus from his dark pants. "How does he know you're not a linen burglar or worse?"

"My ID," Penelope said urging him to stay low.

Shamus ducked down.

"We only have a few minutes," Penelope said. "So, what do you say? You'll keep me in the loop, right?"

"We'll give it a try," Shamus said. "There has to be a quid pro quo here. It's not a one-way street."

Penelope nodded. "I already surmise from your movements that Madison Wills and Bill Carroll are two people Blake mentioned to Meg."

"Madison isn't a murderer."

"Oh please. She wears six-inch heels, skirts tight enough to constrict blood circulation, and enough make-up in one day to fill six potholes. That's not somebody who's leading with honesty. Besides, she flits."

"Flits?" Shamus asked.

"From man to man. You know, whoever can do the most for her at the moment."

A clicking noise. They ducked. It had come from Jeff's direction. Someone was opening washing machines and dropping the lids closed.

"That's Jeff's signal. We need to go," Penelope whispered. "Follow me."

"Why all the cloak and dagger?"

"You haven't met the manager," Penelope replied as she began moving. "He's a jackass."

They skulked their way to an exit door and pushed. Once outside, they began slipping in the snow, grabbing to save each other, and fell into laughter.

"Go," Penelope said when they reached a side entrance to the hotel. "Better I'm not seen with you."

He glanced at her feet. "Are you going to tie those laces?"

"Just go!" she said, a smile in her eyes.

As he entered the hotel, Shamus brushed snow off his shoulders. The bartender noticed him, picked up a napkin from the bar and waved it.

"Your sister wants you to meet her and a friend at MOMA."

He'd need his coat, so he headed to the suite. As he entered, he noticed the phone message light blinking. It was from Judith.

"I did not, repeat, did not hire a team without a boss. I understand that you are delayed due to issues affecting your sister. Nevertheless, we need to hear from you at least every other day. Harrison and I are not used to slipshod work. Call me as soon as you get this message."

Police Interview: Aaron Saffron

"Like any large group, we have all kinds, but not murderers. I can't get my head around that. Some editors think too much of themselves. They tend to lord it over the others. Stan was like that. Blake not really. His main vice was working with Stan. No doubt, he was hoping to replace Stan as editor someday. They couldn't pay me enough to work one day for Stan Evans, let alone for years."

CHAPTER SEVENTEEN

On his way through the lobby, hurrying to MOMA, Shamus saw Tim Baron walking toward him, waving.

"You are Meg Doherty's brother," Baron said enthusiastically outstretching his hand.

"I am indeed," Shamus said, meeting Baron's hand.

"Tim Baron."

"I know," Shamus said. "I was impressed with the calming speech you gave in the midst of chaos the other day."

"As an elder statesman in this field, I felt some responsibility to put the events in perspective so young people would not lose the opportunity to share their work. That's what these conferences are about, along with identifying and encouraging scholars with promise. Like your sister."

"I'm rushing off to meet Meg now at MOMA."

"I won't delay you further," Baron said. "Only to say that in my capacity as one who has seen much over the years, it is to Meg's benefit to continue on the path she has chosen."

"Which path is that?"

"I've seen many young people make choices that derailed their success. They failed to put offenses behind them and move on."

"I don't follow."

Baron placed a friendly hand on Shamus' shoulder. "I simply wish to save your sister future misery. If you would pass along my advice, I'm sure it will make sense to her. She understands the politics of our field. She is very astute."

"You want her to keep quiet about something?" Shamus asked, puzzled.

"Only to be judicious. There will be many people pressuring her to speak ill of others. I am merely advising that she not fall prey to their self-serving machinations."

"Who might do that?" Shamus asked.

"Consider my words the protective counsel of someone who has been around a long time, one who admires your sister and her work," Baron said, smiling benevolently. He spotted someone across the lobby and signaled a greeting. "I must go. I look forward to meeting again."

"But wait," Shamus said as Baron stepped away.

"Another time," Baron called without turning back. "Another time very soon."

Shamus walked briskly up West 53rd Street, his mind dwelling on Baron's enigmatic message. His thoughts were interrupted by a woman of about sixty-five exiting MOMA. Curls of blonde and gray protruded from the edges of her black, Russian style shapka. Shamus stopped in his tracks. His heart raced. The woman turned, looked past him and attempted to hail a cab.

Several taxis passed her by. Exasperated, she threw up her hands and began to walk. Shamus looked through the large glass doors into the museum. Meg and Rashid were waiting for him in the lobby. Meg had a cell phone to her ear. Shamus' phone rang. He muted it and moved quickly out of view.

About fifteen yards to his left, the woman was attempting to navigate large puddles and salted patches of ice in shoes meant for less inclement weather. He followed her.

She proceeded along 53rd Street and down the escalator to the 5th Avenue subway station, paused to remove a card from her wallet and then headed for a row of turnstiles.

There was a booth where Shamus could buy a ticket, but a dozen passengers were already lined up. He quickly headed for a bank of MetroCard vending machines. He slid a dollar into the slot of one, but the currency reader rejected it on two tries, so he took a credit card from his wallet. He glanced back over his shoulder. The woman had stepped onto a downward escalator. The machine beeped and insistently blinked for his zip code. Cursing to himself, he entered 0-6-8-7-7. What seemed like several interminable moments passed before a card popped out of the dispenser.

By the time he reached the turnstile, the woman was out of sight. He swiped the MetroCard, but the reader seemed to sense his lack of familiarity and rejected it. He tried again with no luck. *Please swipe again,* the display instructed. Shamus threw his hands up.

"Give me that," demanded a woman waiting in line behind him. She took his card, flipped it over, breathed on it, brushed it briskly against her coat and handed it back to Shamus.

"Now try it," she insisted.

It worked. Once through the turnstile, Shamus turned to thank the woman, but she'd joined hundreds of other passengers hurrying to their destinations.

He worked his way to the escalator and looked down the long, steep descent. There she was. He tried to maneuver his way past people on the escalator, but only managed a snail's progress.

Finally, he reached the platform for downtown trains. The woman was nowhere to be found.

Spotting a stairway, Shamus decided to try it. He climbed the steps to a much seedier, smaller subway platform.

Standing on the yellow caution strip near the edge of the platform was the woman, reading a book. As if sensing eyes on her, she looked toward Shamus. He turned away and began studying a subway map on the wall. A loud screeching noise presaged an approaching train. The doors slid open and the woman waited while passengers spewed from the car she'd chosen. She stepped aboard. Shamus jostled amongst the crowd trying to get onto the car behind hers. By the time he reached the door, the train was packed. A few passengers moved just enough to let him squeeze in. Avoiding eye contact per New York City subway etiquette, he nodded in gratitude. Looking up, he saw ads for condoms, breast augmentation, skin care and one for rental referrals in a part of town where the monthly rent for a two-bedroom apartment with a river view would surpass his crew's monthly payroll.

The woman was standing near the door of her car holding onto a pole along with several other people. When the train reached its first stop, she exited. Shamus followed her through a tunnel-and-escalator maze, this time to the IRT 6 local stop where he waited for her to board and then got on at the other end of the same car. The train's first stop was Grand Central Station where the women got off and moved adeptly through the crowd. Shamus bumped and tripped his way along until he spotted her standing, as before, on a thick yellow warning strip beside a track.

The number 4 train, a downtown express, was announced. The woman moved further onto the yellow strip even as the loudspeaker announcement advised passengers to not do so. Shamus felt like rushing over and pulling her back.

Nearly silent by comparison to the deafening E train, the IRT 4 Express pulled in. The woman boarded. Shamus did so one car back.

The train sped past stops for Astor Place, Bleecker Street, Spring Street and Canal Street on route to lower Manhattan and its Brooklyn destinations. When the train descended under the East River, she buttoned her coat. At Borough Hall station, she disembarked. Shamus followed to the street and the busy center of Brooklyn Heights.

She disappeared onto Henry Street lined with lovely houses. Shamus would gladly own any of them. He hastened to the corner just in time to see her climbing steps and entering a white-painted brownstone.

He watched her shadow on the bay window curtain as he'd done years ago when his father had been beside her. Shamus had been eleven. He could once again see his father looking longingly into her eyes.

A woman walking two miniature white terriers approached him. "Are you lost?"

"Sort of," Shamus stuttered. "I'm looking for the subway station. I was going to knock on a door for directions."

"You're not far off track," she said smiling. "Go to the end of the block and turn left. Keep walking. You can't miss it."

"Thanks," Shamus replied. He waved awkwardly as she continued to walk.

He lingered a few moments longer. Should he ring the woman's doorbell? What would he say? *Do you remember me?* Instead, he walked. At the subway, he located the Manhattan bound platform. He sat on the train wondering why he'd stalked her. The past was the past. Nothing could erase what his father had done, the secret they'd harbored from Shamus' mother, and the distance between them that had never diminished.

At the MOMA entrance, Shamus leaned against an area of glass covered with a poster. He needed a moment to recover from his journey. If he tried to act nonchalant with Meg and Rashid, they'd notice his pretense. He drew in a deep breath and let it out slowly before entering the museum. He checked his phone. Meg had tried to reach him three times. He rang her.

"It's me Meg," he said, attempting to sound contrite.

"Where have you been? I've been calling you."

"I got held up. Where are you?"

"On the second floor in the Kandinsky exhibit," Meg replied, still an edge to her voice.

"I'll be right there."

Meg studied his expression when he arrived at her side. "You look like you've seen a ghost."

"I'm not as young as I used to be," Shamus said, winded.

Rashid joined them, studying Shamus' coat.

"It's snowing harder out there now," Shamus said. "My jacket was soaked in no time."

"Unpredictable weather. It doesn't suit me," Rashid said, conspiratorially. Well, we're all here now."

Meg shook her head. "Sticking together I see."

"What?" they said in unison.

Meg rolled her eyes and headed over to admire the first of Kandinsky's four panels painted in 1914 for the Park Avenue apartment of Edwin R. Campbell, the founder of Chevrolet Motor Company.

Shamus nodded in gratitude to Rashid. "I bet you're a lousy liar too," he whispered.

"It is hard to find worse," Rashid replied with a wink before he and Shamus joined Meg.

"Did you know Kandinsky coined the expression 'nonobjective' to refer to a manner of painting that depicts no recognizable objects?" Shamus asked.

"No," Meg said, impressed.

"Color mattered most to him."

"I can see that," she said. "But these painting do have recognizable objects."

"Kandinsky would deny that."

"I didn't know you were an art connoisseur."

"There's a lot you don't know about me."

"Is that right?" Meg said with a dubious smile.

They entered a room where a throng had gathered around Vincent van Gogh's *The Starry Night*. A genial, senior docent was stationed next to the painting, allowing visitors to step right up to it and briefly inhale its genius. This was the work of a man dismissed by his father and all but one of his siblings, taunted by children who thought him a freak, obsessed by love yet so often tragically alone. Shamus stood transfixed. He wondered if this painting had emanated from the depths of Van Gogh's being during one of his darker periods. As others walked on, Shamus lingered entranced by the swirls and contrasts, eerie beauty and delicate detail.

When they left MOMA, it was dark and lightly snowing. Meg's cheeks reddened from the cold; her eyes brightened. Rashid breathed in Manhattan's icy magic. Leafless tree branches adorned with miniature white lights, obscure an hour earlier, now reached their glowing branches skyward like secondary characters boldly stealing the show. Cars and taxis moved rhythmically, cooperatively. Buildings glistened. Rainbow hued pigeons, heads bobbing, dexterously scurried and fluttered in a precarious dance with preoccupied pedestrians.

"No place quite like it," Shamus said.

Rashid slowly nodded as he looked up transfixed by snowflakes bright against the darkening sky, some joining like starlings in harmonic formations, upward and downward, inward and outward, as if having practiced together for years.

CHAPTER EIGHTEEN

Meg sat in a 2nd floor alcove designed to enable privacy at large conventions. She contemplated the meaning of Tim Baron's advice. Shamus had passed it on with concern that she'd quickly deflected. "Tim is so sweet," she'd said. "Brilliant as they come, he is also like a second father at times."

Shamus had offered an alternative. "Sounded to me like he wants you to keep your mouth shut about something."

Meg had smiled. "Maybe" she'd said, warding off discussion. "I'll ask when I see him."

What could Tim have meant? Meg wondered as she now sat alone. It was like him to be protective toward young colleagues, as he'd been with Mitchell when Stan had maligned his work. Perhaps Tim was advising her to avoid excessive revelations to the police about the backstage activities of academic conferencing. Tim would protect their field from any and all threats. If he knew what Stan did to her, or thought he might, he'd be concerned for her, but she wouldn't be his first priority. A few years ago, accusations of harassment or worse at conferences were generally dismissed. Rumors rumbled around for a while, but nothing substantive came of them. The culture protected predators. Now, in the #MeToo era, if one senior professor were to be accused of sordid behavior, how long would it take for others to come under scrutiny? Heads could roll. Slight infractions, possibly by Tim when he was younger, could be put under a magnifying glass. Leading scholars might be toppled from their lofty perches. Tim could not abide that.

Meg opened her briefcase slowly. The silk scarf was still there, crumpled now. She shuddered and pushed it down. Her fingers brushed against a small envelope. She slowly removed it. The front was blank. She held it in her lap. After a deep breath, she opened it.

"There you are!" Wesley exclaimed. "Have you been avoiding me?"

"Didn't see your name on my avoid-at-all-costs list," she said, dropping the envelope into her briefcase, snapping it closed, and managing a smile.

"Thank goodness for that," Wesley said as he took a seat beside her.

"I'm just finishing up what I'll say at the division meeting a few minutes from now," Meg said pleasantly, "and at the assistant professor group tonight."

"Skip the second one," Westley abruptly enjoined.

She looked directly at him. "Why?"

"Everyone knows that you've been through a lot. There's no need to be a hero."

"I'm not trying to be a hero."

"Hey," Wesley said gently. "I was just thinking of what's best for you."

"What if one of them took the plan too far?" Meg asked.

"C'mon Meg. You don't really believe that happened."

"Why not?"

"There's no way."

"You remember how some of them were talking at the end of the Philadelphia conference last year," Meg said. "They were tired of the nudging process. Sending complaint letters to publishers was too tame a strategy for them. They wanted Stan gone one way or another."

"Get a grip, Meg. They didn't mean murder."

"How do you know?"

"Okay. Just listen to me." He placed a hand on the arm of her chair.

"Don't patronize me, Wesley. You know better."

Wesley stiffened and pulled his hand back.

"You and I helped start that group," Meg said. "If one or more of them murdered Stan and Blake, we're partially to the blame."

"No one in the group murdered Stan or Blake. They wanted Evans to stop deciding their futures. That's all."

"We hardly know some of the new members. I haven't shared my concerns with anyone other than you, but omission is nearly the same as lying. Besides, how long before one of them talks to Jeffries?"

"Don't show up at the meeting," Wesley said as he stood. "You already have tenure. It's a group for the aspiring, not for the arrived."

Meg watched him stride off. *What had just happened? They were supposed to be on the same team. Besides, no one had the right to keep her away from any meeting.*

"You seem preoccupied," came a voice from behind Meg as she walked to the first meeting. She looked around. It was Penelope.

Meg sighed and continued walking. "I wondered if you'd given up on me," she said. "I was beginning to feel insignificant."

Penelope kept apace. "Your brother asked me to leave you alone."

"Clearly, you decided to ignore him."

"I'm not here to pester you. I just noticed how intense you look and how annoyed your friend Wesley seemed back there."

"Are you also a spy?"

"My job is to be vigilant," Penelope replied.

"I'd call it intrusive."

"Sometimes."

Meg stopped and looked at Penelope. "Wesley and I have philosophical differences."

"We have those in journalism. Only we just call them arguments. They're usually about things people on the outside would find ludicrous. But, to us, of course, they…"

"Did you want something?" Meg interrupted.

Penelope took a business card out of her blazer pocket and handed it to Meg. "I doubt you'll use it. I seem to rub you the wrong way, but just in case."

"Fine. I have to go now to a business leadership division meeting," Meg said as she began to walk away.

"I'll be attending too," Penelope said

Meg stopped.

Penelope pointed to a nametag on her jacket. "You see, I'm registered for this conference, so it's all on the up and up."

Meg glanced at the nametag before noticing Penelope's untied runners.

Penelope shrugged. "I brought some good clothes, but I forgot shoes."

"We're not formal here," Meg said, beginning to walk.

Penelope caught up. "I guess that cuts me some slack."

When they reached the meeting room, there were about 100 people milling about. Several assistant professors were in a far corner arguing, Wesley among them. One of the young men was scowling as he animatedly pointed a finger at another whose arms were folded in resentment across his chest.

"Who are those people?" Penelope asked.

"Young professors probably disagreeing about some research methodology," Meg said—this time with a slight smile.

"Right," Penelope replied.

"Gotta go," Meg said. She headed for the front of the room. Penelope sidled over to a seat near the group and began surreptitiously reading nametags and recording them in her notepad.

One of the young professors noticed Penelope's interest and glared at her before sitting.

"He doesn't seem to like you," Rashid said, smiling from two chairs away.

Penelope looked at Rashid's nametag. "You are from Pacific Coast University like Meg Doherty. In fact, I saw you with her and Shamus in the lobby bar."

He nodded and smiled graciously.

"Did you by any chance sit next to me on purpose?"

"You are a very astute journalist."

"I suppose you're here to insist that I leave her alone?"

"I rarely insist. It is not in my nature."

Penelope smiled, amused. "Well, I'm a reporter and it's not in my nature to leave a person of interest alone even when the request is made by someone as disarming as yourself."

"If I can be of any assistance, perhaps answer some questions without Meg being involved, I would gladly do so to spare her the additional pressure,"

"That's very thoughtful, Rashid. You must be good friends."

"We are. Meg is a very special person."

"Well, she doesn't seem to like me much."

"That will pass," Rashid said with pleasant reassurance.

"What makes you think so?" Penelope asked as she again studied the arguing professors.

"Because I like you," Rashid replied with a broad smile.

"You are a member of a small group."

"I doubt that," Rashid said, smiling warmly before turning to look toward the front of the room. "I doubt that very much."

The assistant professors in the front row were standing impatiently waiting for the meeting to start. One was Sidney Jorgensen of the University of Arizona, Phoenix and another was Arne Phelps of Georgia

Tech. Sensing he was being watched, Jorgensen regarded Rashid with disdain. Rashid knew well that look of smug superiority; the kind he ran from as a child. But no longer. He glared at Jorgensen. Phelps turned and observed the silent exchange. He nudged the frowning Jorgensen causing him to face front again.

Meg called the meeting to order.

"Getting a little ahead of yourself, aren't you, Meg?" Jorgensen sniped. "We can wait for the real chair."

"Chase texted," Meg said. "He's caught in traffic and asked as chair-elect that I start the meeting."

Meg held Jorgensen's gaze until he slowly, resentfully sat.

"Things are tense," Penelope whispered to Rashid.

"Meg can handle it," Rashid said assuredly.

Penelope nodded. "I'm sure she can. But given the rumblings in here, she appears to have a number of detractors."

Rashid audited the room, noting several young professors angrily looking at Meg. Just then a grey-bearded, lean man entered the room and rushed, breathless to the front.

"Thank you so much," the man said to Meg as he removed his coat.

"My pleasure, Chase. We were just getting underway. You haven't missed anything," Meg said as she took her seat.

"Just in the nick of time," Rashid whispered.

Police Interview: Arne Phelps

"I don't know what you're talking about. I'm not a member of any group, let alone one out to get editors. That would be career suicide. Even being here talking to you is risky. Have you talked to Wesley Farnum? He knows Meg Doherty. Maybe he can tell you something."

CHAPTER NINETEEN

Shamus glanced around the lobby. A gray-haired woman sat alone, reading a magazine. His heart raced. Was it her? Had she seen him following her and found him? The woman slowly raised her head. As if feeling his eyes on her, she turned. Their eyes met. He froze and then quickly looked away. Not her.

"You look agitated," Madison said, approaching him.

"Something like that," Shamus said. "It's good to see you talking to me. You know, killing the messenger and all that."

"Actually, you did me a favor. If you hadn't said anything about Blake's list, I would have been blindsided by Jeffries. So, thank you."

"Up for a coffee, then?" Shamus asked. "You might be able to help me."

"Sure."

They found a small, well-used sofa in a corner of a nearby coffee shop and ordered two cappuccinos. They discussed their lives, past loves, anything but the murders.

"Okay. There's something on your mind?" Madison said. "You've gone all around the corral with small talk, but it's in your eyes."

"I've got to work on that."

"It's probably too late in your thirties."

"Shamus nodded and smiled. "You're probably right. Okay. Fine. Do you know about a group of assistant professors who tried to oust Stan Evans from his editorship? My friend, Rashid, heard about them."

Madison's eyes widened. She sat upright. "What?"

"They've been meeting at conferences. I thought you might have heard about them."

"I've tried to put Bret's outburst behind me. Now you tell me a group of professors sharing his anger might be killing editors."

I'm not saying that."

"You're full of good news, Shamus."

Madison grabbed her coat from the back of her chair and fumbled about trying to put it on while still seated.

"I didn't mean to upset you. I don't know much about the group." Shamus reached for one of Madison's hands. She pulled away. "You're shaking."

"Wouldn't you be? I'm facing one threat after the other."

"Why don't you stay in our suite for the next few days?"

"Don't be ridiculous. Your sister won't go for that."

"If she thinks you're frightened, she'll rise to the occasion."

Madison stared at him for a moment. She placed her hands over her eyes, elbows on the table.

"Hey," Shamus said softly, touching her arm. Let's go find out what we can about this group."

She looked at him. "Meg won't tell you about them if that's what you have in mind."

"We'll see," Shamus said. "In the meantime, don't let your imagination run wild."

He instantly realized it wasn't the most astute thing he'd ever said. Two people were dead—both, like her, editors of leading journals. A near stranger had held his hand in the shape of a gun—pointed at her—and then raised three fingers. How far did her imagination have to run to see she could be next?

Back at the hotel, they waited for an elevator. The doors of one opened. It was empty. Shamus followed Madison to the back. They stood in silence. She sighed and looked at him before gently resting her head on his shoulder. He looked at their reflection in the doors. Her eyes were closed. Her mouth was tight, as if fighting tears. *If Meg and Penelope could see Madison now,* Shamus thought, *they wouldn't see a user.*

The elevator doors opened. A young woman was using the mirror on the wall opposite them to tidy a strand of her dark hair. A sense of familiarity, a moment of déjà vu swept over Shamus. His heart raced. It couldn't be. The woman began to turn. His breathing stopped. It was Denise.

Madison felt Shamus stiffen. She lifted her head from his shoulder and looked at his face. His eyes were wide. She followed his gaze to the target of his astonishment and quickly edged away from him. The two of them stood staring at Denise as the elevator doors started to close. Shamus thrust out his arm to stop them and he and Madison exited.

"I didn't know you were coming," Shamus said uneasily.

"I can see that," Denise said with a short smile and a nod to Madison.

"I was upset," Madison interjected. "Shamus was helping me."

"I'm not surprised. He can be very sweet." Denise said, her expression less sanguine than her words.

"Yes, he can," Madison said. She held out her hand. "I'm Madison Wills. You must be Denise."

"Nice to meet you," Denise said with slightly chilled civility aimed more at Shamus.

"Madison is a professor and a journal editor," Shamus said a tad too rapidly. "Meg may have told you that two editors have been murdered. Madison has received threats. So, I thought, well, it just seemed, to me anyway, a good idea to invite Madison to stay in the suite with Meg and me."

"I'll be fine on my own," Madison asserted.

"It's a good idea," Denise said. "Being with other people right now is the smart thing for you to do." She turned to Shamus. "My being here doesn't change that."

"Aren't you going to give her a hug?" Madison scolded Shamus. "She's flown all the way from L.A. to be with you."

Shamus put his arms around Denise and kissed her on the cheek. "Did Meg know that you'd be coming?" he asked stepping back.

"I only decided last night. Rashid sent me a text about what happened. I came to see if I could help Meg. Had I told her beforehand, she would have said she was fine. So, I didn't." She pushed the elevator call button and looked at Shamus. "I'm going to the lobby shop. Why don't you and Madison discuss the details of her stay with Meg? I'll be back shortly."

"There's nothing to discuss," Madison said as Denise entered the elevator. "I'll be fine on my own."

Denise smiled at Shamus as the doors began to close. "Seems you have some persuading to do."

Shamus and Madison stood beside each other feeling chastened.

"Shit!" Shamus said. He slammed his forehead with the palm of his hand.

"I'm so sorry," Madison said looking pained.

"It's not your fault. I probably sounded like a kid caught with his hand in the cookie jar." His eyes widened. "Oh, sorry Madison. I didn't mean to say that."

She chuckled. "You must love her, Shamus. You're an absolute wreck."

Police Interview: Bill Carroll

"You don't have to be Einstein to put two-and-two together here. Yet, here you are quizzing me. This must be those two detectives' first murder investigation. They sure strike me as amateurs."

CHAPTER TWENTY

Meg was taking a soda from the refrigerator when Shamus opened the door to the suite, walked into the living room and collapsed onto the sofa.

"What's up?" Meg asked, sitting across from him.

"Denise is here."

"That's great!"

"She saw me in the elevator with Madison."

"You mean WITH Madison?"

"She had her head on my shoulder."

"That's swell," Meg said throwing up her hands. "Why were you two together anyway? I warned you."

"She's an editor of a bigtime journal. Two senior editors are dead. You saw that guy threaten her. She's frightened. And, like her or not, we might learn some things from her."

Meg looked up at the ceiling, and then at Shamus in reluctant agreement.

"I told her about a group of assistant professors trying to get senior editors to resign. I assume you know about them. Maybe you're one of them."

"Who's your source?" Meg asked.

"You first. Did Madison's name ever come up at one of those meetings?" Shamus asked.

Meg studied him.

"Well, did it?"

"Yes."

"Who mentioned her?"

"A jerk named Jorgensen. I told him in no uncertain terms last year that the focus was to be on Stan. We were going to nudge him out of the editorship. That's all. Not that he or any of them are listening to me now."

"So, Madison could be a potential target."

Meg breathed deeply and looked away.

"I suggested that she stay in our suite until we know she's safe."

"You what? No! Jeffries can find someone to guard her."

"You're usually more empathic, Meg."

"I found two colleagues dead. I'm not myself. Would you be?"

"Sorry," Shamus said. "Of course."

"Even if I were thinking straight, I don't trust her. You know that."

"What exactly has she done to you?"

"It's not about a specific affront. She's just one of those people who does what's best for her. Sometimes others suffer."

"Sounds vague to me."

Meg sat upright. "Never mind. You already invited her."

"Not exactly. She knows I'm checking with you. I thought of it because of what I saw, what we all saw, when that guy, Bret, identified her as the next victim."

Meg nodded. "You're right. I surrender." She held up her hands. Guilty as charged: empathy deficient."

"You're one of the most empathic people I know, Meg. I was just…"

"Going for my Achilles heel?" She smiled.

"Sort of."

"You win. I just want one thing in return," Meg said.

"Name it."

"Take Denise out to dinner tonight. Someplace nice. No hanging around this suite like Sir Lancelot protecting Madison. In return, I'll be on my best host behavior. How's that?"

"I would have asked Denise out anyway."

Meg looked skeptical.

"Fine. I might have invited a few others."

"That's what I mean. Just you and Denise. Okay?"

"I appreciate what you're doing, Meg. And you know how I feel about Denise. But you can't force romance."

"No, but you can give it a chance."

"I need to know something," Madison said looking intently at Meg, placing her suitcase behind the sofa and taking a seat. "Am I one of the targets of the anti-editor group?"

"That's not what it is."

"Whatever you call it. Am I?"

"Not exactly."

"I'm on pins and needles here to learn what 'not exactly' means."

"You've been the editor of a leading journal for a long time and the purpose of the group is to end that practice."

"So, I should be worried?"

"It was very clear from the beginning that our plan was to edge Stan out with letters to the publisher and hope that other long-time editors would get the hint and step down."

Madison smirked. "Stan never would have kept his editorship if you'd spoken up when the ball was in your court."

Meg's brow tightened. She glanced over at Shamus whose interest had been piqued.

"You know what I'm talking about," Madison continued. "That night after your presentation when Stan walked up to you at the dais."

"What's this about?" Shamus asked, looking back and forth at Meg and Madison.

"Nothing," Meg said. "Just a conversation I had with Stan years ago. He had some suggestions on how to get my work published."

Madison, smiling to herself, picked up a hotel magazine from the coffee table and began flipping pages.

Meg rose from the chair and walked into the kitchenette. Shamus edged forward on the sofa, but caught sight of Denise shaking her head, discouraging him from talking to Meg now. He stopped.

Meg placed a kettle on stove. She looked lost in a world of her own.

Shamus turned to Denise. "I wonder if you'd have dinner with me tonight around 7?"

"I'd like that."

They both looked at Madison who was still flipping pages, and then at Meg, her back to them, hands spread wide on the kitchenette counter, looking down.

Denise stood, walked over to Shamus and kissed him on the cheek. "I'll talk with her later," she whispered. "She's upset. Maybe she'll talk to me."

Shamus and Denise had been gone for an hour. Meg had studiously avoided talking with Madison. She'd spent most of the time in her room until hunger forced her back into the kitchenette.

Meg handed Madison a bowl of macaroni and cheese and a glass of red wine before heading back to her room with a tray.

"Tell me about Rashid," Madison said. "Denise mentioned she'd been texting him from California."

Meg turned. "He's my colleague at Pacific Coast University. Why?"

"Just curious," Madison said casually. "Thanks for the dinner. Want to join me?"

"I'm tired, Madison."

"Just for a few minutes."

"Why?"

"I hate eating alone."

"A change of personality and you might suffer less often," Meg said as she placed the tray down and sat on the sofa.

"I guess I deserved that."

"You think? My brother doesn't need to be with us when we share."

"Sorry. Tell me about Rashid," Madison said.

"He's a kind, gentle, bright, honest person, devoted husband and father, champion debate coach, an excellent teacher and one of my dearest friends."

"No one is that good."

"He is, Madison. So, you wouldn't be interested."

"What exactly do you have against me? I mean before I mentioned your chance to end Stan's editorship in front of your brother?"

"You only do what's good for you," Meg replied. "You know you're attractive and you use it with no concern for the people you hurt."

"I see. So, you figure I might go after your friend Rashid, maybe even ruin his marriage?"

"Rashid wouldn't let anyone do that."

"You overestimate people," Madison scoffed. "It's part of your problem."

"My problem?"

"That group you joined to get Stan out of the editorship. Did you really think they'd all be polite and respectful with their jobs on the line?"

"If you mean did it occur to me that one of them might murder Stan and then Blake? No, it didn't. And I don't believe it now either."

"You helped create a gang of professors, and it looks like they behaved just like any other gang."

"That's absurd."

"Then what did happen?"

"A few of us were at a conference dinner one night. We discussed the juggernaut of long-term editorship. People were justifiably angry. There should be term limits. The next day we drafted a letter to Stan's journal publisher demanding that he be removed. The publisher turned us down."

"But it didn't stop there, right? The secret meetings continued," said Madison.

"Most change starts with people talking secretively," Meg said. "That doesn't make them gang members. You didn't get to be senior editor of one of our leading journals without strategic, private conversations."

"Amusing," Madison scoffed.

"Stan and Blake's murders have nothing to do with that group."

Madison shook her head and poked at the macaroni.

"Since we're being so direct," Meg said, "what did you mean earlier about stopping Stan when I had the chance?"

"I was at the session years ago when Stan talked to you. I saw the two of you leave the hotel together."

"So?"

"You were disheveled and bleeding when you returned that night. That pig attacked you, didn't he?"

"You don't know what you're talking about."

"Maybe not," Madison said glibly. "Maybe you got mugged on the street. But you would have reported that. If you had called out Stan when he did that to you, if you had gotten him in real trouble, he wouldn't have remained an editor. His teaching and research career would have suffered too. Also, he wouldn't be dead."

"You don't know what happened that night."

"And," Madison continued as if Meg hadn't spoken, "you would have protected other women. God knows how many he attacked over the last several years," she said smugly. "You could have prevented that."

"What about you?" Meg challenged.

"What about me?"

"You had tenure. Why didn't you speak up if you were so sure he'd attacked me? Where was your concern for other women then? For a graduate student?"

"An accusation from me without your willing input would have been dismissed as pure speculation."

Meg laughed derisively. "Right. That's precisely what it is now."

Madison glared at Meg for a moment and then smirked. "It just occurred to me that I may have underestimated you. Maybe you did make Stan pay—eventually. After all, who was in the room right after he died? Who had a better motive for murder? Poor Blake was probably a loose end. He figured out what Stan did to you, or that pig told him over a couple of scotches. You found out. Blake had to die so he wouldn't spill the beans."

"Shut up, Madison! "Shamus should see you now."

"You suppressed what Stan did to you for years. Lots of women do that. They don't think people will believe them. And they're usually right. Some blame themselves. Others are traumatized or fear their families will find out. Then one day they wake up older, wiser and it all comes rushing back." Madison's eyebrows arched. "Maybe for you it was payback time."

"This is bullshit."

Madison was rubbing her chin and smiling with self-satisfaction. "Jeffries would salivate over this information."

Meg's eyes darkened.

"No worries, Meg. Mum's the word."

Madison walked over to Meg and sat in front of her on the coffee table.

"But look at me."

Meg angrily obliged.

"You made the wrong decision years ago slinking off to your room, crying into your pillow."

"You're more loathsome than I thought," Meg seethed. "And my brother wants to protect you. He should protect himself."

"You're in a bind," Madison said. "I wouldn't want to be you. If you don't fess up and Jeffries finds out, you'll be his number one suspect. That would help a lot of us. If you do reveal your secret, all these long years later, some of us will feel pity. You'd hate that for sure. Others will wonder why you didn't take steps to protect women from Stan. Some men will fear that you've opened a Pandora's box, that women they've wronged will be out for blood now. It's a no win for you."

"And you're here to assure that I make the best decision for you."

"I'm just putting you on notice," Madison said. "Don't think for a moment that I won't use your secret to my advantage if I sense your little group has me in their sights."

Meg rose from the sofa, walked into her room, slammed the door behind her and sunk onto the bed. Madison was worse than she'd imagined. Perhaps she had been the one who'd placed the scarf in her briefcase. Meg struggled to remember whether she'd picked up the scarf from the restroom floor that night…dropped it when rushing across the hotel lobby. She imagined Madison deliciously picking it up. Yet, she hadn't mentioned it tonight when she'd had the chance to prove her claim and enhance her power. That was not like Madison.

CHAPTER TWENTY-ONE

As they strolled along Fifth Avenue, Denise smiled, appreciative, it seemed, of his efforts to leave Madison and Meg's altercation behind them for a few hours.

He guided her around a group of people who had stopped at a curbside just as everyone was about to cross. Two adults and a teenage girl were speaking Chinese. The teenager pointed to her eye with alarm. "My contact lens," she gasped. People froze in place and began searching the sidewalk. A woman holding a small child by the hand slowly knelt. She pointed. The teenage girl shyly stepped forward at the urging of her parents. She picked up the contact lens, looked at the woman and her child, and smiled sweetly. She stepped back to her parents. The three of them nodded in gratitude. Onlookers burst into applause. Then, as if nothing had happened, they moved along.

"That was very considerate," Denise said. "I expected more indifference in the Big Apple."

"Nah," Shamus said. He took her hand as they rushed across the street. "Lots of heart here. It just isn't always obvious." He'd no sooner finished his sentence than a man bumped into Denise nearly knocking her over. He didn't stop.

"Jerk," Shamus said.

The guy turned but kept moving.

"The key is to make people go around you," Shamus said.

"How?"

"Don't look at them. Pretend not to notice people. On the streets of New York City eye contact makes *you* the person who needs to move. So, avoid that. Look past people and they'll go around. Eight out of ten times it works."

Denise followed Shamus' advice, smiling victoriously as busy New Yorkers made way for her.

They reached Rockefeller Center and stopped to watch a curly-haired girl of about 10 on the ice rink captivate the crowd. Dressed in royal blue velvet, powder blue tights, and pristine white skates, she spun into the air and landed perfectly.

"I always wanted to skate like that," Denise said.

"Did you take lessons?"

"Oh yes. My father took me every Saturday for a year. I can get around a rink and do a few twirls, but that's all."

"Had I known," Shamus said, "I would have bought tickets. You'd be down there right now skating with the little girl, giving her a run for her money."

"I'd be lying on the ice," Denise said, "waiting for a chivalrous, handsome guy to help me up."

"I'd punch his lights out," Shamus said, trying to look fierce.

Denise laughed. "I've missed you. *This* you," she said, looking into his eyes.

Shamus took her hand. "I've missed you too."

They arrived at Grand Central Station, and Denise gazed up at the massive, blue ceiling studded with golden constellations and signs of the zodiac. "It's exquisite."

"That entire ceiling was constructed from the wrong perspective," Shamus said. "The model should have been pasted on the ceiling, but instead painters were looking down at it. To compensate, the Vanderbilt family told everyone that the ceiling had been painted from God's view."

"Clever," Denise said. "I've seen photos, but it's more beautiful in reality."

"And if you look over there next to Cancer the crab," Shamus enthused, "you'll see a dirty block area left to show us what the ceiling looked like before the 1998 restoration. It's mostly stained from nicotine."

"I should use that in my medical lectures."

"Good idea," Shamus said as he led her over to the ticket counter. "Supposedly the scheduled train times are always a minute off from the actual departures. Also, if you go over there," Shamus pointed, "you can whisper against the wall and someone at the opposite side of the station can hear you. I haven't done it, but we could sometime."

"It's a date," Denise said squeezing his hand.

They exited onto 42nd Street and headed for Third Avenue.

A tall waiter, dressed entirely in black, greeted them as they entered Osteria Laguna. He graciously took their coats and then guided them to a corner table.

If they closed their eyes and imagined being in Italy, the olfactory experience could not have been more authentic. Oregano, garlic, ripe tomatoes, calamari, and Chianti permeated their nostrils. Dean Martin was crooning softly in the background.

A chair against the wall was offered to Denise. The waiter, white napkin draped over his left arm, poured water from a light blue and gray earthenware jug.

"I am Luigi," he said with an Italian accent. "It will be my pleasure to serve you this evening." His eyes lingered appreciatively on Denise. He lit a table candle and with a slight bow, slipped away.

Shamus watched Denise take in the room. She was beautiful with dark, brown eyes and perfect skin rendered even more stunning by the soft candlelight. Her eyes met his. "You are lovely." He took her hand.

"You're looking quite handsome yourself."

Shamus studied her hand in silence for a few moments. "I'm sorry about earlier."

"I'm not upset about Madison," Denise assured. "She's frightened. I understand that."

"It must have looked like more than that when the elevator door opened."

"I'll admit to having been taken aback for a moment. But no harm done."

Luigi returned. They ordered calamari to share, salads, pastas and a bottle of Montepulciano. When the wine arrived, Luigi offered Denise the first taste and beamed at her evident satisfaction. He lifted her napkin, unfolded it and placed it gently in her lap before taking his leave.

"I think he likes you," Shamus whispered.

Denise watched Luigi serving another couple, paying special attention again to the young woman. "He has wandering eyes."

"Really?" Shamus looked behind him, but Luigi was on his way to the kitchen. He turned back to Denise. "I've always wondered what those look like."

"They glisten and shift ever so slightly while studying the target of their attention. In his case, the movement is charming, brief, and without offense."

"And what do you see in my eyes?"

"Tonight, I see Shamus. The man I fell in love with two years ago."

"I'm an idiot, Denise."

"No. You're just not ready."

"For what?"

"Loving someone. Unless I'm wrong and there's someone else."

"No. There's no one."

Their salads were delivered. Shamus tossed the greens on his plate absently.

"But you've met someone special?" Shamus ventured.

"Yes, I have."

"How long have you been seeing him?"

"Not long."

"A few months?"

"Less."

"He works fast."

"By comparison, indeed." She smiled.

"Got me there."

"You're like lava."

"Slow but hot?" Shamus teased.

"Something like that."

"So, what's his name?"

"Barry. He's a pediatrician."

"I suppose you'll have lots of babies then," Shamus replied off-handedly before placing some greens in his mouth.

"Why?" Denise asked bewildered.

"That's what pediatricians do. I assume it reassures their patients."

"That's quite a stereotype."

"Isn't it accurate?" Shamus asked, not fully appreciative of the thin ice on which he was treading.

"Barry doesn't want children."

Shamus' jaw dropped. "You're kidding. And you don't mind?"

"I'm not marrying him yet," Denise said with an edge in her voice.

"Yet," Shamus said.

Denise shrugged and began eating her salad.

"You love children. Look how great you are with Johnny."

"I love my career too," Denise said intently.

"C'mon," Shamus scoffed. "Two doctors can afford childcare."

"Barry doesn't want strangers bringing up his children."

Shamus' eyes widened. "That's pretty snobbish."

Denise set down her fork hard. "Snobbish?"

"Think about all the people who have to work? They can't say, nose in the air, 'I don't want strangers raising my children.' Besides, child-minders aren't strangers. Children get to know them. And, people raise their own children, childcare or not. Tell Barry that nobody stays home anymore watching the kids every minute. Those who don't work for pay do charitable things, exercise or help in schools while their young children are at daycare, with a babysitter or in an enrichment program."

"You don't even know Barry."

"Look at Meg," Shamus continued, oblivious to her growing irritation. "Johnny goes to daycare, but Meg doesn't neglect Johnny. Tell Barry that too."

Denise flushed indignantly. "I don't believe for a moment that Meg is giving Johnny short shrift. Barry would agree."

"It sounds to me like he wouldn't."

She leaned forward. "As usual, you're engaging your mouth before your brain."

Luigi approached. Denise sat back as he poured some wine into their glasses. He glanced at Shamus, his expression suggesting a change of approach.

Denise fidgeted with her napkin and looked around the room. She was fuming.

Shamus shook his head with self-admonishment. "I'm sorry, Denise. This whole conference is getting to me."

"It isn't the conference," she said, her eyes locked on his.

"What is it then?" Shamus asked. "You appear to be the expert. Tell me."

"You are angry because you don't like me dating Barry. Fine. Why not say so?"

"You're the one who couldn't wait until we worked things out," Shamus snapped.

"This is ridiculous," Denise said. She tossed her napkin on the table. "I'm not hungry."

"Great," Shamus said sarcastically as he signaled for the bill.

"What am I supposed to do, Shamus? Wait until you're sure? Wait until there's nothing going on in our lives to serve as an excuse for delay? Is that what you want?"

"You could have taken a job at Yale or the University of Connecticut," Shamus rebuffed. "Then we'd be together. Yet, I'm the one who's afraid of intimacy."

"So, I'm being selfish?"

"I didn't say that."

"You just did."

"As a doctor, you have options anywhere you want to go. What would I do out in California? Start over?"

"They build and remodel homes in California too, Shamus," she said exasperated. "We've had this conversation many times before."

Shamus threw his napkin on the table.

Denise stood. "I'm going to the restroom."

Luigi arrived. He looked around to see if other diners were listening. "Love is not easy, my friend." He patted Shamus on the back. "But you are, how do you say in English, 'your best enemy'?"

"Worst enemy," Shamus corrected him glumly.

Luigi nodded sympathetically. "Yes, that's right. You are not the first man or the last to be so stubborn." They watched Denise weaving her way through the tables. Luigi leaned to whisper. "Such a beautiful woman will not wait forever."

Police Interview: Belinda Mayfield

"If I were Meg Doherty and had found two dead bodies, I'd be on my way back to California. But she's loyal to this organization. I wouldn't be surprised if the person who murdered Stan and Blake chose to do so when she was around. You know, out of some sort of misplaced animosity, so she'd take the rap. I mean, what else could explain her being there both times?"

CHAPTER TWENTY-TWO

Meg tried to sleep. It was no use. Arguing with Madison had awakened the beast. She could sense the horrific memory of that night forcing its way to the forefront of her mind. She closed her eyes again, pushing back. It didn't work. There was Stan Evans hovering menacingly over her, then crushing her against the cubicle wall, holding both her wrists with one of his hands. His other circled her throat. She fought, but he was insane with anger. He braced his body against hers and covered her mouth before lifting her skirt. She wrenched an arm free and scraped his face with her nails, kneed him in the groin and punched him in the gut. Nothing could stop him. Hatred fueled his advances until she had nothing left.

When it was over, she fell to the floor. He knelt beside her on one knee. "You won't tell anyone. Not a soul. Not unless you want worse next time." He shoved her with his foot like a dead carcass. "No one does that to me. No one walks out on me."

The door creaked open and slammed shut. She remained for several minutes on the cold tile floor in disbelief, hatred of him and self-loathing. Her legs were wrapped around a toilet bowl, like an abandoned, broken doll.

She sat up in the bed, her heart pounding so hard it hurt. Madison had been right about one thing—Stan should have suffered for what he'd done.

But there'd been no witnesses, she reminded herself. She'd also gone willingly to his apartment. That would have been used against her in court, and he would have walked free; time served, at best. Every woman knows that risk. Otherwise, why would so many say nothing?

Before that night, there'd been no doubt in her mind about what *she* would do in such a situation: expose her attacker so that he'd live condemned by others, imprisoned, never able to harm another human being.

Meg breathed deeply. *Had Madison really been in the lobby?* Meg asked herself. She could imagine her leaning against the reception desk, watching as Meg ran to the stairwell.

How different things might have turned out, Meg thought, had Madison come to her aid that night. She brushed away tears. No point in blaming anyone else. She had failed to get past her shock and embarrassment in order to make Stan pay. Humiliating him with a reanalysis of his data and trying to unseat him as editor were feeble forms of restitution. She knew that now. There was only one person to blame for Stan living without fear for years after that night. Only one.

Police Interview: Rod Cranville

"The people here didn't know Professor Evans like I did. He was a genius. And geniuses are temperamental. They're focused. They don't have time for niceties. He withdrew regard as quickly as he gave it. So, I understand the anger, even hatred some people had for him. But there were moments when he looked at me and saw promise. I lived for those."

CHAPTER TWENTY-THREE

Idiot! Shamus told himself as he paced. *You should call Denise, apologize, and suggest a bicoastal relationship, six months in California and six months in Connecticut.*

His mind was spinning with questions. What had he been thinking? He'd stayed at her Santa Monica home a few times only blocks from Palisades Park overlooking Pacific Coast Highway and the beach; just a fifteen-minute walk to the pier, where they'd gone on the rides and eaten cotton candy. They'd strolled up and down Montana Avenue. It was beautiful. You could practically fall out the front door of her condo and into a coffee shop. So, what was his problem? He could use the time when she was at work to generate spring and fall jobs for his crew back in Connecticut, develop the website he'd always wanted, and maybe take a course or two while he looked for construction work in Los Angeles.

If she didn't get a half-year position at a hospital in Connecticut right away, she could take time off. *Why didn't I think of that before? She probably hasn't had a real break in years. She deserves one.*

His cell phone rang. It also buzzed insistently as if familiar with his predilection to ignore it. He begrudgingly looked at the number display. The caller was not someone in his contact list. He was negligent about keeping it updated and so many people who called him were "unknown."

"Shamus here," he said.

"Sounds like you had a bad day," Penelope said.

"Hey. Hi. I just hate phones."

"You wouldn't last long in my job."

"Barely in mine. Clients call anytime nowadays. Pisses me off."

Penelope laughed. "I need to see you."

"Not in that laundry room cabinet. Sorry."

"No. I'm in the corner of the bar looking at the seat where Blake Packard died. Come join me. Now, please."

"What's the rush?"

"There's a late meeting tonight. You'll want to know about it. I suspect your sister will be there."

"No. She's in bed for the night."

"Really?"

"Yes. I checked."

"Well, she must have a twin then, because she walked by the bar three minutes ago."

"Damn it!"

"The meeting is on the QT. That's all I'm going to tell you on the phone. If you're not here in five minutes, I'm gone."

"I'll be there."

He tiptoed through the living room where Madison was asleep.

"What? Who's there?" Madison cried out, startled.

"It's just me," Shamus whispered. "Go back to sleep."

"You scared the crap out of me. What are you doing up? What time is it?"

Madison switched on a light by the sofa. She rubbed her eyes, blinked and looked blearily at him.

"Why did you set up out here?" Shamus asked. "Take my room. I don't mind sleeping on the sofa."

"I don't want to impose," Madison yawned.

"Just go in there. It's not an imposition."

"Maybe tomorrow night," she said.

"I'd argue with you, but I've got to go somewhere. Rashid is two doors down on this side and Denise is two doors past that. If you get spooked, just knock on one of their doors."

"Oh, sure. Like I'm going to knock on Rashid's door. Your sister already thinks I'm after the guy."

"What?"

"Forget it. I'll be fine."

He waited for her to double lock the door before he headed to the elevators. On the way down, a thought occurred to him. *If Wesley was indeed staying with his parents during the conference, why had he been in the elevator the morning Stan was killed? Why had he already been in the elevator when he and Meg stepped in?*

The elevator opened at the lobby. He entered the bar and headed toward the back. Penelope was seated in a booth. Her hair was neatly tied back, tiny curls encircling her face. She was wearing earrings, and a touch of make-up.

"You look very nice this evening."

Penelope shrugged dismissively. "The assistant professor gripe group is going to meet in about five minutes."

"Where did they get that label?"

"I came up with it myself."

"And how did you know about them? More to the point, how did you know I knew about them?"

"I'm an *investigative* reporter," she said. "We investigate. I can't wait around for you to tell me everything."

"Ah. So, what do you suggest?" Shamus asked. "We can't just waltz into the meeting."

"No. But we can find out who does."

"How?"

"I planted cameras above the door."

"That must be illegal," Shamus said.

"It's a public meeting room. Besides, think of all the phone and other recording devices that people bring into conference meetings."

"That's different."

"We're after a murderer. He may go into that room."

"He could also be in Bermuda by now."

"Then why is Jeffries still here? He may be a lot of things, but stupid isn't one of them. If the police are focused on this hotel, then the murderer is likely still here. Jeffries wants badly to land this one because it will make him famous. He won't waste a moment of his time."

"From what I observed at the precinct when his boss was down his throat, it will keep him from getting fired."

"You didn't tell me that you were there," Penelope snapped. "We're supposed to be sharing information. Remember?"

"Why do you dislike Jeffries?" Shamus asked. "C'mon, tell me. I can keep a secret."

"I'm sure you can as long as it doesn't affect your sister or your entourage."

"Entourage?"

"The tall, sinuous professor, the lovely young doctor, and your buddy Rashid."

"That's not an answer."

"Jeffries hates reporters unless they do his bidding. If you want information from him, you have to write the story his way."

"So? That's probably how most detectives want things to go."

"It's dishonest and self-serving." Jaw set, her eyes warned him to drop the subject.

Shamus remained silent.

"Okay. Take the stairwell to the third floor," Penelope said. "The meeting is there. You'll find me in room 307. Keep a low profile."

Without waiting for a reply, Penelope bolted out of the bar toward the stairwell. Her body language had been clear. He could be there or not; it was his choice. He shook his head. He had to hand it to her. She had spunk to burn.

As Meg walked down the center aisle of the meeting room, Wesley, Sidney, Emma and an unfamiliar professor gathered near the podium and stared disapprovingly at her. Clearly, Emma was one of them now—barely out of graduate school, yet edging into the company of the discontented. To Meg's way of thinking, it was a waste. Emma's dissertation had been impressive. It was foolish of her to take sides so early in her career. The dissertation award was a ticket into the inner circle, at least for a while.

Wesley started to walk over to Meg. Sidney touched Wesley's arm and whispered to him. Wesley glowered at Meg. He'd told her not to come. She looked away.

"Fine," Meg mumbled to herself. "Be like that. Let Sidney maneuver you like a puppet."

She scanned the room. A scowling professor whom she'd met briefly the year before was looking straight ahead. She struggled to remember his name. His face was angular, his nearly emaciated body rigid. Whenever she'd seen him, he'd always looked unshaven, lips tight in anger, eyes beads of resentment. His arms were wrapped around a briefcase. She wondered what contents could possibly warrant such protection. Suddenly, he glared at her. Chilled, she quickly turned away.

Shamus climbed the stairs to the third-floor landing. He opened the stairwell door slowly. Seeing no one, he slipped out and found room 307. He knocked lightly. The door opened. A man in his late twenties with unkempt dark hair wearing a wrinkled white shirt gestured for Shamus to enter. Penelope was sitting in front of a computer screen. She turned and beckoned him to take a seat next to her.

"This is Ray DeVito," she said. "He's the king of tech around here. Couldn't do without him."

Ray didn't look up, but Shamus delivered a half-nod greeting, and sat down beside Penelope. "Friendly sort," he whispered.

"Don't mind him. He doesn't like intruders."

"Is that what I am?" Shamus asked bemused. "I recall being invited."

"Not by Ray. But, don't worry. He'll get used to you."

She returned her attention to the computer screen. There were about two dozen young men and women milling around a room.

"Where is this taking place?" Shamus asked.

"Not far from here," Penelope replied.

"Have you seen Meg?"

"Yes. She's there." Penelope turned to Ray. "I need more volume. I can't hear a thing."

Ray tapped away on his keyboard and the volume increased.

"Thanks," Penelope said. "Ray and I have been working together for years. He can hide cameras where even the most seasoned detectives can't find them."

"Good to have that kind of talent working for you."

"Yep," Penelope said. "And lean as he looks, he can beat the shit out of anyone who tries to get in our way."

"Good to know."

Meg appeared on the screen. She was shaking hands with two people seated beside her.

Penelope said, "I'm starting to like her. She's gutsy."

"Oh, she's gutsy alright. Maybe a little too gutsy."

"It beats being a petunia in an onion patch. Look at her take a seat in the front row! She wants them to know they can't just push her out. She was one of the founders of this gripe group. She's asserting her leadership."

"Those three guys over there don't look happy about it."

"One of them is Sidney Jorgensen," Penelope said. "The others are Alex Pate and Ted Arsenault."

"You do your homework," Shamus said admiringly.

"Yep."

Sidney stood and faced the group. "Let's start," he said. The room quieted. "We are here tonight to continue our efforts to remove long-term editors from their lofty perches from which they have blocked the tenure hopes of aspiring assistant professors."

Meg stood.

"It should be said that the original goal of this group was to nudge Stan out as editor," Meg said. "Nothing more."

"You aren't running things here," Sidney said.

"I'm not going to stand by while you or anyone turns a well-intentioned goal into a witch hunt."

"Yes!" Penelope said, punching the air.

"No petunia there," Shamus said in a manner not altogether pleased with his sister sticking her neck out.

"Do you recognize any of the people in the audience?" Penelope asked.

"A few by name and some by sight," Shamus said with his eyes glued to the computer screen.

"Write down the names of the ones you know and where they're sitting," Penelope said as she handed him a pad and pen.

"What's Wesley's problem?" Shamus wondered aloud. "He's glaring at Meg."

"I saw the two of them arguing earlier," Penelope said. "I couldn't make out much of what they were saying, but I heard him tell her not to attend this meeting."

"Ingrate," Ray muttered.

"What do you think of Wesley?" Penelope asked Shamus.

"He's a spoiled, rich kid. Supposedly he is staying at his parent's city apartment during the conference. Yet, the morning Stan was killed he got on the elevator at a higher floor than Meg and me. So, he may well have stayed at the hotel the previous night."

"You don't say." Penelope's eyebrows arched with interest. She looked over at Ray who nodded begrudgingly, as if admitting to some value in Shamus' presence.

Emma stood. "What about the other journal editors that have been hogging their seats for half our lifetimes?"

"She's right," Wesley said. "The imperious Madison Wills for one?"

Emma nodded adamantly and sat.

A nervous young man stood up. "I get my Ph.D. this year. I won't be able to find a job unless my work is accepted by one of our leading journals. If not, I'll be teaching part-time at three different universities to make ends meet. There's more work for this group to do. And now!"

A woman of short stature stood. "Most of you know me. I'm Karina Woods, assistant professor at Rutgers." She looked at Meg. "I have a lot of respect for you, Meg. But I came to this meeting to finish what you started. We need to get editors removed. Like Jonathan just said, for some of us it has to happen now."

"Two of our colleagues have been murdered," Meg said to Karina. "And the killer may be using our group as a cover. We have to consider that."

"Jesus Christ!" Shamus said. He threw his hands into the air. "What the hell is she doing mentioning that? The murderer might actually be in their midst. Is she trying to make herself a target?"

Penelope motioned for him to be quiet.

Shamus leaned over Penelope, placing his hand on the back of her chair. He sensed Ray glaring at him and removed his hand.

"The police know about this group," Meg said, "and that makes us all persons of interest."

"How do they know?" Wesley sniped. "Did you tell them?"

"You know better," Meg shot back.

"I'd like to pop him one," Shamus said through clenched teeth.

"We need to take the debate public," Meg continued. "We can't give safe harbor to a murderer no matter how important our mission. This has to be our last clandestine meeting."

"What it should be is *your* last meeting," Emma called.

Meg retorted with a disapproving frown.

"Anyone who wants to stay in this group, get in touch with me," Wesley said as he jotted his email address on a whiteboard. "I won't share any of your names and the time and location of the next meeting will be kept under wraps by all of us." He looked squarely at Meg. "Anyone who already has tenure is not invited."

Police Interview: Karina Woods

"I only went to that meeting to see what was going on. It was my first time. Meg snapped at me for saying something needs to be done to get close-minded, ancient editors to move on. She's no angel, I'll tell you that. Some people feel sorry for her having found Stan and then Blake dead. Not me. I wonder what she did to deserve it."

CHAPTER TWENTY-FOUR

Meg slipped quietly into her room, past Madison sleeping on the sofa. She closed the door and sat on her bed.

Wesley was the only one she trusted that night after Stan had attacked her. He held her and listened without judgment. He tried to convince her to go to the hospital for a rape kit, but she refused.

"Do you know how many untested rape kits there are in this country?" Meg asked. "Have you any idea?"

"But this is different. You know who did this."

"Wake up, Wesley! Only about three in a hundred rapists are convicted."

Wesley held up his hands in frustration. "Hey, I'm not the bad guy here."

She stared at him, blistering anger almost consuming her. Then she lowered her head. "I'm sorry."

He filled an ice bucket, wrapped some of the ice in a towel and held it on the back of her neck. Then, with a wet, warm facecloth he gently wiped the dried blood from her face and arms. All night, he stayed awake, caressing her head and holding her hand. Near dawn, she slept, knowing he was there.

"I'll check in on you," he promised before leaving. "Call me, and I'll be back here in a heartbeat."

She smiled as best she could, then cupped his wrists. "You can't say anything to Stan. Don't even look at him in an angry way," she pleaded, eyes latched on his. "He can't sense that you know."

Wesley turned away from her and shook his head.

"Do this for me, Wesley," she urged when his eyes had met hers again. "Please, at least for now."

"Listen, Meg. I know you worked too hard and for too long to take the chance that people will think less of you. But they won't. It's him they'll despise, even more than they do now."

She put her arms around his waist, her head on his chest. "Trust me on this, Wesley."

He remained conflicted, arms stiffly at his side, then slowly placed them around her. "Okay. We'll do this your way for now. But if he were here at this moment, I'd kill him."

"Don't say that, Wesley. Don't even think it."

After he left, she leaned against the door feeling more alone than ever before. The world closed in. All previous concerns were absent. There was only now, only this.

She and Wesley never spoke about that night again.

She put her feet up and reclined against the pillows. Once, her father had held up five fingers and told her, "If you have this many enduring friendships in life, you're a rich person." She'd been annoyed by that. Unlike her father and Shamus, she'd been sociable. She was sure she'd have many dear friends for life. But her father had turned out to be right. Priorities, values, partners, proximity and even politics had gotten in the way. Internet social networks provided a semblance of connection, but true intimacy had become ephemeral.

This made losing Wesley as a friend even more painful. *What had happened? When had disagreement become disdain? Why was he suddenly siding with the likes of Sidney, humiliating her in front of someone he'd always despised?* She tried to push such questions from her mind. There were no answers. Obsessing was only making matters worse.

139

CHAPTER TWENTY-FIVE

As a child, Shamus saw a young man stand up in a roller coaster. While friends egged him on, the man waved to people on the ground. Then he wobbled. Trying to regain his balance, he lurched forward and back, arms flailing as the coaster approached a tight curve. His seatmate reached out, but the man keeled over. He bounced off the superstructure, then plunged to the ground. Shamus heard the thud, the screams, and saw the horror on the onlookers' faces. Since that day, vertiginous stairwells, indeed all heights, had posed a problem for him. Growing dizzy, he moved back from the open stair rail and began his descent.

Below, a stairwell door opened and then shut followed by a change in the air pressure. He stopped, listening for footsteps, worried that he might run into Jeffries. Hearing nothing, he resumed his descent, then again paused to listen. Someone was climbing the stairs below him. Gripping the rail, he peered down and saw a man two floors below. In no time, the man appeared on the landing several steps from Shamus. He stood stock still, head down. In his late twenties or early thirties, he was wearing a blue cap, black windbreaker, jeans and runners. Slowly, he raised his head, but the cap cast a shadow over much of his face. Something shiny was in his left hand.

"Shit! I forgot my glasses," Shamus exclaimed as he turned and rushed back up the steps. When he reached for the handle, the man was right behind him. The door flew open, slamming Shamus into the wall.

"My God!" Rashid exclaimed, reaching for Shamus as he fell to the floor. "What happened? Who was that?"

"I don't know. I think he was going to rob me." Shamus grabbed Rashid's arm and got to his feet.

"You must tell hotel security!"

"He might have been exercising or just in a hurry to get somewhere. Why make a mountain out of a molehill?"

"There is no molehill here," Rashid insisted. "That man ran like a rat back to his burrow. Someone else might not be as lucky as you. There is no choice."

Rashid helped Shamus through the door to a bench in the hallway.

"I think he had a knife. I don't know. It could have been a reflection off something else in his hand. It all happened so fast."

"No more stairwells," Rashid said. "What if I hadn't heard your voice? This is New York City. You're out of your element. No more amateur sleuthing, which is, no doubt, what you were doing. Let Detectives Jeffries and Krawski do their jobs. You, my friend, could be dead right now."

After submitting the security form at the front desk, Shamus headed for the lobby bar. Madison and Emma passed by without noticing him. They were squabbling. Just another academic tiff over something inconsequential, Shamus assumed.

The lighting in the bar was brighter than he remembered, undoubtedly a wise post-murder decision by the management. Penelope was sitting in a booth. Arms crossed on the table top, intensely focused and poised for battle, she glared across at Detective Jeffries poking his finger at her like a demented woodpecker.

Penelope didn't flinch. Whatever Jeffries wanted, she was refusing. She pushed his hand away. Jeffries hunched forward, his face only inches from hers.

"Ah," said Shamus, approaching them. "Two of my favorite people."

Jeffries sat back, clearly irritated by the interruption. Penelope looked at Shamus, anger at Jeffries etched on her face.

"I hope I'm not intruding," Shamus said, sliding in next to Penelope.

"The detective is accusing me of withholding vital information," Penelope said.

"I was referring to the time-honored tradition of the press helping with murder investigations," Jeffries snarled.

"I don't share sources. You can lock me up and the story will just get bigger."

"Are you imagining that you're Woodward or Bernstein?" Jeffries huffed. "You're not and this isn't Watergate."

"The press cooperation thing is a matter of debate," Shamus offered much to Jeffries' chagrin. "Withholding crucial evidence could be morally objectionable, and some judges might even consider it a crime. But then there's the First Amendment. So at what point," he asked Jeffries, "does Penelope have a greater obligation to you than to her sources?"

"Kiss my ass, Doherty."

"Detective Jeffries thinks I know something about a group of young college professors who met in secret earlier this evening."

"Were you there?" Shamus asked Penelope, eyebrows raised in feigned innocence.

"No."

"Maybe your sister knows about it." Jeffries said. "I hear they want to force some journal editors out of their jobs?"

"You'd have to ask her."

"I'll do that."

Kathleen Kelley Reardon

"But first," Shamus interjected, "you could ask yourself why a tenured professor would bother with a group like that. Just to save yourself some time."

"Careful," Penelope said. "Detective Jeffries keeps track of affronts. The only ones he forgives are his own."

"Consider yourself warned," Jeffries said to Penelope. "I'm investigating two murders. You don't want to get in the way."

She began jotting in her pad.

"What are you writing?" Jeffries demanded.

"'Consider yourself warned,'" Penelope read back.

"If you print that…"

Penelope wrote again.

"Detective," Shamus said, "there are more productive ways to talk to reporters. She could help you become police commissioner someday."

Jeffries stood, placed his large hands on the table and leaned toward them.

"There is a murderer on the loose. If you withhold any evidence pertinent to this investigation…"

"…You'll be the last to know," Penelope shot back.

Jeffries eyed her, breathed deeply as if composing himself, stood erect and stormed off.

"You were pretty hard on him."

"I have to go somewhere." Penelope said, gathering her things.

He stepped from the booth. She edged past, stopped suddenly and turned. Her eyes met his. "Thanks," she said with a short smile, "for having my back."

As Shamus was waiting to order a Coke at the bar, he noticed Penelope had not gotten far. She was with Ray. Both looked angry.

"You need to talk to Jeffries," Ray was telling her. "You have to get this whole thing behind you."

"Stay out of it, Ray. Just because I shared with you doesn't give you license to fix my life."

"But you're letting your hostility influence your reporting. That's not professional and it isn't you."

"I have to go."

"Look, you're a great reporter," Ray continued. "But you're not being objective. I get that he was terrible at being a father, and you hate him for leaving your mother and you. But if you can't maintain objectivity, you need to get off this story."

"Drop it, Ray."

"I'm only trying to help."

There was a moment of silence, the two eyeing each other. Penelope lowered her head and seemed to be considering an apology. Instead, she squeezed Ray's forearm and walked away.

Police Interview: Ray DeVito

"I have nothing to say except that as a journalist I have every right to be here and you are only badgering me to get at Penelope. I know the story, detective. Penelope's mother got so depressed that she was in and out of hospitals after you ran out on them. Do you have any idea what that does to a child? Haven't you ever had something so bad happen in your life that it sticks in your craw forever? I guess not or you'd take a different tone with her."

CHAPTER TWENTY-SIX

Shamus returned to the hotel suite around 9 p.m. Meg wasn't around. Madison had left a note saying she was going for a swim.

"Alone?" Shamus irritably mumbled to himself.

Not long afterward, he entered the pool locker room. He heard splashing. Suddenly, it turned to frantic slapping. He rushed to the pool area. At the far end, a fully clothed man, face tinged green from the Jacuzzi's reflection was crouched down holding something under water. A woman's arm pushed through the foam grabbing for the man's face.

"Hey!" Shamus ran toward the Jacuzzi. The assailant looked up and scrambled to his feet, the wet floor nearly taking him down. He was headed to an emergency exit. Madison surfaced and clung to the side of Jacuzzi, gasping for breath. Shamus hauled her out.

"I'm all right."

Her assailant was nearly to the door when Shamus caught up, tackled him at the waist, and brought him down hard. The man pulled one leg free and kicked the side of Shamus' face

Shamus caught his foot and jerked hard with a forceful twisting motion, like tearing a cross brace out of a stud wall. The man yelped in pain. He kicked out and delivered a cracking blow to Shamus' jaw, sending him across the wet floor. The man inched toward his prey, this time with a gravity knife in hand. Shamus got to his feet. The glittering serpentine blade caught him in the stomach just as he grabbed his attacker's arm with a grip born of years of construction work. They struggled. The knife flew across the wet floor and skittered into the pool.

Madison drew closer to them, hunched down, phone in hand. "In here! Help!" she called.

Male voices echoed from the locker room. Shamus looked up as the emergency exit door slammed shut. Blood, his own, was oozing down his right leg onto the floor. He dropped to his knees and pressed his hands to his belly. The room spun, he lifted his head, closed his eyes and pitched over into the pool.

A medicinal odor sliced through Shamus' nostrils. He gagged and opened his eyes. Meg was sitting beside the bed looking tired and worried.

"Thank God," she said as a tear ran down her cheek.

"Hey." Shamus managed a weak smile.

Denise came into the room wearing a white lab coat.

"What are you doing here?" Shamus asked, slurring his words.

"That's a fine hello," Denise remonstrated warmly. "It's good to have you back among the living."

Shamus tried to rise then fell right back, grimacing in pain.

"You don't want to do that for a while," Denise said, taking his hand.

"How long was I out?"

"At least three hours," Meg said.

"Mostly due to the painkiller in that drip," Denise explained "It could have been much worse. You're lucky the blade didn't penetrate further. You lost a fair amount of blood and you'll be sore for a while, but you won't require surgery."

Jeffries entered the room.

"He needs to rest," Denise said firmly.

"I won't keep him long."

"It's okay, Denise," Shamus said with a weak wave.

"Tell me about the guy," Jeffries said. "What color were his skin, hair, and eyes? How tall? What was he wearing? Madison Wills is drawing a blank."

"White, about thirty-five, my height, muscular, tattooed wrists, black hair, brown leather jacket. Expensive, I think. And he was as strong as an ox."

"Did he say anything?"

"Lots of grunting. That's all."

Shamus shifted in the bed, cringing.

"And his face?"

"Too much reflection from the Jacuzzi and pool," Shamus mumbled.

Denise shot Jeffries a warning look. He was wearing out his welcome.

"Let's leave it at that for now. But we'll get you and Miss Wills with sketch artists tomorrow and then you can look at some photos."

Meg dozed fitfully in the chair next to Shamus' bed. She couldn't extricate her mind from what happened to him. When that horror was sufficiently bludgeoned for its uselessness, she still couldn't relax. She found herself dwelling on the note from her briefcase. It had been unsigned. Only five words read: *I know it was you.*

Her phone vibrated. She retrieved it from her jeans pocket and looked at the screen. It was Wesley. She answered.

"God, I heard what happened! Are Shamus and Madison okay?"

"Madison went back to the hotel after being treated. She's shaken but she'll be fine. Shamus is doing better now."

"Thank God."

"Which Wesley is this?" Meg asked flatly.

"Guess I had that coming."

"I'm exhausted. My brother could have died. I can't talk now."

"I know. I just wanted to say one thing. I was being stupid and selfish yesterday."

Meg said nothing.

"I'm desperate about tenure, Meg."

"Desperate enough to put a blood-stained scarf in my briefcase?"

"What?"

"Yesterday. Was that you?"

"My God, no!"

"You were the only person with me that night after… I was wearing it."

"Meg, you can't actually think I kept your scarf all these years for some nefarious purpose?"

"I have to go," Meg said. "We can talk later."

"Wait."

"I need to be with Shamus now," Meg insisted.

"But you should know, Meg, that our differences right now don't affect any secrets between us."

Meg was silent.

"Did you hear me, Meg?"

"Yes, Wesley, I heard you."

"I'm here for you. Keep that in mind."

Meg ended the call and stared unsettled at the ceiling. Wesley had protected her secret like an impregnable safe. He alone knew what she had suffered, and the depth of her mortification. She had no recollection of him having the scarf, nor of it being in the hotel room where he'd stayed that night to comfort her. He was more than desperate about publishing. But surely, he wouldn't stoop so low. He was better than that. She sat upright. *Then why had he just told her that her secret was still safe? Why reassure her of that now? Wasn't he supposed to keep it safe forever?*

After returning from the hospital, Meg paced her hotel room. The lack of sleep, the note and her feeling of emotional isolation exacerbated her insecurity about being away from Johnny. Always, her first thoughts in a crisis were of her son, the tenuous nature of life and what it would mean for him if an accident were to befall her. Not being able to see him grow up was the worst nightmare of all. Before Johnny's birth, she'd heard people talk about the bond between parents and their children; that they'd never known such love. She thought she'd understood. But she hadn't, not really.

At least Johnny was with Robert — every bit the father to Johnny he'd promised to be, taking him places when he could get time off from his medical practice. How much Meg wanted him here right now, his arms around her. He'd fly out immediately if she were to tell him that. He'd asked her twice to marry him. Both times she'd asked for more time. Two decades her senior, a failed marriage with Denise's mother, he knew not to rush. She hadn't yet told him about that night. Perhaps soon she would. Until then, marrying him would feel like a deceit. She'd be holding back something that had changed her life. Several times she'd considered telling him. But each time she'd stopped short.

She tapped the Skype icon on her computer. Robert was online, a green check next to his photo. A few rings, and he appeared on her screen with Johnny sitting on his lap. Meg brightened instantly.

"You two look very happy," she said.

"We are, aren't we, Johnny?" Robert said, tickling the toddler.

"Give Mommy a big kiss," Meg said.

Johnny leaned forward, giggled and placed his lips smack on Robert's computer screen. When he moved back, Meg threw him a kiss. Robert reached to catch it and placed it on Johnny's lips. The toddler burst into laughter.

"We went to the park, played on the swings, visited the marine museum in San Pedro and walked on the beach today," Robert said.

"I play ball," Johnny added.

"Oh, yes, that's right. Johnny played ball with another boy at the beach."

"Mommy?"

"Yes?"

"I miss you."

"Mommy misses you too, sweetheart."

"Come home," he said pouting.

"I will, honey. Do you want me to bring home a new ball?"

"Yes," Johnny said bouncing.

"A rugby ball, like Robert used to play?"

"Yup."

A cat walked on Robert's keyboard, pausing to sniff the screen and regard Meg with regal green eyes.

"Hello Sunny," Meg laughed.

"Mow," Sunny replied.

"Seems she misses you too," Robert said, picking up the purring feline and moving her to the side of the computer. Sunny was having none of it. Back she came onto the keyboard.

"She has a mind of her own," Robert said, placing Sunny on the floor.

"I feed her," Johnny boasted.

"She must love that," Meg said. "Will you do me a favor, Johnny? Will you take care of Robert and Sunny for a few more days until mommy gets home?"

Johnny nodded solemnly. "I miss you, mommy."

"I know, honey. Just a few more days."

"We're in good hands," Robert said. "But I'm worried about you and how tired you look, Meg. Denise is keeping me informed of things, but I'm worried."

"I'm okay. I'll call you later. I just need a hug," Meg said, smiling at Johnny who was petting Sunny. "Let's hug."

They hugged their computers and reluctantly signed off, leaving Meg's heart 3,000 miles away.

She sat still, allowing her longing to hold Johnny dissipate somewhat. A part of her was always with him.

Shamus awoke disoriented. The throbbing pain in his head refreshed his memory of the previous evening's events. The pain medicine had worn off and his entire body ached. He turned the flat hospital pillows lengthwise and leaned against them. With great effort he reached for his phone on his serving table.

"Hello?"

"Hi, Madison, it's Shamus."

"How are you? I've been so worried about you."

"More importantly, how are you doing?"

"I feel better. They tell me I didn't suffer any major damage."

"You sure put up one hell of a fight."

"You're the one who decked the guy."

"To be totally accurate, I was decked in the process."

"You saved my life, Shamus."

He was silent for a moment. Then said, "I'm hoping to get out of here today."

"Isn't that awfully early?"

"My face might look like Halloween came early, but the gut wound wasn't deep. They wanted to watch me overnight. I accommodated them. But I can't stay here doing nothing."

"I know the feeling. I'm preparing for a session later today. They assigned me an officer to tag along. Apparently, Jeffries finally thinks being an editor makes me a target. Anyway, I feel safer."

"Do you remember much about the man who attacked you?"

"It happened too fast."

"Why didn't you run away?" Shamus asked.

"What?"

"When I was fighting with him. If he'd knocked me out, he could have killed you."

"Listen to you in a hospital bed worrying about me," Madison laughed.

Shamus turned somewhat to ease the pain. "Just be careful."

She said nothing for a moment. "I won't forget what you did for me, Shamus. Never."

Police Interview: Ted Arsenault

"Look, I don't care what Phelps told you. You browbeat him. Just understand that me getting on editors' shit lists would be career suicide. Literally, my job is in their hands. I seek to please them, not antagonize them. I'm not stupid."

CHAPTER TWENTY-SEVEN

Shamus took a seat in the session room where Madison would soon be presenting.

"Is that seat taken?" Wesley asked, pointing to one next to Shamus.

"No," Shamus said begrudgingly.

"I can sit elsewhere."

"I said it's not taken," Shamus said gruffly. "That means you can sit there."

Wesley stepped around Shamus and sat down. "You don't look good. You should still be in the hospital."

"I'm fine," Shamus snapped.

"Did I do something to get on your wrong side?"

Shamus looked directly at Wesley. "I thought you and Meg were friends."

"We are."

"I saw you and her arguing. It didn't look the least bit friendly."

"We're scholars. We argue about theories and research. It can get heated."

"Right," Shamus scoffed. "I've seen Meg when she gets a bug in her bonnet about some academic topic. This was different."

Wesley looked up at Meg sitting at the panel table talking to a fellow presenter. Shamus' eyes followed. She smiled at them and returned to her conversation.

"See? We're not arguing anymore."

Shamus kept his eyes on the presenters.

"Listen, I seem to have gotten on several people's bad side," Wesley said apologetically. "My parents live part time here in the city. They know about what's happened here. They want to invite you and Meg to a home-cooked dinner tonight. It will get both of you away from this hotel and all the tension. Rashid and Denise are invited too. My parents like Meg. They feel it's the least they can do, given all the both of you have been through."

"Meg won't be up for visiting anyone," Shamus said.

"She refused at first, but then my mother called her. Now she's inclined to go if you will. The food will be wonderful. It's just over the bridge in Brooklyn. Why not?"

"Sorry. I can't leave Madison here."

"Of course not, she's invited too."

Shamus looked at Meg, who was perusing her notes. She did need a break. Besides, he realized, it wasn't his decision to make.

"I'll tell you what. If Meg really wants to go, and not because your mother twisted her arm, I'll go along if Rashid, Denise, and Madison join us. If anyone refuses, we'll have to pass."

Wesley nodded. "Fair enough."

It was decided that getting out of the hotel and eating home-cooked food would be good for everyone. If the evening became less than Wesley had promised, the hotel was a taxi drive away.

"As it turns out," Wesley said with a broad smile when the limo had pulled away from the curb, "my parents suddenly had to go to our Greenwich, Connecticut home. They didn't want to cancel dinner, and so the surprise is that we will be taking a helicopter there." He looked out the window. "It's a clear, crisp night to be in the sky,"

Shamus looked at Rashid who shrugged as if to say, *We're here now. Might as well make the best of it.* Denise frowned in Wesley's direction, shook her head with annoyance, but said nothing. Meg was gazing out the window and Madison gestured half-hearted agreement with Rashid.

They arrived at the East 34th Street Heliport as a sleek, silver helicopter was fighting a sudden icy wind. Their limo pulled in next to several others behind the blast-fence.

"My father has been using this helicopter service for much of his adult life," Wesley said, beaming like a ten-year old boy. "I've flown in them myself many times. On such a clear night, even with the wind, the flight will be magical. You'll see. You've never truly experienced the beauty of New York City, especially in the snow, until you've seen it from the air."

They exited the limo and nearly blew across the helipad to the waiting helicopter.

The interior was posh, a rich cream and indigo. It seemed they were the first to ever set foot in it, complete with that new car smell. Shamus recognized the Sikorsky S-76C. During the summers of his seventeenth and eighteenth years, he'd worked for Sikorsky Aircraft in Stratford, Connecticut. He'd flown in helicopters several times each summer. A pilot had been kind enough to teach him some basics.

The helicopter had two engines. Should one ingest a bird or simply fail, it should stay airborne.

"If this type of helicopter is good enough for celebrities and presidents," Shamus shouted over the whooshing and humming of an aircraft anxious to be in its element, "it should be good enough for a hop to Greenwich."

Meg forced a smile before stepping up and into the helicopter.

"All set?" Wesley shouted to the pilot when everyone was seated. He distributed headsets. The pilot, likely former military by his demeanor and jacket, turned to the passengers and smiled reassuringly.

"Seatbelts please," he said. "You'll be able to hear me if you like. Just flick the switch like so. You'll be able to hear each other when that switch is off. It gets damn noisy up there, but you'll get used to it." He smiled again and winked confidently.

Shamus was seated where he could see the cockpit. The pilot began to lift the collective. A deep flapping noise increased as the rotors slapped the cold air. The helicopter rose slowly, in perfect trim.

Once safely up, they hovered for a moment over the water then dipped to the right. The helicopter straightened, as if in salute, passing by One World Trade Center. A sense of vertigo and butterflies in Shamus' stomach dissipated. Life was tenuous in any case, he reminded himself. People who'd perished September 11, 2001 had gotten their morning coffee and were settling in for a normal day. They may have been thinking of a child at school, an ill parent, anticipating the joy of an engagement dinner, dodging a critical boss or on the verge of a promotion. For them, there was no reason to be fearful, no inkling of what was to come and no larger picture to consider. They weren't up in the air in a helicopter. Yet, their lives were about to end. *When it's your time*, Shamus thought, *it's your time*.

The Statue of Liberty, which he and Meg had visited with their parents, was off to their left. The helicopter tipped as they moved closer. It was spectacular. Veering to the right, they headed up the Hudson River. The Empire State Building upper floors were decked in green for St. Patrick's Day.

From the air, New York City twinkled like a jewel. Shamus watched countless small figures making their way along the streets, traffic moving across both levels of the George Washington Bridge without a hitch, everything going more smoothly than a city of its size had any right to expect.

They were over Westchester County in a matter of minutes, and the Connecticut shoreline soon after. Shamus pointed out his Ridgefield apartment and the various high points of his hometown.

"Isn't Connecticut the first or second wealthiest place in the world? Richer even than Silicon Valley?" Rashid asked loudly.

"This end of the state near New York has a dense concentration of wealth," Shamus replied. "No doubt about it, but there are a lot of people like me living here and certainly further up the 'Gold Coast,' as we call this stretch. It's a small state with everything you'd ever want in beaches, camping, skiing, breathtaking fall colors, and charming small towns largely inhabited by average income people. It's peppered with colleges and universities. We have an excellent basketball powerhouse at the University of Connecticut not far from Hartford. The women's team is consistently amazing. I wish you had time to visit."

"I will make a point of it in case the powers that be at Pacific Coast University decide I'd be welcome to move on."

"They won't do that," Meg shouted.

"You will stop them, I'm sure." Rashid called back with a warm smile.

"I will."

Shamus looked at Rashid and tilted his head in Meg's direction. "She will."

Rashid chuckled. "I would not be surprised."

They were hovering over the Greenwich shoreline. A pink mansion with an expansive lawn to the Long Island Sound appeared to their left. The helicopter maneuvered over the center of the lawn, and gently set down on a thin layer of snow. Mrs. Farnum was standing on the steps wrapped in a light brown mink coat, seeming to be more concerned with how the pilot was handling his job than greeting her son and their guests. She threw up her arms in exasperation.

"I'm afraid the pilot landed a bit close to mother's garden," Wesley said. "It's a mistake he won't repeat after she gets through with him."

It had seemed a perfect landing to Shamus. Besides, as one of his Navy pilot buddies always said, "Any landing you walk away from is a good one." He could see now that Mrs. Farnum's eyes were clenched. Her hands were fists, tight at her sides when she wasn't punching the air. She was calling to someone in the house. The blades slowed. Wesley opened the helicopter door. They ducked and exited, helping each other deal with the cold, pummeling wind coming off the water.

Mrs. Farnum approached like a ferocious fisher cat protecting its territory. Wesley waved for her to stay where she was. She stopped briefly, and then continued toward them. She was pointing at the pilot and shouting. Wesley waved gratefully and signaled for him to take off, much to his mother's consternation.

"It's all right, mother," Wesley said as he reached to hug her.

She pushed him away, her focus still on the helicopter.

"I told him about the garden, mother. He'll give it more room next time," Wesley shouted over the noise. "Just get back inside. It's cold."

"They have no sense, no sense at all," she shouted. "I've spoken to them any number of times. They charge enough. They can get it right."

She stomped past her guests working their way across the snow encrusted lawn. Were his mother alive, Shamus thought, she would have been warmly greeting them, concerned about their time in the cold, endeavoring to make each person feel welcome.

"She'll calm down soon," Wesley said. "She's almost eighty. Some people grow more patient with age, but that was never her long suit. Watch the stairs," he said. "They might be slippery."

"That's another thing," his mother sputtered. "I pay those boys handsomely and here we are risking our lives on icy steps."

Wesley put his arms around his mother and kissed her on the cheek. "That's enough, mother. We have company."

She waved at her son dismissively and strode into the house.

Wesley shrugged as if his mother was just in one of those amusing moods families must endure for the greater good.

Shamus looked over at Meg, Denise and Rashid who were no doubt thinking, as he was, that this was not a good omen for the hospitable evening Wesley had promised. The helicopter was far away now. There would be no early exit this evening, as Shamus usually took from social occasions. In fact, he hardly ever accepted rides to dinner at people's homes. He preferred the ability to leave at will, even from gatherings of people far more personable than Mrs. Farnum.

Madison, still suffering from pain incurred the night before, was having some difficulty with the steps. Shamus, who'd been walking beside Denise, excused himself and limped to Madison's aid.

Rashid joined Denise. "Beautiful home," he said.

"Leave it to you to see the positive," Shamus whispered over his shoulder.

"We are here," Rashid said, gesturing with his arms as if embracing the large estate. "We are not going anywhere. We should live in the moment and make it as pleasant as possible. Mindfulness, my friend, is the key to happiness."

"You may have to remind me a few times this evening," Shamus replied.

"I will do just that," Rashid assured as the three of them reached porch level.

Madison stood up straight, and then tilted slightly. Shamus steadied her. Suddenly he cringed in pain. Denise rushed to his side.

"Come in. Come in," a tall, silver-haired, perfectly coiffed man boomed. "I hope your flight was pleasant. Come in and get warm. I'm Cole Farnum." He reached to shake Shamus' hand. "You must be the brother," he said.

"Yes. Shamus Doherty."

Farnum released his grip. "Welcome, my boy. *Mi casa es su casa.*" Farnum waved his hand across a magnificent sitting room.

"Impressive," Shamus said.

Farnum released Shamus and gathered Meg, Madison and Denise for a tour of his hunting trophies, gun display, sculptures, rare books and paintings. Shamus looked over at Rashid. He suddenly realized that Farnum had not shaken his friend's hand.

Mrs. Farnum, having recovered from her outbursts, offered Rashid a glass of wine. "Are you Indian?" she asked, curiously studying him.

"I am American, but I was born and raised in India."

"So, you are Indian," Mrs. Farnum said.

Rashid regarded Shamus whose brow was slightly furrowed.

"He's American like you and me. My heritage is Irish. His is Indian. What's yours?"

"I am a descendent of the Van Wycks who owned most of New York at one time."

"So, you're Dutch-American," Shamus said.

Mrs. Farnum ignored Shamus. She focused again on Rashid who was smiling warmly as if the entire conversation had been an enjoyable genealogical foray.

"Are you a professor?" Mrs. Farnum asked. "A lot of your people come here to teach."

"I am an adjunct professor, Mrs. Farnum," Rashid replied graciously as Shamus glanced with aggravation at the ceiling.

"That means you teach part time?"

"No. It merely means that unlike your son, I am not on a tenure track. I do not do research. My contract renews every three years. Teaching and coaching the case competition team are my primary jobs."

"Rashid's case competition team just won the New York University championship, mother," Wesley interjected as he re-entered the room. "That's an amazing accomplishment, especially given the caliber of the competition."

Rashid smiled appreciatively at Wesley.

"Wesley, ask Marta to bring some cheese and crackers," Mrs. Farnum ordered.

"She's very busy preparing dinner, Mother. I'll get them."

"Marta will do it," Mrs. Farnum insisted, as she joined the other female hostages of her imperious husband.

Wesley looked at Shamus and Rashid. He shrugged and returned to the kitchen.

"One hundred dollars he doesn't bring the cheese back himself," Shamus said.

Rashid chuckled. "I am not a betting man."

"But what if you were? Would you give young Wesley the benefit of the doubt on standing his ground? I mean, after all, he seemed sincerely concerned about Marta."

Rashid was smiling but remained noncommittal.

The kitchen door opened. Marta entered the room with two trays of cheese and crackers.

Shamus smiled at Rashid. "You were wise not to bet."

Marta held one tray in front of Rashid and Shamus while placing the other on a small table. She looked exhausted but managed a gentle smile.

Rashid graciously accepted the tray. "I will share this with my friend. Thank you."

Marta studied Rashid's warm, brown eyes. Her own brightened with gratitude. A smile flickered across her lips.

"Marta! Don't linger about?" Mrs. Farnum called.

Marta hurried back to the kitchen.

Shamus watched as Cole Farnum's hand moved downward on Denise's back, stopping at the base of her spine, his pinky finger slipping further as he pointed animatedly with his other hand at a large moose head mounted over the fireplace. Shamus started forward. Denise feigned a laugh and pulled herself away from Farnum. She looked briefly over at Shamus and shook her head. He stopped. One more incident of that nature, one more insult, especially to Rashid, and they'd be out of there, Shamus promised himself. He'd pay for a taxi back to the city or they'd all cram into his Ridgefield apartment for the night. The hell with mindfulness.

"Dinner will be ready in ten minutes," Wesley announced.

Farnum glowered "We are quite busy, Wesley. Surely you can see that."

"Sorry, father. I'll let Marta know."

"You are a good son," Rashid said.

Shamus smiled at Rashid. Nowhere in his own social repertoire was this man's uncanny penchant for putting others at ease. It wasn't obsequiousness. Rashid could fight his corner. To do so, however, was not his natural inclination. He would try to follow Rashid's lead, to ignore the Farnums' supercilious commentary, snobbery and egotistical ravings. It would not be easy, but was worth a try.

"We've adopted a *Downton Abbey* theme in the dining room," Mrs. Farnum explained as they all meandered through a sitting room graced by a massive oak staircase. On the far wall was a photo of Rhett Butler carrying a fighting Scarlet O'Hara up nearly identical stairs to her chamber. Apparently, this had been chosen during their *Gone with the Wind* phase, Shamus thought, and somehow survived the remodeling. It occurred to him that at one time he'd considered that particular scene a dramatic depiction of a rebuffed husband's prerogative to take charge of an untenable situation, as John Wayne had done with Maureen O'Hara's challenging character in *The Quiet Man*. Surely, that was the intention of the directors. Now, however, Rhett's overpowering of Scarlet struck him as unsettling at best. He studied the picture until Mrs. Farnum called for everyone to move on.

They entered a lavish dining room. "I would have dressed more smartly had I known we would be in such splendor," Shamus said.

"This is my wife's amusement," Cole Farnum said. "We do not require a white tie."

"It's little enough," Mrs. Farnum retorted. "You have toys everywhere."

"You're right, my dear. You want for nothing," he said for the entertainment of his guests, rolling his eyes.

She shot a look of derision at her husband, instantly extricating him from his callous recreation.

"Your names are in front of the place settings," she said. "Please be seated."

The food was exquisite. Marta, running herself ragged, had done all the work. Wesley had been the one to compliment her. Not once did Mrs. Farnum, who'd yet to share her first name with the group, utter anything other than annoyance and poorly veiled contempt for Marta. The guests compensated, especially Rashid, with smiles and compliments to the gracious, appreciative cook.

"I have heard a great deal about you, Shamus," Cole Farnum said as he chewed on a piece of meat far too large for civil human consumption.

"Positive I hope," Shamus replied, trying to appear oblivious to his host's foul mastication.

He glanced at Rashid. The left side of Rashid's mouth rose a bit. Shamus chuckled to himself. They were of one mind. Here in the flesh was Joyce's Leopold Bloom.

Farnum swallowed hard, choking, his cheeks bulging. Shamus' face constricted with disgust. His gut wrenched in anticipation of regurgitated food flying across the room. Farnum swallowed again, paused and pointed his fork at Shamus who was endeavoring to regain some semblance of social composure.

"I understand you saved Madison's life last night," Farnum said just before putting another large piece of meat in his mouth.

"For heaven's sake, Cole," Mrs. Farnum interrupted. "Cut your meat."

Farnum spit the meat onto his plate. "Yes dear."

Shamus coughed to disguise his initial gag response. He forced a smile. "Fortunately, she had put up a valiant fight. I mostly chased the man away."

"I'd hardly call the punishment you gave him a mere chase," Madison interjected.

"I'm sure Madison and Shamus would just as soon not think about what happened, father," Wesley said. "They're far from recovered. Fortunately, they brought their own doctor along." He nodded at Denise.

"This is my table," Farnum bellowed. "I do not need your advice on how to host it."

The room went silent. Knives and forks no longer clinked. Mrs. Farnum looked over at Wesley, disappointed.

"I was merely..."

"So, you were injured?" Farnum asked Shamus, ignoring his son.

"Yes. I'm not the youth I once was," Shamus said keeping his comment short, attempting to support Wesley's desire for a change of subject.

"And you my dear?" Farnum asked Madison.

She breathed deeply, looked down, and straightened her napkin. "If you don't mind, I'd rather not talk about it."

Wesley, seated next to Madison, placed his left hand on the back of her chair and glared at his father.

"I meant no harm," Farnum said, clearing his throat. "Evelyn and I were worried. Weren't we, dear? We only have one child. So, of course, we're concerned about the series of horrific events that have occurred in his proximity."

Farnum looked at Wesley, whose face was growing increasingly scarlet in anticipation of the topic to follow.

"We had always hoped that Wesley would choose a career like banking or become a lawyer. He never had the grades to be a doctor. We accepted that. But his choice of academia was a disappointment. As Meg well knows, getting tenure is very difficult and politically driven. Our Wesley is not political."

"Father," Wesley said tautly. "They are not interested."

Farnum glared at his son with cold eyes. "How often do we have guests who can shed light on the challenges you face? Surely you won't begrudge your mother and I some insights into the reasons why your chances of obtaining tenure are weak at best."

"I wouldn't say that," Madison said.

"Wesley is a fine scholar and an excellent teacher," Meg said.

Farnum turned his attention to Madison. "You're the editor of a leading journal. Right?"

"Yes," Madison said guardedly.

"Has my son published in you journal?"

"Father!"

Farnum held up his hand, palm out to Wesley, "I will make this quick." He looked directly into Madison's eyes. "Has he?"

"No," Madison answered coolly.

"And why is that?"

"The editor decides whether to accept or reject based partially on the reviews," Madison said. "The competition is stiff. The paper must meet certain criteria regarding topic, quality, potential readership interest, and editorial policy."

"In which capacity did Wesley fail?" Farnum asked.

"Madison cannot reveal to anyone other than the author why an article was accepted or rejected," Meg said to Farnum. "It's not professional."

Farnum smirked. "Easy for you to say."

"If you mean because I have tenure, you're wrong. I've had my share of rejections. I'm also on the editorial board of a journal and know the rules."

"Meg is right," Wesley said in a tone intended to halt the conversation.

Farnum slammed his fist on the table. "You can't fight your own battles. You never have. So, shut up and let me handle this."

Wesley stood. His father did the same. They locked eyes in reciprocal animosity. Shamus stiffened. Mrs. Farnum tapped a knife on her plate and shook her head slightly at her husband. He ignored her. She reached under the table. A buzzer sounded.

Two large men rushed into the room, startling everyone. One was wearing a dark suit, an impeccably pressed light blue shirt, and dark tie. The other man was casually dressed. Both were poised for combat.

"Go away!" Farnum shouted at them waving in the air. "For Christ sake!"

The men held their ground, then guardedly slipped from the room.

Mrs. Farnum cleared her throat. "Please sit down, Wesley dear."

Wesley, still frozen with embarrassment, glanced at his guests, lowered his head and sat.

"You too, Cole dear."

Farnum slowly sat, eyes fixed on his son.

Mrs. Farnum directed a counterfeit smile at Madison. "My husband has a bad temper. But to his credit, he is merely looking for an estimate of Wesley's chances. Apparently, tenure depends on publishing in highly rated journals, of which yours is one."

Madison nodded. "I understand your concern, but…"

"Do you really?" Cole Farnum challenged. "Do you have children?"

"No," Madison replied defensively.

"Then you have absolutely no understanding of the aspirations of a parent for a child," Mrs. Farnum insisted. "You do not know the lengths to which good parents must go to spare their children pain."

Mrs. Farnum's eyes were moistening. If she were nearly any other mother, Shamus would have felt sympathy. But her tears were not for Wesley. They were real, but for herself.

"We have one child," Cole Farnum continued. "His future happiness depends on the whims of people blinded by their own biases and ignorance."

"Is that what you're concerned about?" Shamus asked. "Because he doesn't look happy right now."

Farnum glared at Shamus, then turned to Denise. "And you, my dear. You are a doctor whose father is one of the best surgeons on the west coast."

"Yes," Denise replied.

"I suppose in your case tenure was never an issue."

Shamus bristled. He leaned forward intending to intervene.

Denise's right hand was resting on the table. She raised it slightly, signaling Shamus that she would handle Farnum again.

Shamus sat back.

"Wesley is a brilliant young scholar. He will publish in leading journals when he has a full understanding of what the editors expect. That comes with rejection and determination to do better."

Farnum didn't appreciate her cool confidence.

"And I believe, from what Meg has told me, that he will be tenured soon enough," Denise continued. "Sometimes university politics influence promotions. Luck is part of it. Who you know can play a roll. But your anger here tonight is exceedingly misplaced if you think journal publication is the only criteria for promotion."

Farnum's face was reddening. He looked at Shamus. "I can see in your relationship who will be in charge."

"All right, that's enough," Shamus said, tossing his napkin on the table, cringing slightly with pain. "I didn't come here with my sister or invite our friends so that we might be insulted. Wesley will get tenure or not based on his own accomplishments. Case closed."

Farnum stood. "What right have you to tell me at my table, in my home, what case is or isn't closed?"

"Thank you, Wesley, for the helicopter tour and the invitation to dinner," Shamus said. "I wish we could stay longer, but unfortunately we must leave now."

Meg, Madison, Denise and Rashid stood.

"Sit down!" Mrs. Farnum ordered.

Rashid smiled at Mrs. Farnum. "My apologies for our early departure. We are most grateful for a delicious dinner. I do not know when I have had better, but Madison suffered a terrifying event last night. Shamus is also recovering. We cannot allow them to be upset further."

"Dessert has not been served," Mrs. Farnum asserted.

Rashid smiled stiffly at her. "Perhaps another time."

Wesley stood. "My apologies to all of you. My parents have been out of line."

Farnum's face was aflame with indignation. He walked behind his chair, removed his phone from his pants pocket, and texted. A moment later, his phone beeped.

"The helicopter will be here in five minutes," Farnum announced. He strode toward the doorway. His wife followed him in a huff.

"He is livid about my career," Wesley offered.

Shamus scoffed. "You think?"

"My parents are not pleased with my choice of career either," Rashid said to Wesley. He smiled empathically.

"Remind me not to visit your home then," Shamus kidded.

Rashid laughed. "They would be wanting to ask similar questions."

"But they wouldn't ask them," Wesley said. "That's the difference."

Rashid smiled. "I cannot speak with complete confidence about my mother."

The helicopter landed on the lawn far from Mrs. Farnum's garden. Two unfamiliar men emerged from it. One was likely in his forties and at least 6' 2" tall. Solid like a football defensive tackle, he wore a dark, Hell's Angel's type leather jacket with the collar folded upward. He was scruffily unshaven and sporting a ragged goatee, black skull cap and dark-rimmed sun glasses. His eyes angled menacingly over a broad, pock-marked nose that looked to have been broken multiple times. Across his neck was a chain-link fence tattoo. He lit a cigarette a little too close to the helicopter for Shamus' comfort, puffed and allowed his lower lip to trap smoke before blowing it up into the air.

The shorter, thinner one, who Shamus figured had to be the co-pilot, was wearing a more subdued jacket that was gray and tatty from long use. He offered his approaching passengers an odd smile.

"What's up?" Meg shouted to Shamus over the loud swooshing of the main rotor. "Something wrong?"

"Just recovering from our lovely evening," Shamus shouted back as they ducked and headed for the helicopter.

"Sorry about accepting the invitation," Meg said.

"Hey, it wasn't your fault. Besides, the food was good and free."

"Do you know these pilots?" Shamus asked a few minutes later as Wesley boarded. "They look kind of pissed off."

"Mother probably insisted on a last minute replacement for Jim. He's a highly decorated retired naval commander, a superb pilot, but she thinks he landed too close to her garden."

"Speaking of your mother," Shamus said, glancing over Wesley's shoulder. "It looks like she's calling you."

Wesley looked back toward the house. His mother was waving insistently from the porch. Pointing at Wesley, she gestured for him to come back.

Wesley rolled his eyes. "Sorry. I'll just be a moment."

When Wesley reached the porch, he and his mother immediately engaged in an altercation. Mrs. Farnum crossed her arms emphatically and scowled. Wesley threw up his hands and turned toward the helicopter. He waved both arms to get the attention of the pilots now settling in, shrugged and signaled with two thumbs up for them to take off.

"What the fuck?" Shamus mouthed.

The helicopter rose, jerked abruptly and headed out over the dull gray, frigid Long Island Sound.

After a moment of harrowing disorientation, the helicopter tilted and the lights from houses and streetlamps along the Connecticut coast came into view. The passengers breathed more easily.

"Could be a little bumpy tonight," the co-pilot announced. "There's cloud cover over most of the area and wind is coming in strong from the west. As we go into clouds, you may feel panicked. Sometimes streamlined clouds look like the horizon, which scares the daylights out of some passengers. No worries, though, just giving you a heads-up. Sit tight and distract yourselves."

The passengers' eyes met apprehensively.

"He's just being macho." Shamus said. "They'll rely on their instruments if there are any visibility issues."

"Hank here has seen it all," the co-pilot called. "We call him 'Shrap' for all the incoming fire and metal he took in Iraq as a contractor. Military wouldn't take him. He flies his way. Sit tight. He's not above turning off the transponder and cutting the squawk, as we call it. We may go lost com with Air Traffic Control for a little while. Hank doesn't need some jerk in a tower telling him what to do. He can fly by the seat of his pants. In fact, he's the best natural stick I've ever seen. If it starts to snow or we experience icing, we'll take her lower, skim a few waves perhaps, and find a safe place to land. Again, everything is under control."

Shamus rolled his eyes.

Rashid looked unsurely at Shamus before turning to look out the window.

Suddenly, the helicopter lurched forward. Everyone clenched and grabbed the armrests as it rose rapidly and tipped back. Madison gasped. They felt weightless, as if the rotors had stopped turning before what could only be a deadly drop. The helicopter shuddered and moaned in protest. A red light flashed in the cockpit.

Steady for a moment, the nose fell downward. There was no doubt. They were headed for the water.

Only Shamus' eyes remained open. The helicopter shifted to horizontal mere feet above the sound, clipping the waves and tossing from side to side.

"What the hell was that?" Shamus yelled.

"We're fine," the co-pilot responded with a smirk in his voice. "We just averted a bird strike. I said you're in good hands. Tail rotor is in good shape. Wouldn't want to lose it, though it wouldn't be the first time that's happened. Right, Hank?" The two looked at each other with irreverent amusement.

Rashid was gazing upward. Shamus knew what he was thinking. He and Nida would never have a chance to reconcile. His children would be fatherless.

"We're doing fine now," Shamus tried to reassure his fellow passengers. "The birds are avoiding the storm just like we are."

"We'll be there in no time," assured the co-pilot.

"Are we lost com?" Shamus called.

"Got an amateur helicopter enthusiast here," the co-pilot chuckled.

Hank turned to face Shamus. He smirked. "Maybe you'd like to drive."

"I just asked if we're lost com," Shamus repeated, louder this time.

"We were for a couple of moments there. Squawk is back on now. ATC sees us on their screens."

"Who sees us?" Denise asked tremulously.

"We're in touch with ground authority. Don't worry, we're fine," said Shamus smiling reassuringly, but his effort fell short.

Madison stared straight ahead, a hand clutching Meg's arm.

Without warning the helicopter twisted, groaned and spiraled toward the water, then suddenly straightened again. Madison's face was flushed with fear. She leaned forward as if to upchuck. Meg placed a hand on her back. Denise's eyes were closed, her lips tight.

"It's going to be rough until we land," the co-pilot called to them.

"Declare an emergency with the ATC," Shamus shouted back. "You need to put it down."

"No can do, buddy. We're equidistant from home and there's no safe place to land. I'm radio silent to keep those ATC monkeys off our back while we maneuver our way out of this thing."

Just then the helicopter ascended and pitched violently. The horizon appeared to tilt. Vertigo seized Shamus' senses, sickness his stomach.

"Have you switched to instruments?" he called, his hands tightening on the arm rests in a death grip.

"Nah, nothing to worry about!"

"In two seconds you guys won't know clouds from horizon or up from down," Shamus shouted.

"I said, we've got this, pal," Hank shot back angrily.

Shamus knew that getting out of this mess required a pilot to fly against his own instincts by denying his body's messages and relying solely on what the instruments told him.

"Go to instruments!" Shamus shouted.

The helicopter jerked, twisted and bumped. Madison covered her mouth, stifling a scream, her eyes wide with terror.

They were flying blind.

For what seemed like an eternity, the wind tugged treacherously at the aircraft. At last the pilot began to lower the helicopter above the landing pad. He caught the co-pilot's eye, then took the bird back up and descended again for a drop landing.

After they exited, Shamus held back. He turned to face the smirking co-pilot. They stood eye to eye, each daring the other to make the first move.

"It's not worth it," Rashid called to Shamus.

The pilot shut down the helicopter, exited and pushed his co-pilot away from Shamus.

"If you got a problem buddy, it's with me," he growled.

"Either you're the worst pilot on earth," Shamus shot back, "or Farnum put you up to this."

"I can't help it if you're a sissy," the pilot said.

Shamus turned away, then suddenly spun back. He landed a powerful punch square on the pilot's nose sending him reeling to the ground.

Rashid stepped in front of the co-pilot. "Come on. Let's do this," Rashid shouted, rotating his fists.

Shamus joined him.

The co-pilot regarded them for a moment. He raised his hands, palms out.

"I don't get paid enough for this," he said.

Rashid held his stance until the co-pilot turned and walked away. Shamus glared at the pilot on the ground.

"We need to go now," Rashid said. "We have more than ourselves to consider." Meg, Denise and Madison were shaking from the cold.

The pilot managed to get to his knees, wiping with his leather sleeve at the blood running from his nose.

"Tell Farnum I'd better not see his face again," Shamus shouted as he and Rashid backed away. "Or yours."

Denise hailed a taxi. As they departed, the pilot and co-pilot were arguing, shoving and shouting obscenities at each other.

"Seems the pilot isn't pleased with his buddy's refusal to back him up," Madison said.

"Smart move on the co-pilot's part. There were two of us," Rashid boasted.

"Oh please," Madison said. "That guy could have flattened both of you."

"I do not think that is the case," Rashid replied, indignantly. "He knew he was outmatched by either one of us. There is no doubt about that."

Eyebrows raised, bent forward in pain, Shamus looked at Rashid with a smile.

"What? You do not believe me?" Rashid defended. "The man was terrified. He is lucky to be alive."

Rashid crossed his arms and looked out the window. Shamus watched his friend for a few moments noting a slight smile form. They had been outmatched. No question. The punch had indeed come from intense anger. Nevertheless, its impact had been beyond expectation. Perhaps on this night, Shamus considered, religious or not, he owed one to the Man upstairs.

Police Interview: Ruth Carroll

"My husband Bill and I have been in this field for a very long time. We are highly regarded scholars. Never has anyone been harmed, let alone killed, over a journal rejection. You're gathering the low-hanging fruit if you fall for that ruse."

CHAPTER TWENTY-EIGHT

Shamus spent the remainder of the taxi ride considering options for revenge. He could drop off everyone at the hotel and locate the Farnum's Brooklyn home where he could break a few windows. It was a ludicrous plan, but tempting.

Entering the hotel lobby, Denise took Shamus by the hand. "I could use a drink," she said.

They both ordered Johnny Walker Black on ice.

"How are you doing?" Shamus asked.

"Shaken up. You?"

"Angry."

"Do you think they were a couple of wild cowboys out for fun at our expense?"

"Cole and Evelyn Farnum do not take insults lightly."

"No. You don't really think they arranged it? We could have been killed."

Shamus squeezed Denise's hand with a comforting smile. "Let's try to put tonight behind us for the next hour or so."

"Agreed. Especially since I go back to L.A. tomorrow morning. A patient needs me."

"Can't your father handle the situation? Give you a little more time here?"

"I wish he could, but she doesn't like my father. I'm sure you remember that feeling from when you first met him. He has a gruff exterior."

"It'll pass as soon as she finds out how smart he is," Shamus said.

"We haven't had much time together," Denise said, "and there's something I need to know before I go."

"What's that?"

"Is there a future for us?"

He studied her intense expression for a moment, smiled warmly and took her hand. "I want to work on the bi-coastal idea. We could spend six months in L.A. and six months in Connecticut."

She looked into his eyes wistfully. "I don't think it will work."

"It will," Shamus insisted.

"I wish you were right, Shamus."

"So, you're going to marry Barry?"

"No. I care for him," she said. "We share an interest in medicine and he's a good person."

"But?"

"But…" she sighed. "He isn't you."

"I don't want us to end."

"Me neither."

"Then what?"

"I think we start by seeing each other more often," Denise said. "If that turns out not to be enough, we'll take it from there."

"It won't be enough. I can tell you that already."

"But you aren't ready to move to California if the university won't allow me flexibility, right?"

Shamus couldn't believe his own silence. She was beautiful, smart and caring. He must be crazy to not drop everything and follow her to California. "I do love you, Denise."

"Yes, you do. But love has levels."

Shamus sat back, gently releasing her hands. "I thought it was all in or out. That's why they call it 'falling' in love."

She shook her head. "I don't think so."

"What level are we on?"

"Maybe three."

"Out of ten?" Shamus asked, eyes wide.

"Out of five."

"How do you know?"

"I'll spell it out for you," Denise said. "If tonight had any benefits, it's that being close to death elicits priorities. Makes you think of what's missing. My romantic side needs to hear from the bottom of your heart that you love me. That you can't imagine living without me. Frankly, you're not saying those things."

"But…"

She placed a finger on his lips. "Not now."

"There isn't anyone else for me," Shamus said.

"Penelope likes you."

"She's dangerous," Shamus kidded. "Besides not being you, she has a guy who is mad about her. She just hasn't noticed yet."

"Madison is definitely attracted to you."

"She flits."

"Flits?"

"Yep. Like a bee from flower to flower."

Denise chuckled. "I've never thought of you as a flower."

"There's so much to learn about me." He smiled warmly.

She looked at him for several seconds, then stood. "I have to pack."

"Please sit," Shamus said, touching her arm.

She leaned over and kissed him. Their lips released, but she stayed close. She kissed him again, longer this time, stood slowly and touched his cheek. Then she collected her coat and began to walk away.

"Denise," Shamus said.

She turned back.

He stood and walked over to her. "From the bottom of my heart," he said taking her hand. "I can't imagine…"

She touched his lips and smiled with moist, relieved eyes. He placed his arm around her waist as they walked from the lobby, into the elevators and made their way to her room. They stopped just inside the door, their eyes tenderly taking each other in.

"You want to be swept off your feet, right?" he said with a mischievous smile.

"Who doesn't?" Denise replied, gently playing with a wave of his hair.

Shamus nodded and then whisked her off her feet.

Denise tossed her head back laughing as he twirled her around.

"Level three?" Shamus said as he carried her into the bedroom. "Are you sure?"

"Maybe four."

"We'll see about that," he said, lowering her onto the bed. He leaned over her, studied her face, her eyes, and then gently kissed her neck. Their eyes met. She cradled his face with both hands and drew him to her.

The next morning, Shamus walked Denise down to the lobby. He was missing her already. He hailed a cab for her and stood watching until the taxi merged into traffic and out of sight. When he went back into the hotel, Jeffries was standing at the reception desk watching him.

"Love is a beautiful thing," Jeffries said.

"Spying as usual," Shamus said.

"Let's take a walk," Jeffries replied with no room for rejection.

They entered a coffee shop across from Central Park. Shamus ordered a bagel with cream cheese and a coffee. Jeffries followed suit. Outside the window beside their table, people were enjoying the first hint of spring.

"Madison ditched the officer guarding her when you people went on a joy ride to Connecticut," Jeffries said sharply.

Shamus' eyes widened. "Shit!"

"He could become a beat cop again or even lose his job if that happens again. As it is, I ripped him up one side and down the other."

"I'll talk to Madison. It must have slipped her mind."

"Tell her we don't have to protect her," Jeffries huffed.

"I will."

Jeffries sipped his coffee. "Fortunately, your sister stayed in touch with Officer Tamayo after the plans changed. Otherwise, they'd be on my shit list too. I figured four of you wouldn't risk my wrath by taking off permanently. But that's not the point."

Shamus nodded, wondering how much more Jeffries knew about the prior night and who'd been filling him in.

"Have you been able to recall anything else about the guy who nearly killed you and Madison?"

"No." Shamus looked out the window as a woman with five leashed dogs of various sizes awkwardly struggled by, trying desperately to keep the larger dogs from stepping on a toy poodle that clearly considered himself in charge.

"No detail is too small," Jeffries continued. "And when something comes to you, and it will, I'm the only person you tell."

"By which you mean skip Penelope."

"You don't want to obstruct this investigation, believe me."

Shamus held out his wrists to be cuffed.

"It won't be funny if it happens."

"Don't worry." Shamus said. "You're growing on me."

"Is that right?"

Shamus nodded, bit into his bagel and looked outside again. A man was sitting on the nearby bench. Shamus sat erect and swallowed hard.

"What?" Jeffries said, glancing in the same direction.

"You see that guy?"

"Yeah. What about him?"

"Look at his watch."

"It's a Rolex," Jeffries said. "Big deal. This is midtown Manhattan."

"The guy had a gold and stainless one."

"What guy?"

Shamus looked at Jeffries exasperated. "What guy do you think?"

"You're telling me the guy who tried to kill Madison was sporting a Rolex?"

Shamus nodded. "And, now that I think about it, he was wearing a large, silver ring on his left hand."

Jeffries removed a pen and pad from his jacket pocket and jotted down a few notes.

"It didn't have a stone. Maybe a crest. He hit me with it."

"Think hard, Doherty. I need specifics."

"I'm thinking!" Shamus shot back. "It all happened fast. After he slashed me, I was focused on staying alive."

"Okay," Jeffries said, waving his hands, testily erasing the issue. "More later. For now, tell me what you know about the pissed off professors bent on unseating editors."

"Probably as much as you know."

"Such as?"

"From what I understand, they were supposed to pressure journal publishers to replace Stan and some other editors who'd overstayed they're welcome. The young professors are desperate to get tenure. They want to loosen the grip of long-term, set-in-their-ways editors."

"Editors as in plural?"

"Yep," Shamus said.

"Is Wesley Farnum in the group?"

Shamus hesitated. "Could be."

"Don't be coy with me, Doherty."

"Why should I throw him under the bus?"

"He's a desperate guy," Jeffries said. "Desperate people do desperate things. As I heard it, his parents expected him to become a doctor or a lawyer, not a professor with no hope of tenure."

"Hardly a reason for murder."

"The guy isn't getting any younger. He doesn't want mommy and daddy to get their Dolce & Gabbana's in a knot over his failure."

"So, he kills two people?" Shamus scoffed.

"Desperation fuels hatred. I've seen it countless times in my line of work."

"What about the other members of the angry young professor society?" Shamus asked. "Have you checked them out?"

"Detective Krawski is on it."

"Any of them on your list?"

"They are."

"Who?"

Jeffries smirked. "I don't know what it's like in charming Ridgefield, Connecticut, but here one hand washes the other. Why don't you do some more thinking about the guy with the Rolex and then maybe we'll share secrets from our diaries?"

"Mine has one of those little keys," Shamus said with a half-smile.

"Cute." Jeffries said.

They stepped outside and walked toward Central Park. Patches of green were peeking through where snow had begun to melt. People had taken up residence on benches, eating breakfast and enjoying the warm sunlight. Children were piling snow on a snowman whose stone eyes, nose and mouth had given way to the inevitability of spring. A little boy struggled to fix the snowman's sad mouth. Shamus smiled and turned back to Jeffries who was transfixed on a skateboarder weaving precariously among pedestrians. When the boy of about twelve got close, Jeffries flashed his badge. The child toppled off the board, stood, mouth agape, grabbed the board and ran.

Jeffries smiled. "Another menace to mankind stopped in his tracks."

"It must feel good to right the world like that even if the bad guy was just a kid."

"There are perks to this thankless job."

Jeffries assessed the area as if looking for more lawbreakers.

"Why don't you apologize to her?" Shamus said out of the blue.

"To who?"

"Penelope."

"Why the hell should I apologize to her? Have you read her stories in the *Times*? You'd think I was the killer."

"You and she have a history."

Jeffries glared at Shamus, then looked away. "Stay out of it."

"People fuck up," Shamus said. "My father did. Maybe you did or maybe you didn't. I've learned the hard way not to carry grudges. Distancing yourself from people who love you is just an excuse for not doing the hard work of healing wounds."

"You've been reading too many Hallmark cards."

"She was just a child. She saw her mother get hurt. She got hurt. You don't want my advice, that's fine. But it looks to me like you or both adults involved screwed up big time and you never paid the piper. That's all."

"You're crossing a line, Doherty. Let's be clear. We're not buddies."

"I'm just trying to do you a favor."

"It was a long time ago. Too much water's gone over the dam."

"Maybe not," Shamus said.

Jeffries' phone buzzed. He took it out and retrieved a text. "Gotta go," he said, casting Shamus a nod and taking off in the direction of the hotel.

Shamus watched the detective disappear into the crowd. *He's a tough guy for sure, a cop's cop*, Shamus thought. *But what happened with Penelope and her mother years ago wasn't because the guy didn't care.*

Meg had gone to bed after the hellish helicopter ride, and twice she'd awoken having dreamed of the scarf around her neck and then, suddenly, across her face as Stan slammed her into a wall. Slowly, she rose from the bed, crossed the room, and opened her briefcase. She looked for a few moments at an edge of the buried scarf, as if touching it might bring back more memories than she could bear. Then she lifted it and draped it across her wrists. If she could look at it for even a few minutes without shaking, she might deny the sender his or her power.

She gazed into the large bureau mirror. Before that night, she'd felt strong and capable. No obstacle could halt her career progress. She feared nothing and no one. Was that same woman looking back at her now? "You are who you were," she said to her reflection. "You can't let him, or anyone, take that feeling away. You've mourned long enough. It's time to get ahold of yourself again, to be strong, to deny anyone the power to diminish who you really are."

She knew that path would be strewn with obstacles. She'd get lost again, no doubt. But this morning would be a start back to who she'd been. Johnny would not grow up with a damaged mother. She would face her demons for him and for herself.

CHAPTER TWENTY-NINE

Jeffries' unfinished personal business with Penelope reminded Shamus of his own. He'd managed to largely put the woman he'd followed to Brooklyn Heights out of his mind. That is until this morning. Two days remained of the five-day conference. He exited the coffee shop, walked up 53rd Street and boarded the subway.

As it sped along, he wondered why he'd criticized Jeffries about his personal life. What had gotten into him? His modus operandi in relationships was to avoid delicate subjects, certainly not to confront or probe. Yet he'd presided as judge and jury over another man's seeming parental malfeasance. It was a wonder Jeffries hadn't taken a pop at him. *He would have been within his rights*, Shamus admitted to himself. He wasn't a parent. But he knew parenthood made even the strongest, most self-assured people insecure. He'd seen it among his friends and in Jeffries' eyes. For parents, failure was always looming just over the horizon.

When Shamus reached the brownstone, he ascended the steps and checked the names on the mailboxes. He was about to push the buzzer for apartment one when a boy exited the building in a rush. Shamus caught the door. He walked a few yards, hesitated, and then knocked.

He sensed someone looking through the security eye. He smiled. Locks clanked and clunked. Silence followed. Part of him wanted to run, like he had that night.

The door opened slowly.

Her eyes were bright, almost turquoise, alert, and studying him. She smiled and moved back, gesturing for him to enter.

"I'm Shamus Doherty."

"I know," she said with a tender smile as if he were a boy again. Stepping aside, she gestured that he could enter.

"You are Loretta?"

"Yes, dear. How did you find me?"

"I saw you outside MOMA a few days ago. I followed you.

"I sensed a shadow that day," Loretta said with a short smile. "But I'm getting older now and decided it was just my imagination."

"I didn't want to intrude."

"Come in. Sit down." She pointed at a floral sofa. "I'm glad you changed your mind. You're not intruding."

Shamus walked into the living room, allowing her to take his jacket.

"Please sit," she said. "I'll get you a lemonade."

"I'm fine," he said.

"It's no bother. I'll be back in a moment."

She went into a bedroom. When she came out, her slippers had been replaced with shoes. She crossed over to a tiny kitchen and opened the refrigerator.

A curio cabinet in the far corner captured Shamus' attention. He approached it. On the top shelf were Hummel figurines, Lladro ballerinas, children and angels like his mother had occasionally received from his father. Silver framed photos of relatives and one of her as a child adorned most of the other shelves. As he approached for a closer look, his heart stopped. One of the photos was of a young man in his late twenties. It was his father.

"I should have removed that photo," Loretta said as she came back into the living room. But then I never expected you to visit."

She placed two lemonade filled glasses and a dish of cookies on a tea table. She sat, placed her hands in her lap and waited for him to join her on the sofa. "You're wondering, I imagine, why your father is so young in the photo. He was certainly older when you saw us together."

A moment passed as Shamus again studied the photo. He nodded.

She sighed. "I don't suppose the story can hurt anyone now."

Shamus had never considered that there might be a story other than the one he'd allowed to shape his life for so many years.

She handed him a glass of lemonade as he sat. "I heard about the accident that took both your parents. I'm so sorry."

"Thank you," Shamus replied.

She looked at his father's photo as if asking for his permission and then began. "We were high school sweethearts."

She rose, walked to a desk, opened the top drawer, and took out a book. She returned and sat next to Shamus. It was an old high school yearbook preserved to near perfection. As she slowly opened it, the binding creaked in complaint releasing a slight musty odor of years gone by. Loretta flipped through pages, stopped at one, smiled and turned the yearbook so Shamus could see it more clearly. He examined black-and-white photos of young faces filled with promise. His eyes halted at a familiar one. It was his father.

Loretta turned the pages to a full-page photo of his father in a football uniform poised to throw the ball. Shamus recalled the stories his father and mother had shared of spectacular wins and tragic losses. They'd smiled at each other as if only they could fully appreciate the intensity of a time and place where townspeople's joy and despair rode on the outcome of each high school game.

Loretta turned to other photos of Shamus' father in the photography club, then the chess club and with the National Honors Society.

"Your mother didn't go to our school," Loretta said. "She went to St. Mary's, but I remember her at our football games and how she looked at your father even then. He hardly noticed her. She was two years younger. A child in our eyes. An immense chasm existed between seniors and sophomores. I suppose that's not so different today."

Loretta turned the pages to a photo of herself sporting a cheerleader's outfit and leaping high into the air, a pompom in each hand.

"You were stunning," Shamus said.

"Yes," she said as if drifting back to that time and admiring someone other than herself. "I was."

"I mean you still are lovely," Shamus stammered.

Loretta laughed and patted his hand. "That's sweet."

Another page was marked by dried flowers. She and his father were dancing. Her head was on his shoulder, the two oblivious to their surrounding classmates. His father wore a white tuxedo jacket with a flower in his lapel. Loretta was elegant in a gown of layered lace.

"The gown was pale green," she said. "He loved it." She smiled ruefully and closed the book. "You see, Shamus, your father once loved me, and I loved him. We were engaged for more than a year after high school. We parted over something silly. About six months later he began dating your mother. They broke up and we resumed dating. We fell in love again. He placed the diamond back on my finger. It was the happiest day of my life."

She looked at Shamus. Her eyes were glowing. She glanced down at her left ring finger and straightened a diamond ring. "It was a long time ago. Are you sure you want to hear a bunch of old stories?"

"I do," Shamus said.

Loretta smiled. She stood, walked over to the desk and put the yearbook away. "A month later, your mother called him. She was pregnant with you."

"What?"

"Your father was an honorable man," she continued, returning to sit beside Shamus. "He did the right thing. He left me and married your mother. It broke his heart and it broke mine."

"That isn't true!"

"I don't mean to imply that he didn't feel deeply for your mother."

"But it's you he really loved. That's what you're saying."

"I believe that he loved us both," Loretta said softly. "And I understood his decision. I nearly died of heartache, but I understood.

"You never found someone else? Never married?"

"No. A month after they married, I discovered that I was also pregnant with your father's child."

Shamus threw his arms into the air. "What kind of man does that? I mean..."

"We were to be married shortly and wanted children early." She paused as if wondering whether to say more. "I think he and your mother had only been intimate once. She was quite religious. Her parents forced her to tell him."

He looked for some hint of lying in her eyes. It wasn't there.

"I let him go. I kept my secret from him."

"Why?"

"Shamus," she spoke softly, evenly, "What good would it have done to tell him?"

"He had a right to know! He might have helped somehow."

"What would that have meant for you and later for your sister? How could he have managed two families? In those days it would have caused a scandal. There would have been no end of gossip deeply hurting your mother and father, me, their child and mine to say nothing of our parents."

She closed her eyes tightly for a moment. "No. He could not be told," she said as if reassuring herself. "Any right he had to know about the baby paled by comparison to the harm it would have caused."

Shamus shook his head. "Women have so many secrets."

"Perhaps we think more than men about how the truth will be received. Sometimes the fear of seeing disappointment in the eyes of a person you love is a heavier burden than remaining silent."

Shamus sighed. He looked down and slightly shook his head. They sipped lemonade for a few moments, Shamus glancing at his father's photo. "How did the night at the railroad station come about?"

"We ran into each other on the train. The moment was intoxicating. He was only going to walk me home. What happened afterward was wrong. We felt young again. We picked up where we'd left off. He loved your mother. When I looked out the window and saw your sweet face enraged by our transgression, I slid to the floor drowning in self-loathing. We'd caused the very pain I'd avoided for so many years."

"He could have told me about your past. Then maybe…"

"How?" she said. "Think about it. What would you have thought and felt at such a tender age?"

"He lived a lie after that."

"He was ashamed. I suspect he told your mother. A few months later, I saw her at the grocery store. We chatted. The truth was in her eyes. She had every right to hate me. Somehow, she didn't."

"You could have hated her years earlier."

"For a while I did. I'm no saint, Shamus. But I knew there was no way I could tell your father about being pregnant. Your mother likely suspected. But she kept her suspicions to herself. She was always pleasant to me. You and my son used to play in the park when you were very little. You might remember him."

"Richie," Shamus said, his eyes wide with recollection.

"You were playground best friends." She produced a photo from the side table near her. It was of a young man in uniform, a Bronze Star and Purple Heart mounted on either side of the frame.

"He was disabling a landmine in Afghanistan when he died."

"I'm so sorry," Shamus said, holding the frame, feeling something of her loss.

"Richie was fearless. He would want me to be as brave as he was." She put the picture down and went on, "I have a granddaughter. She's five. Her name is Emily."

"Does she live in the city?"

"In Danbury, Connecticut. I see her twice a month. My daughter-in-law hasn't remarried. Even if she does, she'll make sure I continue to see Emily. She is a lovely person and a wonderful mother."

Silence ensued for a few moments, then she said, "I'm sorry for what we did to you that night, Shamus."

"My father and I hardly spoke after that," Shamus said.

"He simply didn't know what to say."

Shamus looked up toward the ceiling.

"There are things we do in our lives for which there is no going back. They simply can't be set right by words," Loretta offered. "I'm sure he felt that way."

"Maybe."

"He did try. Your father tried to write a note to you."

"He did?"

"He showed me a draft when we spoke briefly on the train about a year after the night you remember. I still have it."

"He gave it to you?"

"No."

"You stole it?"

"In a manner of speaking I did. He crumpled it and threw it into the trash bin at the railroad station. I wanted something that he'd written, even if not to me. So, I took it."

Shamus remembered that bin—He'd hidden behind it, so excited at the prospect of jumping out to surprise his father.

She walked over to the desk, removed an envelope and brought it to him.

Shamus stiffened. "If he didn't give it to me when he was alive, I shouldn't have it now."

"That's up to you, but it is yours. Open it or throw it away. He wasn't a perfect man. He was, however, a better man than you think."

Shamus hesitated and then gently took it from her. "There were so many times when he could have said something about your history together."

"Perhaps you have never lived a lie or held a secret to protect someone you love. Maybe you've never felt deep shame."

Shamus looked away, letting his eyes close briefly.

"I was going to tell him about Richie that night. Your father looked out the window. He saw you. I'd never seen such pain on a man's face. He grabbed his things and ran out of the house."

"So, I ruined things for Richie too."

"No, Shamus," she said, placing her warm hands on his upper arm.

"Had I bicycled home, not followed the two of you, not climbed the tree and watched you and he kiss, all of our lives would have been different. Better."

"Had we not walked from the station, allowed ourselves that forbidden time together, a little boy would not have had his heart broken, and a loving father would have gone home and played with him. That would have been better."

"Not for you."

"Oh yes. It would have been. I lost him again that night. The pain was excruciating and made all the worse knowing that you'd been hurt. Richie had my dad while he grew up. They were inseparable. It was your pain that haunted me."

She lifted the cookie dish. Shamus declined. She put the dish down and closed her moist eyes. After a moment, she made herself smile with a strength that comes from years of moving past pain. "I've been reading in the newspaper about the conference your sister is attending. Meg was mentioned as having found a murdered professor." Her brow furrowed in sincere concern. "And then another man was killed. How is she?"

"It's always hard to say with Meg. She seems to be doing as well as can be expected."

Loretta nodded.

"We got away from it all last night and visited the parents of one of her friends. Wesley Farnum. You may have heard of the family. I'm sure their attendance at upper crust gatherings makes the news here."

"I used to work for them. I was exhibit director at MOMA. They lured me away with promises of freedom to design their offices and homes. They never paid what they owed before letting me go. I gave up a career on a promise from those awful people."

"Did you get your job back at MOMA?"

"It was too late. I'd been replaced. I work part time there. It helps make ends meet."

"Did they ever give you a reason for being fired?"

"One of Mrs. Farnum's turtles went missing."

"What?"

"Not real ones, though she says the love she has for them came from a real turtle she had as a child. She collects expensive turtle paintings, pottery, pins and antiques. She has turtle jewelry with various stones. Even solid gold turtles. They're everywhere in her bedroom, their library and her home office. Mr. Farnum convinced her to keep the living room clear of them, but if you look closely, you'll find a few."

"Did they even ask if you'd taken it?"

"The Farnums don't discuss, they dictate. The turtle pin probably fell from a shelf. One of 'the help,' as she refers to people who work there, may have knocked it over when dusting. Or, the loss may have been a complete fabrication. Evelyn Farnum isn't above that, I'll tell you."

"From what I've seen, I wouldn't put it past her either."

"She had Mr. Farnum fire me. He liked my work. But she is the one who owns most of their fortune. He does not cross her."

"She probably didn't want to pay you."

Loretta nodded. "I never met Wesley, but it's hard to imagine two such creatures raising a good person."

"He's spoiled, but he has some redeeming features."

"That's good."

She patted her knees, and stood. Shamus did, too.

"I hope you found what you needed here today. Some closure. Though I find that concept highly overrated. Some things in life are never resolved. You blame yourself, wish you'd done this or that, worry incessantly about what others think and then, God willing, you learn to live with what happened. You wake up one day and understand that the past can't be changed. The path you travelled is behind you. There is no value in hatred or revenge. Finally, the demons get bored with you. Most skulk away. A few remain, lurking, waiting for your weak moments."

She squeezed Shamus hand. "Don't be a stranger. "Come meet Emily when she visits or when I'm in Danbury. After all, you're her uncle."

"I'd like that very much."

"Make it soon," she said. "I may be moving."

"Why?"

Loretta scanned her apartment wistfully. "Life moves on," she said before turning to Shamus with a warm smile.

Shamus decided not to pry into her reasons for leaving a place she clearly loved. He hardly knew Loretta, yet she'd been a part of his life for a very long time. As he passed by the mailboxes, he noticed a pile of unopened envelopes stamped with the words "EVICTION NOTICE: UNPAID RENT" in red.

CHAPTER THIRTY

As Shamus walked along the sidewalk, the skies opened. He ran under an awning, hoping the torrent would lighten again. His mind was latching onto renewed disdain for the Farnums. They'd deprived Loretta of the job she loved at MOMA and a salary good enough to hold onto a rent-controlled apartment. The rain had not let up. He stepped out into the deluge. At the subway station, soaked to the skin, still angry, he descended to the Manhattan bound side.

Leaning against a pillar, his mind drifted again. Loretta was not the person he'd expected. For over two decades he had thought of her as evil, but she was the antithesis of that. He touched the letter in his coat pocket feeling the years of emotional energy wasted that could never be retrieved. If his father were still alive, Shamus thought, things would be different. They'd argue, but that would be better than interminable silence and regret.

Then there was his mother. His wrath and his father's unwillingness to address it had burdened her with more pain than she'd already borne by knowing what had happened between his father and Loretta. He could see that now. But, as Loretta had said, that path had been walked. No matter how many times he looked back, nothing could be changed.

When Shamus entered the subway car, there was standing room only. He grabbed hold of a pole already steadying at least five other passengers and inched his hand upward until sure of offending no one.

He looked though a small window to the adjacent car. A man in his late thirties wearing a brown leather jacket was glowering at him.

"Shit!" Shamus muttered. A woman with a stroller gave him a sideways glance. "Sorry."

She nodded, diverting her eyes after a don't-do-it-again look.

He peered through the window: no brown leather jacket. Perhaps he'd been imagining things. After all, there must be thousands of men wearing the same jacket in New York City, and just as many peeved by crowded surroundings.

A seat near him became available. Shamus gestured for the woman with the stroller to take it. Another woman nodded at Shamus and then smiled at the gurgling baby. A few other passengers grinned, amused by the baby's gleeful smile. Then, one by one, each returned to a dour expression.

Shamus glanced into the adjacent car. It leaned. He hadn't been imagining things. There was the familiar face. He reached for his phone to call Jeffries but stopped. *What if he isn't the guy? And how would I explain being in Brooklyn Heights?*

At the Lexington Avenue stop, the crowd was too thick to see much. He got on the escalator. Halfway up, he looked back. The man was sporting a Yankee's cap, head down, pushing his way through a crowd at the base of the escalator.

As Shamus stepped off the escalator half of him was in fight mode, the other in flight. The latter had almost won out, then he had an idea. He left the station and darted across the street. The man emerged looking around. Their eyes met. Shamus lifted his phone and took two photos. Madison's attacker, Rolex and all, was on record. The man scowled and stepped into the street. A taxi barely missed hitting him. Then, a bus crossed his path. He kept advancing. Shamus slipped into a crowded diner, headed to a booth in the back and called Jeffries.

A police car screeched to a halt outside the diner. Shamus stood. Customers stopped ordering and eating. Two officers guardedly emerged from their car. A siren sounded and then another car pulled up. The first two officers to arrive searched outside. The other two entered the diner. Shamus remained still until Jeffries and Krawski emerged from an unmarked car. Krawski signaled to Jeffries that he'd handle the exterior. Jeffries entered the diner, reassured customers that the man they were after was far away and then walked slowly to the back of the diner.

Jeffries sat across from Shamus.

"That was quick," Shamus said. He signaled a waitress to bring two coffees — one decaf — as the detective glared at him.

"This should help," Shamus said, holding up the photo. "It's him."

"Christ, Doherty. You took his photo while he was looking right at you?"

"He was across the street."

"Oh, that makes all the difference," Jeffries mocked. "Are you out of your mind? You could have gotten yourself killed."

"I was in danger anyway."

"How long was he following you?" Jeffries asked as he tore open a sugar packet and dumped half of it into his coffee. "What are you doing here?"

"Took a subway ride to think."

"Right," Jeffries said, eyeing Shamus as he lifted the mug.

"I did."

"Where?"

"Lots of places."

"You had nothing better to do today? No need to keep an eye on your sister or Madison?"

"You already have them covered."

"Still," Jeffries countered, "it seems rather frivolous to go off on a joy ride under the circumstances."

"It wasn't a joy ride. Haven't you ever gotten away to clear your brain? To think straight?"

"No," Jeffries retorted.

"You should try it," Shamus said as he lifted his mug. "Besides, what does it matter where I go? I'm not a suspect."

Jeffries stood. "I'll need those photos."

"Already sent to your email."

"One of my officers will take your sorry ass back to the hotel. Stay there until you hear from me."

"Suits me fine." Shamus sipped his coffee.

"You're pretty flippant for a guy who just looked death in the face."

"There are cops everywhere. One at my table. I haven't felt this safe since I was back in Ridgefield."

Jeffries eyed Shamus for a moment, checked his phone for the photos, and walked resolutely from the diner.

CHAPTER THIRTY-ONE

When Shamus entered the suite, Madison was reclining on the sofa with an ice pack held to her head. Rashid looked out from the kitchen area.

"You are just in time," Rashid said. "I make the world's best jasmine-lemon tea."

"Smells great. I'd like some."

Shamus sat down near Madison.

"I don't want to talk," she said. "My head is killing me."

Rashid served the tea.

"No surprise after what you've been through. I have only one question. Have you been able to recall anything about the guy who attacked you?"

"I was too busy worrying that he was going to kill you."

"He's not your average thug," Shamus said. "He had on an expensive leather jacket, a Rolex and a large, silver signet ring."

He took out his phone, opened it to one of the photos, and placed it on the coffee table.

Madison's eyes grew large. "My God! Where did you get this?"

"So you remember him?"

"No. I mean, sort of, I guess. Is that him?"

Shamus nodded. Rashid leaned in to get a look.

"What the hell were you doing that close to him?" Madison asked.

"I spotted him watching me."

"You stopped to take this photo?" Rashid asked, amazed.

"It was a spur of the moment decision."

Rashid cast his friend a skeptical look.

"Those are his eyes," Madison said. "Even from this photo I can tell. He glared down at me in the jacuzzi. His eyes are two different colors. One is blue and the other gray." She sat up. "I didn't remember that until now. My God! And, I've met him. It was after my session. He complimented me on my presentation. I mumbled an apology for it having been a bit too long, and he said, 'The appropriate response is to thank me.' I was taken aback, but then I realized he was right. He'd taken the trouble to compliment me, so I should have been gracious. I thanked him. He looked at me kind of eerily and walked away."

"Had you ever seen him before?" Rashid asked.

"No."

"Did you see him talking to anybody else?"

"No. Oh, wait a minute. There was a graduate student standing next to me who looked surprised—as if she thought he was out of line."

"What's her name?"

"I've seen her in our division meetings. She has long, black hair and bangs. Her skin is very pale, kind of an Adam's Family Letitia look."

"Serina Frost?" Rashid offered.

"That's her!"

"Where can we find her?" asked Shamus.

"She was at my poster session," Rashid said. "Her questions were very astute. I think she gave me her card." He reached into his pocket and produced a small stack of business cards. "Here it is, with her mobile number."

Rashid handed it to Shamus.

"I'm going to call and ask her to meet me."

"I'm going with you," Rashid said.

"Jeffries should be doing this," Madison objected. "You don't know what you're getting yourself into."

"I'm only going to ask her if she knows the guy," Shamus explained. "We'll tell Jeffries if we learn anything."

"There will be no heroics," Rashid assured Madison.

As they headed for the door, Shamus stopped. "Madison, did you remember to tell the officer guarding you that we were going to the Farnums' home for dinner last night?"

"I think I mentioned that we'd all be going out for dinner. I can't remember."

"That's not good enough. It's his job to tag along. Jeffries told me that if you ditch him again, he'll wind up on foot patrol—if he's lucky."

"I'll apologize," she said with a brief wave as she retrieved a magazine from the coffee table.

"It's serious," Shamus insisted.

Madison sighed. "Okay. Got it."

"Shall we go?" Rashid asked.

"Make sure Jeffries knows it wasn't his fault. And let him yell at you."

Madison indifferently flipped pages of her magazine.

Shamus waited for her to look up—to demonstrate reasonable concern. She didn't. *If Meg were here,* Shamus thought, *she'd be looking right at me, her eyes saying, "I told you so."*

CHAPTER THIRTY-TWO

Shamus tried to phone Serina. No answer. He texted, asking that she call him. The elevator opened to the lobby level. Sessions were ending, so Shamus and Rashid had to weave their way through a thick crowd.

"Hey," Shamus called to Emma who was chatting with another woman.

Emma looked over at them and smiled, less than enthusiastically.

"Did you give another presentation just now?"

"No," she said glancing around as if looking for an escape route. "I sat in on one."

"This is Rashid. He is a professor at Pacific Coast University with Meg. His case competition team just won the NYU tournament."

"That's wonderful!" Emma said, reaching to shake Rashid's hand.

"They are a special group of young people," Rashid replied appreciatively.

"Rashid is modest," Shamus said. "He's a marvelous coach. And he also won the top poster session award."

Rashid gave him a cease-and-desist look.

Emma's eyes widened. "Congratulations!"

"Thank you," Rashid said.

"Have you seen Serina Frost?" Shamus asked. "Meg wants to talk with her about a paper. It came in second for the dissertation award you won. Apparently, Meg thinks it has publication potential."

Rashid glanced disapprovingly at Shamus, then quickly back at Emma with a smile.

"That's very considerate of Meg," Emma replied stiffly.

"My sister is very encouraging of young scholars."

"Yes, of course," Emma said.

"She knows your paper will be published given that it won the dissertation award or I'm sure she'd be talking with you too."

"Serina just presented. She's likely still there talking to people." Emma pointed. "The room is three doors down that way. She presented her dissertation paper, so I'm surprised Meg didn't go to the session given her interest."

"She had to be elsewhere."

"I see."

Shamus nodded awkwardly. "We're going to head over to the room to catch Serina."

"My congratulations, Emma," Rashid said. "The Top Dissertation Award is an honor portending a very impressive academic future."

When she was out of earshot, Rashid said, "You cannot go around making up such things about publication! Your sister will be furious. You have nearly promised that she will help Serina publish her paper. I would not wish to be in your shoes when she finds out."

"She'll understand."

"You are not an academic. The people around you publish or perish. Their futures are not to be toyed with. It is beyond reckless."

"Didn't I say Meg wants to help her publish, not that she'll guarantee it?"

"You must not go near that line. Do not offer Meg's help lightly."

"Fine," Shamus said. "You're right."

They entered the session room Emma had pinpointed. A young woman was enjoying the appreciation of about five people. Her captivating green eyes seemed focused intensely on each person to whom she spoke, causing some to linger, to extend their moment of exclusivity. She had long, ebony eyelashes and perfectly shaped thin eyebrows that rose in welcome to each new admirer. Peeking from beneath the cup sleeves of her simple, white silk blouse were the edges of brightly colored tattoos.

"Perhaps you should sit down," Rashid said. "At the very least close your mouth. You look as if you've fallen into a trance."

"Well, she's unusual. It threw me a bit."

"Yes. She is an exotic beauty," Rashid said as they watched a beaming Serina hold a woman's hand with both of hers as if thanking her for a particularly flattering compliment.

As they approached, Serina was saying a few parting words to Mitchell Avery. She looked up at Shamus with a brief glimmer of recognition before turning her attention to Rashid. "Good to see you again," she said enthusiastically.

"It is my pleasure," Rashid replied with a slight bow of his head. He added, "This is Shamus Doherty."

"You must be Meg's brother," Serina said brightly.

"Yes," Shamus replied, reaching to shake her hand. "I wish we'd heard your presentation. It must have been terrific given the number of people gathered around you when we arrived."

"Thank you."

"We're here because you may have seen someone yesterday talking to Madison Wills after the session. He criticized her for not accepting his compliment on her presentation with a simple thank you."

"Oh yes! I remember."

"Do you know him?" Rashid asked.

"No," she said. "But my friend Emma does."

"Would that be Emma Richards?" Shamus asked.

"Yes."

"Anything you can remember about him could be helpful," Rashid said.

Her eyes widened with concern. "Does this have anything to do with the murders?"

"We don't even know who he is," Rashid replied. "He just struck Madison as odd."

"I agree," Serina said. "He gave me the creeps."

"Did he have a nametag?" Shamus asked.

"Yes. It read in capital, block letters: 'REB'. There was no university or business mentioned. When he finished talking with Madison, he looked at me as if annoyed at my eavesdropping. To offset my discomfort, I pointed at his nametag and piped up, 'Does that stand for rebel?' He smirked. Turns out it stands for Erebus."

"The Greek god of darkness," Rashid said.

"Yes," Serina replied, impressed.

"How did you know that?" Shamus asked. "How would anyone know that?"

"I am a case competition coach. We study persuasion, beginning with the ancient Greek philosophers. You naturally learn about their deities."

"Naturally," Shamus mocked good-naturedly.

"I couldn't help but wonder what kind of parent names a child after darkness," Serina said. "As if reading my mind, he said the name was given to him in prison. Clearly, he was trying to unnerve me. I didn't respond. He glared at me, turned and walked away leaving a chill in his wake."

"You were kinder than I would have been," Shamus said.

"People test each other at conferences and say some odd things to speakers. Some get angry at your point of view, or an imagined insult to theirs. It doesn't pay to be rude. I treat their comments as informative."

"I would stay very far from that man," Rashid offered.

Serina picked up her briefcase. "Emma should be able to tell you more. I saw her with him in the lobby last night. He looked angry. His face was a couple of inches from hers. Emma noticed me and forced a smile. He shot me a warning glare. I just kept walking."

"Do you happen to have Emma's phone number?" Shamus asked. "We saw her earlier, but she may have vanished by now."

"Yes," Serina said, then hesitated. "I'll get it." She took her phone from her briefcase just as Rashid took his from his pocket. She found the number and showed it to Rashid. He entered it into his phone.

"Please don't tell her I gave you the number. We're conference friends, but I don't know her well enough to be sure she wouldn't be annoyed."

"We will be judicious," Rashid promised.

"By the way," Shamus interjected, "my sister wants to talk with you about where you might publish your dissertation. She'd like to help."

"Really?" Serina said, eyes wide.

Rashid frowned, then busied himself with his phone.

"She enjoys mentoring promising young scholars like yourself."

Rashid stepped further away.

"I'll call her later today, if that's okay," Serina effused. "I can't tell you how much this means. Thank you."

"I can't make promises for her, but surely only good can come from it," Shamus said.

"Even her advice would be a gift."

They watched as Serina nearly skipped from the room.

"She will float for days," Rashid said. "Fortunately for her, and you, Meg will speak with her. She will keep your promise. But, as I advised, she will not be happy with you."

Shamus shook his head. "It had to be done. I'd already told Emma that Meg wanted to help Serina. The stories had to match. I went easy, though. Made no promises. She understood that."

Rashid sighed. "I hope that is the end of it. I'll say no more as clearly my advice is falling on deaf ears."

"Nothing you say falls on deaf ears," Shamus said, placing a hand on his friend's back. "Your wisdom is always welcome. I was in too deep this time. But next time, I'll heed your words to the letter."

Rashid smiled, shaking his head as they walked. "I will be waiting with bated breath."

Police Interview: Mitchell Avery

"Yes, Stan Evans was more than dismissive of me and my work. Tim Baron put him in his place. Stan thought he was God's gift to social science. What kind of full professor shreds a graduate student in front of hundreds of people? The way I see it, you reap what you sow and that's exactly what happened to him."

CHAPTER THIRTY-THREE

Emma was walking alone, talking to herself, preparing for a speech.

"We meet again," Shamus said as he and Rashid caught up with her. "Did you find Serina?"

"We did," Rashid said pleasantly. "Thank you."

Emma smiled and began to edge away. "I'd love to talk, but I'm presenting in a few minutes and need to go get settled at the dais and make sure my notes are in order."

"It will only take a minute," Rashid said, affably.

"I really can't…"

"Serina mentioned seeing you last night," Shamus said. "You were talking with a man we need to find."

"Who?"

"The guy you were seen arguing with," Shamus insisted. "He goes by 'Reb'."

"I haven't a clue what you're talking about. Besides, who I speak with is my business."

"I need his full name," Shamus said, his tone sharpening.

"We are not accusing you of anything, Emma," Rashid reassured her. "He may pose a danger to Madison. Surely you wish to protect your mentor."

"He followed me from the bar and insisted on taking me out for coffee. I told him to leave me alone."

"Serina saw it differently," Shamus said.

"I really don't care what she saw." Emma scoffed.

"May I ask whether you had ever seen him before that time?" Rashid asked.

"No."

"You're lying," Shamus said.

Emerging from the crowd, Wesley joined Emma and shot Shamus a fierce look.

"What's the problem here?"

"This doesn't have anything to do with you," Shamus said, his eyes intent on Emma.

"Clearly, Emma doesn't want to talk to you."

Two other men joined Wesley. Shamus recognized them. They had been at the meeting that he and Penelope had surreptitiously observed.

"Who are these goons?" Shamus asked. "Friends of your family? Pilots perhaps?"

Ignoring Shamus, Wesley said, "I'll escort you to your session, Emma."

"I'd appreciate that."

She brushed past Shamus and went into the session room, entourage in tow.

"She was lying," Shamus said.

"Can you blame her? Perhaps this man is dangerous," said Rashid. "You might have considered that before pressuring her so hard."

"What am I supposed to do, pussy foot around?"

"Let me try again. You are a foreigner in this academic culture. There is much you don't understand—hidden alliances you fail to consider. A moat surrounds this castle. Tread lightly with people like Emma who the princes fear may reveal too much, or the drawbridge will surely be slammed shut."

Jeffries was sitting at the lobby bar having a Coke when Shamus and Rashid approached him. He gestured for them to sit and signaled the bartender for two more Cokes. "Do you two have something to share? Otherwise, I'm pushed for time."

"It's not something you can take to the bank," Shamus said.

"Just tell me."

"There's a professor named Emma Richards. She's a rising young star. As we speak, she's presenting her award-winning dissertation work. Apparently, she was seen with the man who stalked me. Also, having seen his photo, Madison remembers him coming up to her after her last presentation. She recalled him having two different colored eyes and acting oddly."

Jeffries sat up a little straighter. "And?"

"A graduate student, Serina Frost, was standing next to Madison on the dais. She also thought he was acting weird. She noticed his nametag. It read 'Reb,' short for Erebus, Greek god of darkness."

"What the fuck?"

"Right. My thought exactly," Shamus said. "But that's what he said."

"Serina doesn't know him," Rashid added. "But she recalls him having a conflict with Emma in the lobby the other night. Emma insists he was just some stranger pestering her."

"You don't believe her?" Jeffries asked.

"No," Rashid said.

"But you don't know for sure?"

"Are you not listening?" Shamus asked.

"How's this?" Jeffries said in a mocking tone. "You two have solved the case. I'll tell my detectives to take the rest of the day off. Two more murder cases solved in the Big Apple by a construction foreman from a suburb state and a left coast professor. Happens all the time."

"Sorry," Shamus said. "I'm agitated."

Jeffries remained silent, studying Shamus, seeming to cool.

"We are trying to help prevent more murders," Rashid said.

"You're both out of your depth. I appreciate the tip, but now leave the rest to me. You've avoided being killed so far. Next time you might not be so lucky." Jeffries stood, tossed a twenty on the bar and walked away.

"We should heed his advice about the danger," Rashid said. "But we will find this man."

Shamus turned to Rashid. "What's this 'we'? I thought you were peeved at my heavy-handed ways."

"Indeed I am," Rashid said as he stood. "It is not an entirely new feeling in your presence, my friend." He stifled a smile. "I suspect, however, as before, it will pass in due time."

Meg arrived at the door of the banquet room where hundreds of her colleagues were gathered for a pre-dinner cocktail party and awards ceremony. She was wearing a striking emerald green velvet jacket, ivory satin blouse and gray skirt.

A group of graduate students called to her. Mitchell Avery was with them, along with Rod whose eyes were still strained. Meg joined them. Mitchell introduced her. When she turned to Rod, he nodded and walked away.

"I'm surprised he's still here," Mitchell said to Meg. "He's a wreck. I would be if my mentor had been killed."

Meg nodded, her eyes following Rod as he took a seat by himself in a dark corner of the room. "He looks lost."

"You were there right after two murders," blurted a female student.

The others looked embarrassed for her.

"Ashley has a way with words," Mitchell said apologetically.

"I'm just stating the obvious," Ashley defended. "Nobody wants to talk about it when you're around, but two times you just missed spotting the murderer. It's just weird."

Mitchell frowned at Ashley and shook his head slightly.

Ashley was not deterred. "I would have died. I mean really died. You must be made of steel."

Meg smiled graciously. "I should mingle a bit. Good to meet all of you," Meg said, turning to leave. "Especially good to see you again, Mitchell. I've heard many good things about your presentation under fire."

"I have Professor Baron to thank."

"Tim doesn't rise to help just anyone. He sees promise in you. So do I."

Meg touched the beaming Mitchell's arm and took her leave. She passed by Bill Carroll who was speaking loudly, beer in hand.

"There she is," he bellowed.

Meg turned. "Hello Bill."

She began to walk. He grabbed her arm with a beer soaked hand. "Join us," he insisted.

Meg cast her eyes downward at his offensive hand. He released her.

"Look at you," Carroll said. "I didn't expect to see you out partying and looking so festive."

"Unfortunately, I can't stop to chat," Meg offered to the others. "I have plans and I'm running late."

"So, we're not good enough for you," Carroll laughed. One of the onlookers walked away.

"What's going on here?" came a familiar voice from behind Meg. She turned. Tim Baron smiled at her before glaring at Carroll.

"Bill is a bit wasted," Meg said. "I'm handling it."

"No doubt you are," Baron said. "There's just something very offensive to me about a senior professor with no manners."

"Oh, the civility police have arrived," Carroll scoffed. He held his glass high.

"Run along," Baron said, "while you still have a smidgeon of dignity."

"Have it your way," Carroll said with an exaggerated bow that nearly toppled him.

The inebriated professor made his way over to another group, clearly not pleased to see him.

"He's a hopeless bully," Baron said to Meg.

"That he is."

Baron glanced appreciatively at Meg's outfit. "You look stunning this evening."

"Why thank you, Tim. You're looking rather dashing yourself with that bright blue bow tie."

"Just a bit of fun."

"Shamus gave me your message," Meg said.

"The intent was a positive one."

"You want me to keep something to myself for the good of the field. Is that it?"

"For your benefit as well."

She smiled slightly. "Does it have to do with Stan?"

Baron looked around for eavesdroppers and his eyes met hers. "I think you know." He touched her elbow sympathetically. "Please excuse me, Meg. I hate these ludicrous parties, but I must make the rounds."

"Tim…"

"I have said all I can," Baron interrupted. "Anything additional would be unseemly."

Meg stood contemplating the word "unseemly" as Baron moved on. It made her feel unclean somehow.

"My, my," Wesley said approaching Meg. Then his eyes widened. "What the hell are you doing?" he whispered. "You're wearing the scarf. The blood stains are visible for Christ's sake."

"Whoever left it in my briefcase expects me to be terrified. I'm not giving him or her the satisfaction. I'm done with that."

"You're going to give Jeffries a reason to suspect you of murder. He'll know dried blood when he sees it. He'll find out what happened years ago. Have you lost your mind?"

"Someone is going to recognize this scarf," Meg said looking past Wesley, scanning the crowd. "I'll see it in his or her eyes."

"And then you'll do what?"

"People are looking at us, Wesley. We can talk later."

He blocked her path. She looked directly into his eyes and he reluctantly stepped aside.

A group of senior professors to her right were discussing a research presentation given earlier in the day. They noticed her and quieted. She began to walk. People stepped from her path. A few nodded. A cluster of vaguely familiar faces were arguing murder theories. They turned in unison, accusatorial, as if characters in a dream. The floor seemed to undulate; the room grew warm. She searched for the nearest exit. There, in the doorway, was Tim Baron, watching her, noticing the scarf, looking ominously displeased.

CHAPTER THIRTY-FOUR

Shamus bought two bagels and coffees to bring back to the hotel. Meg was sleeping later than usual. He'd considered knocking on her door to see if she'd like to come along. Instead, he'd let her sleep.

A limousine pulled up next to him just as he reached the hotel. Cole Farnum stepped out. He was wearing a long camel hair coat. Two men exited the limousine behind him. They stood with their arms crossed, eyes forward.

"I'd like to invite you to our city apartment," Farnum said. Our Connecticut house needs a remodel and your team may be right for the job. Let's go discuss it."

"Bullshit," Shamus said and kept walking.

From around a corner, no more than twenty feet from Shamus, another of Farnum's security goons appeared.

"There are more like him," Farnum said. "Get into the limo."

"No thanks," Shamus said, starting to walk again. "Had enough of your kind of transportation the other night."

Farnum nodded toward the car. It drew slowly beside Shamus. The driver stepped out. He was huge.

"A man in my position can get a lot done, my boy. Power talks in New York City. No one is going to hurt you. All I need is an hour of your time to discuss the deal."

Shamus looked down, chuckling derogatorily. "The deal?"

"Don't toy with me, Doherty."

Shamus sipped his coffee. He dropped it and the bag into a trash bin, turned to Cole Farnum and smirked. "This better be good," he said as he entered the limo.

The limousine pulled up in front of a traditional large white brick house attached on both sides by ones of equivalent opulence. The driver exited the vehicle first, followed by the two oafs who'd been staring at Shamus since they'd begun their journey. A large black door to the front of the house opened slowly. Shamus looked for a person, but no one appeared. Farnum waited for his door to be opened and exited the limousine. He gestured for Shamus to follow.

Off white marble steps, broad at the base, swept indulgently to a landing beneath a graceful portico of matching marble. Shamus endeavored to appear unimpressed, which Farnum observed with a patronizing smile. They entered the house. Farnum led Shamus up the stairs lit by a massive antique chandelier. Shards of light danced across the high ceiling like carefree ballerinas.

"Where is Mimi," Farnum called, his brow furrowed.

"Coming, sir."

A slight, dark-haired, young woman dressed in a maid's outfit descended the steps arriving like Wendy on a flight from Neverland. She dipped in deference before taking their coats, and rushing delicately up the stairs and out of sight.

"She's impressive," Shamus said.

"Ah. She's all right." Farnum grumbled and waved dismissively. "She's lasted longer than most. They're all of lax habit if you ask me."

"Who?" Shamus asked.

Farnum looked at him as if an explanation was unwarranted.

"Ah," Shamus said sarcastically, "the help."

"Watch yourself," Farnum warned him.

"Hey, I can call a taxi and head back to the hotel."

Farnum glowered. He was about to give Shamus a piece of his mind when a woman's voice called.

"Cole, what's keeping you?"

Suddenly Farnum roared with laughter and tossed his head back as if Shamus had told a marvelous joke. He smiled broadly and put his arm around Shamus' shoulders.

"That's just my way, son. It's gruff. I'm working on it. Mrs. Farnum finds it distasteful. My apologies."

They ascended the remaining steps and entered an expansive, lavishly furnished living room. Shamus half expected a museum docent to sweep in at any moment followed by intrigued tourists.

Mrs. Farnum was seated on a plush white sofa. As they approached, she regally extended her hand. Shamus moved to take it, clearly unsure of the protocol. She pulled her hand away.

"Let's not be formal," she said, appearing disappointed by his ungainliness. "Come. Come. Sit."

She pointed to a light blue chair, no doubt an antique. Shamus sat. Over a sumptuous, grey-speckled marble fireplace hung a Jackson Pollack.

The room was impeccably clean. If there was a speck of dust, Shamus could not find it despite the sunlight pouring in through white gossamer curtains over pristine glass. He felt an urge to place his hand, palm out, against one of the windows if for no other reason than to provide a hint of human imperfection. He could never live like this.

Mimi arrived with a tray of tea and coffee, cream, sugar and scones. She placed it gently on a small table in front of Mrs. Farnum and hurried away.

"How good of you to come," said Mrs. Farnum.

"Your husband is very persuasive."

"Indeed," she said with a knowing smile. "We got off on the wrong foot the other night. It happens."

Shamus was about to speak, to add his own twist to her understatement.

"Some tea or coffee?" Mrs. Farnum offered.

"Either," Shamus said, glancing around the room.

Mrs. Farnum poured tea. Shamus struggled with the delicate cup and saucer decorated with tiny turtles. He sipped and then placed the set on his own small table, where he intended it would remain for the duration of his visit.

"Are you an admirer of turtles?" Mrs. Farnum asked hopefully.

"I had one as a child," Shamus said.

"Did you hear that Cole?"

"Yes dear."

"They are the abode of an ancient deity in Mayan art and culture. Hence the protective shells," Mrs. Farnum explained with exquisite pleasure. "Your cup has an emerald green conch shell and matching body, gorgeous markings with flecks of gray. It's one of my favorites."

"You know what you need, Doherty?" Farnum interrupted to his wife's displeasure.

"Cole doesn't like my turtles," she said petulantly.

"He can hear about them another time, Evelyn."

Mrs. Farnum stiffened, shot her husband a disparaging glance and looked away.

"A touch of Midleton Very Rare whiskey is what Shamus needs," Farnum said.

"It's too early," she insisted.

"Nonsense, dear. Doherty here is Irish. Midleton is Irish."

Farnum exited the room and returned with the long, slender Midleton box. He removed the unopened bottle and poured two healthy amounts into crystal glasses before handing one to Shamus.

"To your health," Farnum said, holding up his glass.

Shamus returned the gesture and observed as Farnum downed the whiskey in one gulp.

Shamus emptied his glass. Farnum eagerly poured again.

"That will do, Cole," Mrs. Farnum said emphatically.

Farnum put down the bottle. He sat on the sofa beside his wife. "I told Shamus that we plan to remodel our Connecticut home."

"Indeed we do."

"We have studied your work and would like to receive a bid from you," said Mrs. Farnum.

"Do you have some drawings here?"

"I do," Farnum replied, as if the timing was not yet right to produce them.

"Can I see them?"

"Of course. I will retrieve them shortly."

"I see."

"You know," Mrs. Farnum said, "we once hoped that your sister and our Wesley might marry."

"And now?"

"I'm afraid your sister has broken our hearts and Wesley's as well."

"How did she do that?"

"You don't know?" Mrs. Farnum asked, eying her husband as if they'd practiced what was about to be said.

"No, I don't."

"She could have helped Wesley publish in a leading journal as second author, but she changed her mind. Halfway through the project, he reneged on their agreement."

"She must have had a good reason."

"It's too bad. She could have been a very wealthy woman. Her child would have gone to the best schools."

Shamus laughed derisively. "You don't know Meg very well if you think that would impress her."

Mrs. Farnum scowled at Shamus then seemed to think better of her demeanor and forced a smile. "If she chooses to do so, she can still help Wesley."

"And you brought me here thinking I'd ask her to do that?"

Sipping her tea, Mrs. Farnum peered over the cup at her husband.

Farnum cleared his throat and sat more erect. "Evelyn hesitates to say outright that we have been very kind to Meghan. We have overlooked elements of her background such as having a child out of wedlock."

Mrs. Farnum looked downward and then over to her right side as if someone had expelled flatus.

"We are not the type of people who take kindly to being treated with disregard when we have been generous," Farnum said.

"I see," Shamus said standing. "Just so we're clear, my sister wouldn't marry your son. I don't say this because he isn't smart enough, but because he isn't good enough for her. Or for her son."

Farnum nearly leapt from his chair, chest puffed out and eyes livid. "You just lost a very lucrative construction contract."

Shamus smirked. "There's not enough money in the world for you to hire me."

His host's jowls quivered with anger. "Get out!" Farnum bellowed.

"Wait!" Mrs. Farnum said, stretching her arm out between the men. "Cole, we are forgetting our manners here."

Farnum glared at his wife, rage emanating from every pore.

"Would you ask your sister to reconsider?"

"Why doesn't Wesley ask her himself?"

"Some matters are delicate and more difficult for young men. We believe, upon reflection, your sister may decide that she acted rashly. Of course, being asked by the right person could make all the difference. She might even allow him to be first author, which would help his tenure chances immensely."

"Thank you for the tea," Shamus said with an amused smile. "I'm afraid I have promised my friend, Rashid, that I will stay clear of all things to do with publication. Apparently, I know very little about it."

"My wife is quite serious," Farnum said. "You have not given her an adequate answer. That is unwise."

Shamus stepped forward until he and Farnum were only inches apart. Mrs. Farnum lifted a porcelain bell.

"There's no need to call your goons. I'm just letting your husband know that should my sister ever feel intimidated or threatened, nothing on this earth would stop me from making him pay dearly."

"Get out!" Farnum shouted.

His guards rushed into the room. Farnum held up his hand and they stopped.

Mimi rushed into the room looking horrified. She shook her head, advising Shamus to go no further, hurried off and returned with his coat.

"Do not call me again," Shamus seethed. "And you, Mimi, should find another job. You're better than they deserve. Far better."

Shamus descended the stairs. Once outside, he hailed a cab. He sat in the back inattentive to the world passing him by. People like the Farnums made him sick. How his sister had come to be even loosely connected to them was more than he could fathom. At a stop light, Shamus opened a window, leaned out, waited until there was no one close by and spat.

CHAPTER THIRTY-FIVE

Shamus arrived at the suite. Meg looked up. He placed a fresh bagel and a coffee on the table in front of her. She smiled.

"Thanks," she said. "That was thoughtful."

"I have an odd question," Shamus said, taking a seat across from her. "Take it at face value. I'm not implying anything. I just don't understand the inner workings of journal acceptances and rejections in your field."

"Okay," she said. "It's complex, but go ahead."

"Could you have helped Wesley in some way? I mean in terms of publishing?"

"Where is this coming from?"

"Just bear with me. Did you ever publish together?"

"He asked me to co-author a research paper. He didn't do his share of the work, so another professor helped get it finished. She became second author. Wesley was third."

"What was his excuse?"

"There was a string of them."

"Did you tell him that you were going to move him to third author?"

"We'd discussed his lack of involvement and he saw the final draft before it went to a journal."

"I mean did you give him a chance to change his ways with full knowledge of the consequences?"

"What is this all about?"

"I just wanted to know if the Farnums were lying."

"Don't tell me," Meg said. "Did Cole Farnum phone you?"

"No. He showed up in a limo with his hit men. They insisted I go with them—supposedly to talk about remodeling his Greenwich house. He wouldn't have let up, so I went."

Meg studied her brother's face for a moment and then shook her head. "Authorship isn't about who wanted to do research and write a paper. It's about who actually did those things."

"I know a lot less about publishing than I do about hatred. It festers."

"Oh please, Shamus. Wesley is no murderer. I told you that."

"I'm not talking about Wesley. The Farnums nearly killed us the other night."

"They're not murders," Meg replied. "They're self-important and obnoxious."

"You don't get it, Meg. They have one child who, in their estimation, is failing at life because the right people haven't helped him."

"Like me?" she returned. "I tried to help Wesley."

"They think you purposely didn't."

"They're wrong."

"I'm not taking their side, Meg."

"It sounds like you are."

"I don't think you understand hatred," Shamus said. "What it does to people like the Farnums."

"Oh please," she said standing. "I have to go."

"Wait." Shamus reached for her. "I didn't mean…"

She pulled away, but stopped at the door. Her eyes met his. "Someday I'll tell *you* about hatred. Then we'll see which of us knows more."

Shamus was standing silent, mouth agape, arms outstretched, wondering what the hell had just happened, as Meg opened the door and left.

CHAPTER THIRTY-SIX

Party in 707—U. of Oklahoma! read the text from Rashid. Shamus texted back that he'd be there. As he left the suite, he couldn't shake Meg's anger from his mind. Never before had he seen her like that. *What had he said? How had he said it? What exactly had set her off?"*

Music, people, loud conversation, and laughter were spilling out of room 707 into the hallway. Shamus would like nothing better than to turn on his heels and flee, but he went inside. Seeing no one familiar, he made his way to the bar. He stood there sipping slowly on water.

People were crowded cheek to jowl. The occupancy had to be way past the fire limit, Shamus thought. When some raucous people queued up at the bar, the space juggling became too much for him. He walked over to a window and looked out at the skyline.

"You're a sight for sore eyes."

Shamus turned around. It was Penelope in a close fitting, half-backless dress with matching three-inch heels.

"These shoes are killing me," she grumbled as Shamus stared in admiration. "I never wear heels."

"Why tonight?"

"Are you some kind of simpleton? To fit in of course."

"Fit in? With whom?"

"Forget it," she huffed.

"Has Ray seen you in that fancy getup?"

"What does that have to do with anything?"

"You do know he's nuts about you, right?"

"He is not. It's professional admiration."

"Then let's go see what he thinks of us together with you looking so fine and all."

She rolled her eyes. "Let's pass on that."

"Hope we don't run into him," Shamus continued with a smile.

"He's busy tonight."

"That's a load off my mind."

"Are you through entertaining yourself?" Penelope asked, hands on her hips.

"Sorry. It's the crowd and the heat of this place."

"Sure it is."

Shamus raised his hands. "I surrender. Guilty of taking humor too far."

"Guilty of not being funny," Penelope said.

"You're right. I give in. Have you seen Wesley?"

"No. Why?"

"I had an unwelcome encounter with his parents today. They were about to offer me a job if Meg would publish with Wesley, letting him be at least second author."

"In their world money can buy anything. If parents can buy university admission for their kids, why can't professor's parents buy tenure?"

"There are several committees in tenure decisions, lots of hoops, but I wouldn't put it past them to try. Wesley would be furious. In fact, I'd like to find out what he thinks of them trying to bribe me on his behalf."

"Not much, I suspect. He's not like them," Penelope said.

"Speak of the devil."

Shamus nodded toward the door. Wesley had arrived and was headed for the bar.

"I'll be right back," Shamus said. "Don't go anywhere."

Moving from the window, he saw Meg approach Wesley. She said something to him, and they left the room. Shamus worked his way through the crowd and peered out the doorway. They were arguing. The noise from the party made it impossible to make out just what Meg was saying, but Shamus managed to catch the gist. It was about Wesley's parents. Shamus heard his own name mentioned. Wesley shook his head emphatically, but Meg was having none of it.

"Stop!" Wesley demanded loudly, gripping Meg by the shoulders. "I have no control over what my parents do. It changes nothing!"

Meg grasped his wrists and forced his hands to his sides.

"We can't talk here," she said before abruptly walking away.

Wesley watched Meg for a few moments seeming to consider his options. He breathed deeply, slapped the wall and followed after her.

"C'mon," Shamus said, returning to Penelope and leading her out the door.

"What's up?"

"Meg and Wesley were arguing and then took off."

"So?"

"Trust me. We need to find them."

"They're probably doing the party rounds," Penelope said, trying to keep up with him in heels. "There's another one on the mezzanine level."

As the elevator doors opened, Jeffries stepped out. He looked Penelope up and down.

"I almost didn't recognize you."

She brushed past him into the elevator, her arms crossed.

"Lovely, isn't she?" Shamus offered, following her.

Penelope glared at Jeffries as the doors began to close.

"I didn't say she isn't. I mean, yes. Shit!"

"Another man at a loss for words around women. You have to feel for the guy."

"Right," Penelope quipped.

Jeffries kneed one of the elevator doors and it opened.

"Sorry," Shamus said. "No time for chat," He pushed the door close button.

Jeffries blocked the doors with his body. "I suppose you're on your way to celebrate," Jeffries said looking at Shamus.

"Celebrate?" Shamus asked.

"You mean your sister hasn't shared her latest achievement with you?"

"Okay. Spit it out."

"She's a master," Jeffries chortled. "You've got to hand it to her. She finds two editors dead and days later she's about to be named the new editor of their journal. Pretty smooth."

"She wouldn't do that!"

"Ask her yourself," Jeffries taunted as the doors bumped their way to a close.

Shamus was doing a slow burn.

"He's pulling your leg," Penelope said. "Meg is probably just a candidate for the editorship."

"What benefit would Jeffries get from lying?" Shamus asked.

"The benefit to him is that he irritates you. Maybe he causes a rift between you and your sister. He has nothing on the murderers, his boss is peeved, her boss is apoplectic from what I hear, so he's trying to get under your skin just because he can."

"And then there's the press," Shamus said looking accusatorial. "He's fairing pretty badly there too."

"So, you've read my articles."

"A couple of them anyway."

"I report what I find."

Shamus eyed her skeptically.

"What?" Penelope challenged.

"Nothing."

"Tell me."

Shamus gave his better judgment a chance to intervene. It didn't. "We all have bad childhood memories. But we grow up. We move on or everyone suffers."

"Is that so?"

The elevator reached the mezzanine level. Penelope stomped out.

Shamus caught up with her. "Listen," he began.

"No. You listen," she said, eyes blazing. "That man deserted my mother and me. We served our purpose when he wanted to look like a stable family man. Once he got promoted, he discarded us. My mother never got over it."

"I only meant..."

"He doesn't deserve sympathy. And you couldn't possibly understand."

"You're right," Shamus said. "Of course. I'm sorry."

Penelope looked away.

"I'm working on my interpersonal skills," Shamus said, "but as you've seen tonight it's nearly hopeless."

"It's not all you. Just seeing him makes me crazy." She held his eyes for a moment. "Truth be told," she said with a short smile, "I suspect that someday some woman will learn to live with your limited interpersonal skills."

"Well, thank you Penelope. That's very kind."

"Against her better judgment, of course."

People were packed in like sardines at the University of Santa Barbara party.

"Swell," Shamus groused as they wormed their way through the crowd outside the door.

"Snap out of it," Penelope said, taking hold of his arm. "You can't walk in there looking like it's a funeral. Put on your party face."

"This *is* my party face."

Well into the room, Shamus nearly gagged on an intense amalgam of colognes and perfumes. Excusing himself, he went into a bathroom and splashed cold water on his face.

When he returned, Penelope had disappeared. A woman suddenly pulled him into a conga line that snaked about the room and out into the hallway. His hands were on the waist of a huge man. The line turned at the end of the hallway and headed back. Shamus broke away at the door, feigning life-threatening exhaustion.

He went to the bar for some water. Bill Carroll was bragging to graduate students. Madison spotted Shamus and gestured for him to join her. Shamus pointed to the bartender and mimicked drinking. She nodded.

He sipped on a glass of ice cold water, contemplating whether to join Madison and her growing retinue. He caught sight of Meg talking to a smiling Serina. There was no sign of Wesley. After tipping the bartender, he made his way over to them.

"Where have you been, Meg?"

She smiled over a simmering residue of anger.

"You look happy," he said, turning to Serina.

"Meg is going to help me publish in a leading journal, which is more than I'd let myself hope for after you and I talked."

"Well, I guess that'd please any young scholar."

"It's an impressive paper," Meg said with an encouraging smile for Serina.

"Thank you," Serina effused. "If you don't mind, I'm going to go mingle a bit." She nearly floated across the room to share her good news.

"Still sore at me?" Shamus gingerly inquired.

"She's bright and very pleasant, so I don't mind helping her. But don't do that again."

"I meant about the hatred thing."

"These conferences make everyone jittery even when no has been murdered," Meg replied, clearly ending the discussion.

They watched as people surrounding Serina were shaking her hand and hugging her.

"It should be easier to help her publish now that you're replacing Stan Evans as editor."

"Who told you that?" Meg whispered sharply.

"Hey, it's not like I gave away your phone password."

"I haven't accepted the offer," she said.

"Who else is in the running?"

"As far as I know, no one."

"I thought you were smarter than to even discuss it with the publisher at this time."

"Leave it, Shamus. It's my business."

"Jeffries is making it his. You need to decline the offer."

"I already told the publisher that I'm interested."

"Now you can tell him you've changed your mind."

"No."

"Then I'll tell him. Where is he?"

"Listen, Shamus, an opportunity like this rarely comes along. It will mean a great deal when I go up for promotion to full professor. Besides, I'm not your teenage daughter. End of discussion."

"If you were my teenage daughter, you'd be grounded, Meg. This isn't worth risking your life."

"Whoever killed Stan and Blake—if it had anything to do with the journal—was targeting editors who'd rejected hundreds of submissions. I don't have a track record of rejecting anyone's paper. I'm not a threat. I would be a welcome change."

"Detective Jeffries may not think you killed anyone by yourself, but he hasn't ruled out the possibility that you were in on it. This makes it look like you had something to gain. That's called a motive."

Meg looked up at the ceiling for a moment shaking her head. "Fine. I'll ask the publisher to postpone all discussions about the editor position."

"And not to identify you as one of the candidates."

"Stop now, Shamus. That's enough. I get it."

"You're angry again. What is that all about?"

"Forget it," Meg said. "There's the publisher. I'll catch you later."

Meg moved toward a tall, erudite looking man with well-coiffed gray hair. As she approached, he smiled broadly and reached out to shake her hand.

Shamus turned to find Madison beckoning impatiently for him to join her group.

He wended his way through the crowd. Madison smiled warmly, placed her arm around his waist and introduced him to her admirers. He shook some hands, made a few quips about the beer being warm, and retreated into silence punctuated only by the occasional requisite nod and cordial half-smile.

After the others had moved on, Madison turned to him.

"You are miles away. What's on your mind?"

"I'm recovering from the conga line."

She laughed. "I saw that. You're such a good sport."

"I was shanghaied."

"Sometimes we get a little carried away at these parties."

"I'll say."

"If you do good work in academia, socializing helps you get ahead. Everyone here knows that. I'm sure it's the same in your line of work. You must have to schmooze potential clients."

"Never had to conga with them," Shamus said, making Madison smile. "But I take your point."

A professor tapped Madison on the shoulder. They began chatting. Shamus caught sight of Wesley speaking to an eerily familiar man. He was holding Wesley's arm firmly. As if sensing a pair of eyes on him, the man looked at Shamus.

"See you later," Shamus said to Madison.

As he moved, the man darted out the door. Shamus started to follow him, but Wesley intervened.

"Can I get you another beer?" Wesley asked.

"No thanks," Shamus said trying to step past him.

Rashid, catching Shamus' eyes, handed his glass to a surprised student, signaled that he'd take care of things, and swiftly exited the room to follow the man.

"If you're angry at me, I can't blame you," Wesley said. "Meg told me what my parents tried to do. I can only apologize. They don't think I can live my life without their interference."

"Who is the guy that just had you in an armlock?" Shamus asked.

"Some drunk jackass looking for an argument. Apparently, he had an entirely different perspective than the one I advanced in my presentation."

"I guess you meet all kinds," Shamus said facetiously.

"It's a party. What can you expect?"

"Your father holds a grudge against Meg for not getting you published."

"My father is misinformed."

"You think so?"

"Of course."

"Even after she listed you way down in third author country?"

"That's in the past."

"Even so, Wesley, it must have stung."

"She was senior author. It was her decision."

"So then it couldn't have anything to do with why you grabbed Meg by the shoulders earlier?"

"I don't remember that."

Shamus moved in, his face just inches from Wesley. "I do. I place that with you lying about the guy who just left and missing our little helicopter ride. Three strikes, Wesley."

"Mother insisted that I stay. She was in tears about how the evening ended."

"In tears, my ass. She had a motive—protecting you."

"The weather was bad."

"Seriously?" Shamus retorted. "You expect me to believe it was all coincidental?"

"You seem to enjoy getting in people's faces and making accusations all in the guise of protecting your sister. Meanwhile, you haven't a clue as to what's really bothering her, what's really causing her pain. Maybe you should come down off of your high horse and start there."

"She found two dead bodies."

"That's what I mean. You don't know what's really going on beyond the murders. So, you assume a lot. Try asking Meg to come clean with you. Maybe then you'll get off my back."

Shamus watched Wesley storm out of the room. Madison was looking at Shamus. He shrugged for her benefit as if Wesley had proven himself an idiot. When she turned away, he stood still for a few moments digesting the conviction in Wesley's words and tone. He looked over at Meg who was talking to some people. Her eyes met his, puzzled, before Shamus turned and walked to the bar.

He ordered another beer and tried to reach Rashid by text. After a few minutes, he tried calling him. No luck. He looked up and saw Bill Carroll coming toward him.

"I see you're making the party rounds." Carroll slurred, holding up his beer glass in a sloshy salute.

"Get lost, Carroll."

"Looking for your sister?"

"No."

"I don't hold a grudge," Carroll said as he tripped on the leg of a bar stool. Shamus stepped back, but the beer splashed from the floor onto his pants. Carroll laughed and slapped Shamus on the shoulder spilling more beer.

"I'll tell you a secret," Carroll whispered sloppily. "Your sister is on Jeffries' list. So, you see, I'm in good company."

Shamus stiffened. Before he could reply, Penelope appeared at his side.

"Let's go to the next party," she said.

"Who is this lovely young thing?" Carroll's prurient gaze moved from her toes upward, halting in a lurid smile.

Penelope's face contorted with disdain.

"And you're cuter still when you're angry," Carroll mocked. He covered his mouth with a hand, took an exaggerated scan of the room, and whispered. "We're not supposed to say things like that to women anymore. I might get arrested for harassment. They might throw me in jail. Harassment jail."

Shamus stepped closer to Carroll.

"I've got this one," Penelope said, without taking her eyes off the leering professor.

Carroll laughed derisively. "She doesn't need you, Doherty. Maybe she wants a real man." He moved closer to Penelope and reached out to touch her face. Penelope grabbed his arm, twisted it, lunged forward and flipped him. With a thud, Carroll landed, dazed, on the carpet.

"We're in the same karate class," Penelope said to the gasping onlookers. "I guess this time I won." She headed for the door.

"I thought we were ignoring him," Shamus said, tagging along. "Where'd you learn that move?"

"It's a big city. A woman needs a few arrows in her quiver."

Shamus nodded appreciatively. "How many arrows do you have left?"

"You don't want to find out."

"I'd say you're right."

"Not to change the subject, but who was that guy your friend Rashid followed out of here?"

"How did you know he was following somebody?"

"As I said, I'm an *investigative* reporter. Observing is what I do."

"You're damn good at it."

"Thanks."

"I'll tell you while we look for Rashid. I tried texting him and calling but no answer."

"My guess is that he silenced his phone to avoid being noticed," Penelope said.

"That could be, but I sure as hell wish he'd get back to me."

CHAPTER THIRTY-SEVEN

Meg fell onto her bed exhausted. Shamus was right. She'd been snappish—rude even.

She removed her jacket and the scarf, lowered her head onto the pillow and slipped into sleep.

She was in an audience of vaguely familiar people. On stage were men in white coats preparing for what looked like surgery of some type. She sat back in her chair. The woman seated to her left was voraciously eating popcorn and sipping soda. A man at her right was loudly and laboriously opening a candy bar. She looked around. Bill and Judy Carroll, Wesley, Serina, Emma and Madison were seated in the same row, all facing forward. None of them had noticed her. At the very end of the same row, a man turned and looked directly at her. It was Tim Alan. His expression was stern and accusatory. He suddenly waved with a smile. He gave her a thumbs-up and mouthed the words "good luck."

Meg returned a puzzled wave and the professor looked forward. She shuttered. The room was cold. She rubbed her arms. Why had Tim done that? Why were all these people here? Why am I here?

Suddenly, two large men were behind her. They lifted her. She struggled and called out. No one looked her way. Everyone was eating and sipping drinks. The men dragged Meg down an aisle amidst loud laughter and conversation drowning out her screams. A handkerchief was stuffed in her mouth. Meg elbowed one of the men. The handkerchief slipped. She bit the hand of someone who'd tried to replace it. Blood spurt into her eyes. She was nearly blinded for a moment before the pain of a hard slap caused her body to go limp. Another blow and the room went black.

She was up against a cold, steel wall when she awakened - her arms and ankles locked by clamps. Her colleagues were just as they'd been moments before—awaiting something, looking at the stage where she was now shackled. She looked out at them through a large glass across the front of the stage. She called to Wesley. He turned to chat with others.

A clanging sound brought her attention back to the glass enclosed room. Medical equipment was being rolled toward her.

"They can't see or hear you yet," a familiar voice echoed eerily through a sound system.

"Let me go," Meg called.

"I don't think so," the same voice snickered. "We can't disappoint all those people."

Meg looked again at the audience. They were laughing and staring at the glass as if a cartoon was being shown.

"Where am I?"

"She doesn't know where she is," the voice mocked.

"Tell me."

"Shortly you'll figure it all out. There won't be any need to tell you."

Her wrists and hands were unclamped by two large, white-clad men. A moment later, she was lifted onto a cold, steel gurney. To her horror, she was wearing a surgical gown. Nothing else. A strong odor of rubbing alcohol abraded her nostrils.

"Relax," another white-clad man said as he approached the gurney from her left. Only his eyes were visible through a plastic visor. They were cold and maniacal. "I'm well trained. There will be no slip-ups. What we are about to do is only what you deserve. It's the revenge of all those people out there who you kept in the dark for years. Look at them."

Meg turned to the audience. Most were leaning forward as if a long-anticipated event was about to begin.

The man pointed. "Emma over there wouldn't have been harmed if you'd spoken up. That's why she hates you."

Emma had been laughing. She stopped suddenly and looked at Meg with revulsion.

"Serina could have been spared as well," the man accused.

Serina's dark eyes latched onto Meg's with cold contempt.

"But you were quiet as a church mouse, Meg. So, people suffered."

"I'm so sorry," Meg called to Emma and Serina.

"Too late," came a familiar voice to her right. "You didn't stop me." She blinked, disbelieving. The eyes now peering down at her through a visor were those of Stan Evans. "Your selfishness put you here."

She looked to her left again and studied the man's eyes. It was Blake.

"I didn't know what else to do?"

"She didn't know what else to do," Blake mocked out to the audience.

They roared and derided in unison like evil munchkins: "She didn't know what else to do."

A large machine began ominously descending from the ceiling. Metal arms replete with knives were aiming at Meg, glittering in the bright lights. Stan reached for the first knife, Blake for another. They sneered down at her, raised the knives high and plunged them into her chest.

She sat up, shaking with the residual terror of a vivid, horrific dream. Her alarm was beeping insistently. She scanned frantically about the dark hotel room. A bathroom night light was flickering erratically. She sat still, freezing. Mocking cries of *"She didn't know what else to do"* repeated in her head. Had Emma and Serina been attacked by Stan? Reality and fiction were equal combatants as she tried to shed the horror from her muddled mind. Even as sharper images dulled, she could feel the cold gurney and see the knives lowering. Her wrists ached from being dragged to the stage, yet they looked normal. She stood, picked up her briefcase, and walked unsteadily from her bedroom.

"I need to talk with you," Madison said from the sofa. "I've been waiting for you to wake up. Whoa, what's the matter with you? You're as white as a sheet."

"Nothing. Tell me what you want."

Madison took a folded piece of paper from the coffee table and handed it to Meg. "It was taped to our door. My name is on the front."

Meg sat and examined the paper. It read, *You're next.*

"Did you tell Jeffries?"

"Not yet."

"What are you waiting for?" Meg asked testily.

"I have my own solution."

"You can't be serious, Madison. This is a death threat. You need major police protection."

"I don't think the people who killed Stan and Blake give warnings. It may well be a hoax. Somebody taking advantage of the situation."

"You can't know that, Madison."

"I didn't know you cared."

"This isn't funny."

"I'm going to do something that I should have done sooner," Madison said.

"What?"

"Give in. I'm going to publish Wesley's most recent paper. The threat is likely from the disgruntled assistant professor group you helped start."

"No. I'm sure it isn't."

Madison held up her hand, palm facing Meg. "I'm going to throw them a bone and give them a sign that I'll meet their publishing demands. Otherwise, one or more of them might just act on the threat."

Meg's forehead tightened.

"I'll be helping Wesley revise the paper he presented earlier this week."

"That's the worst paper he's written."

"It'll be stellar when I finish editing it."

"But Wesley didn't write that note. That's not his writing."

"It doesn't matter. All of them will see this move as a victory. They'll back off."

"I'm telling Jeffries if you don't," Meg said, moving to stand.

"I can hurt you!" Madison shot back. "You know that."

"Why did you tell me about the note if you don't want my help?"

"So you'll look pleased for Wesley when I announce his windfall. If you look angry, people will notice and wonder what's up."

"I won't be there."

"You will. And you won't tell Jeffries. Because if you don't cooperate, I'll tell people what Stan did to you."

Meg's eyes were latched onto Madison's, hateful now.

"Don't underestimate me," Madison pressed.

"You're a piece of work."

"People will wonder why you didn't make Stan pay. If he pulled that crap on other women after you, they'll hate you. Hell, even if another puffed up misogynist got rough with one of our female colleagues, people will blame you. By the time I finish spinning the story, there will be no pity or sympathy for you, only anger and disgust."

"You don't actually know what happened that night."

"I do."

"Stan's version?"

Madison smirked. "As if Stan confided in me."

"Blake's then?"

"What difference does it make? Do this and I'll recommend you for editor of Stan's journal."

"That's already in the works."

"I can stop it," Madison threatened icily. "You know I can."

"Go ahead," Meg countered. "Give it your best shot."

Madison stood ominously and pointed her right index finger at Meg. "This is going to happen. That paper is going to be accepted. In fact, I'll add one by Sidney and another by Emma for good measure. Their little group's opposition to me will wash away like a sandcastle at high tide. If you are the least bit negative about their good fortune, you'll look like a jealous bitch. And that's nothing compared to what will be said about you when your secret comes out." Madison smirked. "Maybe I'll have Wesley reveal it. He's desperate to publish."

"He doesn't know…"

Madison cackled. "Oh, please. He knows. You told him. He hasn't shared your secret, but he's a piss poor liar. Get near the subject and his expression tells me all I need to know."

Meg looked around the room uneasily.

"You're not in my league, Meg. You're angry. Anyone can see that. But, unlike me, you have a bothersome conscience. Even if you could endure the pity, blame and ignominy of that night being revealed, you'd surely crumble were your brother to find out. And I'll make sure he does. Worse than that, the news will give Jeffries the motive he's been seeking—a reason for you to have killed Stan."

Meg's eyes closed. She breathed deeply.

"Right," Madison said, sensing victory. "Just make sure you appear delighted when I make the announcement."

Madison walked to the door and stopped. Their eyes met.

"Don't think for a moment I won't follow through on my threats, Meg. You know me better than that."

Shamus and Penelope entered the lobby. They caught sight of Meg sitting alone, her expression dark. He whispered to Penelope that he'd find her later and then gingerly approached Meg. Pulling a chair close to her, Shamus accidentally knocked her keys off a small table between them. He picked them up, again noticing the turtle etching on the flash drive. He placed the keys on the table.

"We're both stressed," Shamus said gently. "Whatever you don't want to tell me is none of my business, but I'm here if you need to talk."

"I'm going back to California." She looked at him, expecting resistance. When it didn't come, her face softened. "I miss Johnny."

"Of course you do," he said with a hug.

"I've never been away from him this long."

"I'll go back with you."

"You'll lose that building contract."

"Fuck the contract."

She smiled slightly.

Shamus searched her strained eyes. "What else is going on?"

"You wouldn't understand."

"Try me."

Meg looked long at Shamus and then downward.

"He attacked me," Meg said flatly.

Shamus shot upright in the chair. "Wesley?"

She looked up. "No."

"Who?"

Meg hesitated. "Stan."

It took a moment for Shamus to take this in. His brow furrowed before his eyes sought an explanation.

"It happened at a conference like this. I was young and feeling out of my depth. He invited me to his suite to work on a paper. I was flattered."

"You went to his hotel room?" The question and tone of disapproval had slipped out. He wanted to yank it back.

"Yes, Shamus," she said sharply. "I went to his room." The volume of her voice had risen. "Does that mean I should have been attacked? That I deserved what I got?"

"No, of course not. I didn't mean that."

"At conferences, professors meet in lots of private places to work on projects," Meg defended. "He invited me to work on a journal article with him. I was over the moon. He was far senior to me, established in the field. When he suggested his hotel, I didn't even think that maybe…"

Meg stopped and looked into Shamus' eyes. "I knew it," she said tossing her hands in the air and letting them drop hard into her lap.

"You knew what?"

"That you'd be like this."

"Like what?"

"Forget it," she said, looking away, biting her lip.

Shamus sat bewildered. "Meg," he said softly. "I'm here for you."

Tears filled her eyes. Shamus desperately wanted to hold her, to apologize for not knowing what to say.

"My secret is no longer mine alone or I wouldn't be telling you."

"You should be telling me. I'm your brother."

Meg looked at Shamus.

"I want to help," Shamus said. "Tell me what I can do."

"Blake knew," Meg said. "He told me in the bar before he was killed. I assume Stan bragged about it one night when they were working together. Men do that."

"Only men who are pigs."

Meg nodded.

"Meg, did Stan...?"

"He choked me," she interjected. "He nearly killed me. What else matters?"

"You're right. Of course."

She looked down. "I don't want the details in your mind. It's better that way. Trust me."

"He should have paid publicly," Shamus said. "He should have lost his job and his editorship. He should have been blamed and shamed, forced to skulk off into oblivion."

"Meg looked at him. "You're saying I should have turned him in to the police, right?"

"Well, I only meant…"

"He would have denied it," Meg said. "I would have looked like an idiot for believing he wanted to publish with a nobody, for going with

243

him to his room, for trusting him. I *was* an idiot. After it happened, I was traumatized. I knew if word got out, I'd be mortified. How would I have gotten up in front of my students? Think about it!"

"Right. I just…"

"You see, if my own brother believes that I should have turned Stan in to the police, that's what others will think if the word gets out now. When it happened, I feared not being hired. I hated the thought of our parents knowing. Mostly, I feared losing you."

"You wouldn't have."

"I might have. We weren't close then."

"But we've been close for two years. Why did you wait until now to tell me?"

"Where would I have fit it in, Shamus? While putting Johnny to bed should I have said, 'Oh, by the way, I was attacked by a man I trusted.'"

"Of course not."

"When we were enjoying a dinner out in Los Angeles? Should I have ruined it with the truth? Remember, this happened years ago. Women weren't speaking out then. There were no congratulations on offer for stepping forward, no 1,000 Facebook likes for bravery. Besides, even if it happened today, it would be hard to tell people. I felt stupid, betrayed, and disgusted with myself. And that's just the half of it."

"What's the other half?"

"Violated, Shamus. I felt dirty if you must know. His hands had been all over me. Do you understand? Do you?"

"Jesus Christ, Meg. You were young. You can't torture yourself."

"Too late. I have tortured myself. And being at these conferences brings it all back. I turn into a different person." She leaned forward, elbows on her knees, hands holding her forehead.

Shamus' heart was thumping. He wanted to throw the vase beside him across the room.

"I wanted him dead," she continued as her eyes met his again, saturated in misery. "Before he was killed, hardly a night went by that I didn't envision him in a car accident, the seatbelt stuck, him burning to death, or being killed in a robbery. I saw him bleeding in dark alleys, falling from cliffs…"

"Easy. I get it." He placed his hands on hers.

She pulled away. "I wanted revenge, Shamus," she said, every muscle of her face taut. "Once I got past wanting to crawl into a hole and never come out for being so stupid and then for not saying anything, I wanted revenge. You see, you were wrong; I do know about hatred. I wanted him to suffer and to pay. I'm glad he's dead."

"How did you manage to keep this to yourself all these years?"

"Women do it all the time."

"I know, but not…"

"Not someone like me, right?" she snapped. "Not someone with options, with a career ahead of her, a level of credibility the police might respect."

Shamus placed his right hand on his forehead for a moment. His mind was swirling with images and questions.

"You're wondering if I killed him."

"No Meg. I'm not." His tone was emphatic.

She clenched and unclenched her hands. "I didn't kill him," she said faintly.

Shamus' eyes closed with relief.

"My effort to remove him as an editor was a warning to him. I wanted to be sure that if he had thoughts of hurting other women, he wouldn't act on them because the price would be high. The loss of his editorship was just a start. I wasn't going to skulk off and do nothing. He knew that."

"I'm sure he did."

Meg looked down again.

"You did the right thing."

"There are two of me, Shamus. One lives in this world, the other in the aftermath of that night. I can't explain it better than that. I know I've snapped at you repeatedly. I'm sorry. If I let go of the hatred, I'm afraid I'll fall apart."

Shamus watched as she gazed distractedly about the lobby before looking at him.

"Madison knows," she said.

Shamus' eyes narrowed. "How?"

"Apparently, she saw me come back to the hotel that night. I was a bloody mess."

"She did nothing to help you?"

Meg shook her head.

"But now she plans to use what she knows. Somebody sent her a threatening note today telling her she's the next target. She's freaked. So, she plans to publish papers by Wesley, Sidney and Emma to appease the assistant professors targeting her editorship. She thinks one or some of them wrote the note. If I oppose her, she'll tell everyone about that night. She might have Wesley do it."

"Jesus Christ! Did you tell him?"

"You should have seen him that night," Meg said, ignoring Shamus' tone. "I don't know what I would have done without him. And he has never said a word to anyone, never threatened to tell even when he's been livid with me."

Shamus looked up at the ceiling, his mouth half open. He sighed, composed himself, and then looked at Meg.

"He won't do what Madison wants," Meg insisted. "But that won't stop her from finding a way to carry through on her threat. I'm going to have to keep quiet and let her buy people off with publications."

"And that's all it will take to dismantle the assistant professor group?"

"It's a start. She'll exact promises from the three of them to do all they can to end it. They'll fall in line. Others will think their chances of publication have improved and so she just might pull it off."

"And what if they had nothing to do with the murders or the note?"

"I told her to tell Jeffries."

"I'll talk to her."

"You won't!"

Shamus stiffened. "I don't mean as a friend."

"I know her better than you do," Meg said. "She can't sense that you know her plan."

Shamus studied his sister's adamant expression for a moment. "Okay. Fine," he relented. "We'll do it your way."

They sat in silence for several moments. Meg stood. She looked at him. "I'm sorry," she said. "I never wanted you to know."

He looked up into her eyes and stood. "I'm your brother, Meg. I'm sorry for not always being there for you, but I'm here for you now."

A tear ran down Meg's cheek. "I know," she said. "I know."

He pulled her close and held her.

Police Interview: Serina Frost

"Yes, I did see Emma with that man. They were arguing. They seemed to know each other. She was scared. I don't know why. He looked menacing. Creepy. What was she doing with a guy like that? Emma doesn't take crap from anyone. She's smart. But that night something was wrong."

CHAPTER THIRTY-EIGHT

Shamus and Meg returned to the suite. He was wracked with guilt for not having been the person she could have told rather than a disinterested brother with his heart and mind hostage to the past.

"Shit!" he uttered, pacing. His mind turned to that night. *What had that animal done?* His hatred for Stan Evans seethed hot. Were he alive, he would tear him limb from limb.

There was a tap at his door. He waited a moment, regained his composure and opened it.

"I have to go to one more party," Meg said, eyes still strained.

"You don't have to go," Shamus said.

"I do. It's where Madison will make the announcement. If I don't go, she won't be assured of my cooperation. I can't risk that."

"I'll join you. Just let me try to reach Rashid."

Shamus tried by text. No luck.

"You look worried," Meg said.

"His phone battery must have died. Or maybe he's at the party and can't hear it."

"There really isn't any need for you to go," Meg said. "I'll be fine. And if I see him, I'll call you."

"I like parties. You know that," Shamus said, attempting some levity. He grabbed his jacket off the bed and walked with her to the door.

"I should have told you," Meg said as he reached for the door handle.

Shamus dropped his hand and looked at her. "I like to think that back then I would have risen to the occasion. That I would have been supportive. I hate to say it, but I understand why you couldn't be sure of that."

"I shouldn't have put any of this on you, Shamus. It happened to me. Lots of siblings go through times when they're not talking. That doesn't make you responsible. It's enough that I carry it around blaming myself. Don't you do it too."

When they arrived at the boisterous University of Massachusetts party, Wesley was off in a corner surrounded by grinning people. A man slapped him on the shoulder. Two women kissed him on the cheek. Clearly, Madison had told him of her plan.

Sidney Jorgensen approached Wesley and vigorously shook his hand. Someone raised a smart phone and took photos of the two men beaming.

Wesley caught sight of Meg, smiled broadly and waved for her to join them. She contrived a smile for Wesley's benefit, nodded to Shamus, and joined the celebration. Wesley embraced her. Sidney shook her hand as if past antipathy had vanished into thin air.

Shamus had no patience for such hypocrisy no matter how seemingly necessary. He walked to a corner where he could be alone and watch for Rashid.

"Come with me," Wesley said, taking Meg's hand.

They walked across the room to where Madison and Emma were celebrating the latter's victory. Meg hugged Emma before managing a brief smile for Madison.

"Isn't it wonderful?" Emma effused, her eyes on Meg.

"It is indeed!

Shamus watched Meg. It made him sick to think of what she'd been through. *Was it the reason why she hadn't married? Was it why she'd chosen to be a single mother? Had that night of horror scarred her forever?* He sought a window to spare him the images and hatred crowding his mind. *How had Meg gotten through it—alone?*

"You look very distracted," Madison said as she drew close to Shamus.

Shamus yanked himself back to reality. "I'm getting sick of these parties and all the sycophants."

"Does that include me?" she asked coyly.

"Sorry, I'm too tired for vacuous banter."

"That's what parties are all about, Shamus."

"Tell Meg I went back to the room."

A shriek of joy erupted from behind them. A young woman was jumping up and down.

"Looks like you made her day too," Shamus quipped.

"She is Sidney's co-author. He just informed her of their mutual good fortune. Too bad you're in such a morose mood. You could enjoy their happiness as your sister is doing."

"I'm just not that big a person."

"What's bugging you?" Madison asked. "I mean other than your general dislike of events like this."

Shamus looked hard into Madison's eyes. She'd done nothing for Meg that night. That's all he needed to know.

"Go enjoy your victory," Shamus said, moving to leave.

"Victory?" she snarled.

"I'm out of here. This isn't a game I care to play."

"I see Meg told you about the note and my solution."

"She told me a lot more, Madison. I'll expect to see that you've left our suite by the end of today. I'm sure there are a lot of people celebrating in this room right now who'd be glad to have you as a guest. Who knows what else they might gain?"

250

With Madison glaring at him, Shamus edged through the crowd and left the room. But she came out after him.

"What did Meg tell you?" Madison demanded.

"You know damn well what she told me. I helped you, warned you about Jeffries' list and invited you to stay in our suite when you seemed terrified. At the time, I didn't accept Meg's insight into the type of person you really are. I pressed her to be understanding of your fear. All that makes me feel rather sick right now."

"Go to hell," Madison spat. "And take your sister with you."

She strode away, fists clenched.

"You go to hell," he said under his breath. "The sooner the better."

Shamus arrived in the lobby looking for Rashid. He tried reaching him by phone again. No luck. He took the elevator to the laundry, planning to work his way up from there. When he stepped out, he saw a sea of white as laundry workers, including Penelope's spy, Jim, were looking down. Shamus approached. Rashid was lying on the floor, moaning, blood oozing from his nose and the back of his head.

"God, what the hell happened?" Shamus gasped as he knelt beside Rashid.

"Somebody beat the crap out of him," Jim said. "Looks like he came out of the elevator and got cold cocked and then some. There's blood on the wall there. He may have a concussion or worse."

"The ambulance is here," a woman called as she ran toward the group.

"I lost him," Rashid muttered.

"Never mind that," Shamus said. "The ambulance is coming. You'll be fine."

Rashid's eyes fluttered.

"Hey! Rashid. Stay with me."

Two EMTs rushed in scattering the onlookers. Shamus backed away as they worked and then moved Rashid onto a gurney. Shamus followed them into the ambulance.

Rashid slowly reached a hand up, looked into Shamus' eyes and patted his shirt pocket. Shamus reached in and removed a thick, gold chain.

"It's his," Rashid managed to say before closing his eyes.

One of the EMTs nudged Shamus out of the way. "Sorry," he said. "You can sit over there."

As he moved, the gold pendant and broken chain slipped from Shamus' hand onto the floor. He retrieved it. The back read 22 carat gold. He turned it over. Blood covered something rough to the touch. Shamus wiped the pendant with his thumb. He squinted and turned it around slowly. Sparkling up at him was a raised turtle's shell encircled in what appeared to be multicolored gems.

Rashid was admitted to the hospital. Shamus returned to the hotel having been advised that Rashid needed tests and rest, not company. Exhausted, he took a seat in a lobby alcove to avoid running into anyone. He removed his phone from his jacket pocket and dialed.

"Hello?" Loretta said as if not used to receiving calls.

"Loretta. It's Shamus."

"I'm so pleased to hear from you,' Loretta said warmly.

"I called to ask you a question, if you don't mind."

"Yes, of course."

"You said Mrs. Farnum rewards people who work for her with jewelry. Specifically turtle jewelry."

"Yes. That's right. And if people do big things for her or she favors them for some reason, she might even give them expensive gold jewelry. If they do a particularly reprehensible chore for her, they get jewelry bedecked with precious or semi-precious stones."

"Meg has a turtle etched on her key ring flash drive," Shamus said hesitantly.

"That's one of the cheap gifts, Loretta scoffed. "Mrs. Farnum probably made a big thing of giving it to Meg as Wesley's friend. She expects a big to-do about such junk gifts. If she really liked Meg, she'd have given her something much nicer than a flash drive."

"Thank you, Loretta. You've been very helpful."

"Wait," Loretta said. "After you left, I couldn't get the Farnums out of my mind. I hope you're staying clear of them. They're used to getting what they want. One time, Mrs. Farnum insisted I attend a charity ball with them. While people from a nearby table were dancing, Mr. Farnum snatched their stuffed teddy bear centerpieces. Imagine that. Mrs. Farnum already had two from our table, but she told her husband that she wanted more. They could have purchased the entire teddy bear factory, but that wasn't the point."

"Strange."

"It's how they think. They consider themselves superior to other people and above social norms and rules in general."

"You have to wonder how people get like that."

"Be careful Shamus. You and Meg should not get in their way."

After he hung up, Shamus took out his phone and located the photo he'd taken of Reb. He zoomed in on the signet ring. It was blurry, but Shamus would bet his next several paychecks that the design was a turtle.

The next morning, Shamus called Rashid's hospital room. Meg was there and answered.

"How's he doing?" Shamus asked.

"Much better, thank God. Nida is on her way here."

"You called her?"

"Yes. She's beside herself."

Shamus said nothing, honoring Rashid's wishes.

"I know what they're going through," Meg said. "Rashid told me. But Nida didn't sound like it's over. Far from it."

Shamus could hear Rashid asking for the phone.

"Hello, Shamus," came Rashid's strained voice.

"Hey, how's the hero?"

"There will be no books written about me, my friend. He got away."

"I never should have let you follow that guy."

"It was not your fault. Tell me about the chain and pendant. Have you shown it to Detective Jeffries?"

"Not yet. It has a turtle engraved on it as does a signet ring on the guy who nearly drowned Madison. Apparently, Mrs. Farnum gives such jewelry to people who do favors for her and her husband."

"I'm still groggy," Rashid replied, "but are you saying that the Farnums were involved in the murders?"

"They had a motive," Shamus said. "They also had the means."

Detectives Jeffries and Krawski were not at the hotel. They were at a high rise on Fifth Avenue dealing with another case. Shamus grabbed a cab. He entered the atrium lobby.

Jeffries greeted Shamus as if the visit was an imposition. Officers were coming in and out giving the detectives updates on a murder-suicide that had occurred in one of the condominiums. From what Shamus could gather, a married couple's argument had gone very wrong. Cops were everywhere. Detective Krawski was dealing with a growing group of journalists.

"What do you want?" Jeffries asked. "I'm really tied up here."

"My friend, Rashid, was attacked in the conference hotel. He's in the hospital."

"I heard," Jeffries muttered grumpily, eyeing an officer having difficulty blocking an agitated journalist from entering the building.

Shamus waited until Jeffries returned his attention to him. "The man who attacked Rashid and the one who attacked Madison and followed me in the subway have something in common."

"Yeah. What's that?"

"If you look at the left hand of the man in the photo who you'll remember goes by Reb, you'll see a signet ring engraved with a turtle. That same engraving is on this pendant."

Shamus held it out.

"It must have come off during the struggle with Rashid. He gave it to me in the ambulance. Anyway, Mrs. Farnum gives turtle-engraved jewelry to people who work for her. She's mad about turtles. Seriously expensive jewelry like this chain and pendant goes to people who do important or distasteful jobs for her."

"How do you know about Mrs. Farnum's thing for turtles?" Jeffries asked.

"A former Farnum employee."

"A disgruntled one I imagine."

"Someone you'd trust," Shamus said.

"You know me that well?"

"I do."

Jeffries signaled Shamus to follow him to a less crowded area.

"Okay. So, you want me to believe that the Farnums are somehow involved in the murders of Stan Evans and Blake Packard. And, correct me if I'm wrong, these near octogenarians allegedly did this to help their son get tenure. Right?"

"Pretty much," Shamus said.

"I'll have this pendant and chain checked out, but you're really reaching here."

"The Farnums had everything to lose if Evans and Packard remained editors," Shamus insisted. "Wesley is their only child. He hadn't a prayer of publishing in Evans' journal prior to his death and

Packard was a threat too. The Farnum legacy is wrapped up in Wesley's success. You know that already."

Jeffries studied Shamus. He looked away to think for a moment. "Fine. I'll send two detectives over to talk to the Farnums."

"You and Detective Krawski should go. This is your case. The Farnums won't respect junior detectives."

"We can't be in two places at once. Now get the hell out of here, Doherty. We're on it."

Shamus found Penelope in her laundry room storage cabinet office. He shared the Farnum theory, reminding her that it was no more than that and certainly not ready for her newspaper's readership. He shared Jeffries' reaction, expressing frustration at the detective not going to see the Farnums himself.

The next morning an article appeared on the front page of *The New York Times* city section. The headline read: *Little Progress in Midtown Hotel Murders.*

The article proffered that key lines of investigation appeared to be on hold while the NYPD focused its resources on a high rise murder-suicide. Untold millions of city revenue dollars from conferences were being put at risk. An unnamed professor had been taken by ambulance to the hospital after a violent altercation. The article referred to a credible source who had provided Detective Jeffries with a promising lead that he then passed on to junior detectives.

Meg came out of her bedroom dressed professionally with briefcase in hand. Shamus was reading Penelope's article, shaking his head. Jeffries would surely know who'd been talking to Penelope and there would be hell to pay.

"You know that turtle you have on your flash drive?" Shamus asked.

"Yes," Meg replied.

"The man who almost drowned Madison and nearly killed me has a signet ring with a turtle on it. A man who would have attacked me in the hotel stairwell had Rashid not shown up, and who was the one who nearly killed Rashid, wears a gold pendant with a turtle. It was a gift from Mrs. Farnum. His turtle also has gemstones meaning that he is one of her favorites."

"You didn't tell me about somebody coming after you in the stairwell."

"You have had enough on your mind."

"How do you know about a pendant and Mrs. Farnum's love of turtles?"

"Rashid gave the pendant to me in the ambulance. It came off the guy during the fight. The turtle thing took a little research."

"So based on jewelry, you're implying that the Farnums hired murderers?"

"I'm sure they'd do just about anything to help their son get tenure."

Meg regarded her brother as if he'd just arrived from another planet. She took a seat across from him. "Why would they send someone to hassle or harm you in a stairwell?"

"To make sure I didn't pick up the scent. Maybe to encourage us both to leave the city. Who knows? But those turtles aren't a coincidence."

"Murder is not something parents do to get their professor children published. I get that you're really angry about that wild helicopter ride. Me too. I wouldn't be surprised if the Farnums had a hand in that. But not in murder."

"I don't expect you to believe me."

"Does my flash drive make me a murder suspect?"

"Of course not. It's not laced with gemstones. Mrs. Farnum gives cheap flash drives to unimportant people."

"Really? And how do you know that?"

"More research. Anyway, I told Jeffries about the turtle connection."

"And what did he say?"

"He listened, but he was preoccupied with a murder-suicide on Fifth Avenue. After he sees Penelope's article in today's *New York Times*, that might change." He handed her the paper.

Meg scanned the article.

"Answer this," Shamus said. "Why was the same guy I saw in the stairwell and who put Rashid in the hospital talking to Wesley at the Santa Barbara party?"

"What?"

"Yes. Obviously, Wesley knows him."

"Still, I don't see…"

"It's a little too coincidental," Shamus said.

"I'll ask Wesley who he was talking with at the party," Meg said. "I'm sure there's a reasonable explanation."

"I'll tag along."

"Not necessary."

Their eyes met. When they were younger, he could stare her down. Not this time.

Meg didn't need to find Wesley. He found her in a busy hallway. Gone was his celebratory countenance. He was angry. He walked her to a corner behind a large fichus plant.

"Great, Meg. Just great!" Wesley was standing red-faced, staring down at her.

"What?"

He threw his hands up chuckling sarcastically. "Go ahead. Tell me you didn't know detectives were going to pay my parents a visit today."

"What did you expect?"

Wesley stepped back, slack jawed. "So, you admit it."

"No. I didn't know. But the police aren't stupid, Wesley. You suddenly have a journal acceptance from Madison shortly after a threat to her life. I'd say you and anyone associated with you will be paid a visit. That's what NYPD detectives do. They find links."

He leaned closer. "Bullshit! This has your brother's fingerprints all over it."

"My brother isn't a detective," she shot back.

"He thinks he is. My parents are worried that they're being accused of murder! Two murders! They're not getting any younger. This could give my father a heart attack."

Meg caught sight of Shamus quietly positioning himself behind Wesley.

"Listen," Meg said, "there are two guys, both creepy, both wearing jewelry with turtles like this." Meg held up her flash drive. "As you know, your mother gave me this."

"Oh please."

"Listen to me," Meg insisted. "One of these guys nearly accosted Shamus in a stairwell and put Rashid in the hospital. The other almost drowned Madison before attempting to kill my brother. You were having a tiff at the Santa Barbara party with one of them."

"Ah. See. Your brother told you that."

"The point is that it happened.'

"You know my parents. They're pompous, overbearing and impossible at times, but they're not murderers. Since I refused to leave the conference, they sent a bodyguard. He may have run into your brother in the stairwell. Those guys always look threatening. That's their job. At the party, I told the guy to get lost, and that I didn't need him following me around as if I were twelve-years-old."

"Apparently, he then went and beat up Rashid," Meg said.

"That's absurd."

Meg took out her phone and accessed the photo Shamus had taken. She held it up. "This guy nearly bashed my brother's face in after Shamus tried to stop him from drowning Madison. Does he look familiar?"

"No." Wesley pushed the phone away. "So, let me get this straight. My elderly parents arranged to have Stan killed, right? Supposedly by one of these thugs. When that wasn't enough, they had Blake killed just to be sure no one would block my publication in the journal. They put a scare into your brother in a stairwell for reasons I can't fathom and nearly had Madison drowned."

"Works for me," Shamus said as he approached them.

"If it isn't the brother," Wesley snarled.

Shamus gestured for Meg to stand beside him. To his consternation, she held her ground, eyes intent on Wesley.

"I wasn't going to hurt her."

"You weren't? You seem to have scared Madison enough to publish one of your papers."

"It wasn't me."

"Ah. So, you know about the threatening note," Shamus said sarcastically.

"Shut up," Wesley shot back.

"I think we're through here," Shamus said to Meg.

"I'm not," Wesley interjected. He turned to Meg. "Did you ever get around to telling your brother our secret?"

Meg's eyes widened, then clenched with anger. "Tell me you're not going to stoop that low."

"Quid pro quo, Meg. Find a way to get Jeffries to leave my parents alone. You owe me that."

"She owes you nothing," Shamus growled.

Wesley held Meg's eyes, ignoring Shamus. "Don't test me," he said before storming off.

"If his parents had anything to do with the murders, he's not aware of it," Meg said.

"How did you get that from what he just said?"

"A murderer, even an accomplice, isn't sad."

"I didn't see sad," Shamus scoffed. "I saw angry and arrogant."

"All three were there," she said, watching Wesley turn a corner. "You weren't looking for sad."

"He just threatened to tell me what Evans did to you. That's low."

Meg nodded slightly. "His back is against the wall. His parents are obnoxious, but they're still his parents. He drew the only weapon he had: the secret he's kept for years." She looked directly into Shamus' eyes. "The thing is, and this is big," she said, "he could have used it right then and there, but he didn't."

Shamus was deep in thought as he crossed the hotel lobby. Meg giving Wesley a pass didn't require him to do so. He hadn't seen an ounce of sadness in Wesley's expression. The guy was livid. He'd been crowding Meg; crouching menacingly like a hawk over its prey. *She'd seen what she wanted to see. And who could blame her?*

As he passed the coffee shop, he saw Penelope and Jeffries at a table near the door. He stepped from view, still able to see them. Jeffries reached a hand out and covered Penelope's left hand. She stiffened and tried to pull away. But Jeffries held on. He seemed to be pleading with her.

Penelope held his eyes with a fiery gaze. He spoke again, his body language contrite. She tugged her hand back and looked away.

"I tried to see you many times," Jeffries insisted loud enough for Shamus to hear. "Your mother wouldn't have it."

"I don't believe you."

"Your mother wasn't well. You know that. She wouldn't stay on her medication."

"Your quick departure made her more ill."

"I'm sure it seemed that way at your age, but I tried to stay. She wanted me gone."

Penelope went silent, refusing to look at Jeffries.

"I loved you and your mother."

Jeffries stood slowly as if wanting to say more. Shamus pulled back. Penelope was refusing to look at Jeffries, who waited a few moments before closing his eyes with a sigh and walking away.

Shamus had considered entering the coffee shop to sit with Penelope. He thought better of it and headed to the suite. Forty winks would be a godsent, Shamus thought as he fell onto the bed. A two-pillow sleeper by nature, he grabbed a third from the other side of the bed and endeavored to fluff all three. It was useless. Some wizard of economy in hotel management had decided to skimp on, of all things, pillows. Shamus raised up and punched them before lying back and turning on his side. He would fill out the customer satisfaction card this time. That was a promise. At last, he dozed.

There was a woman traversing the rocks, long floral skirt lifted slightly, her dark, curly hair blowing in an inconstant breeze. She paused, unaware of his presence, to dip her toes in the crisp, clear water. He leaned from a bridge at first and then sat on the shoreline watching her sort pebbles, placing treasured ones in her skirt pocket. With childlike precision, she hopped again across the stones. Her profile was lovely, as always. He smiled, considered waving to Denise, but paused. She was looking at him, but he could not see her face. He leaned forward willing her to come into focus. She was smiling. He could at least see that. Then, he noticed her eyes. It was Penelope.

Shamus woke with a start, then leaned back against the headboard and closed his eyes. He felt a cold twinge of disloyalty surge through him. But it had been a dream, he told himself. Stress does odd things to dreams.

He glanced around the room and halted at his father's letter on the bureau. He stood and walked over to it. Buying time, he studied himself in the mirror. The man looking back was only a few years younger than his father had been when he'd written the letter to his son. Shamus studied the envelope and held a tremulous hand above it for a moment. He picked it up, returned to the bed and opened it.

Shamus: I have tried many times to write to you and as many times I've failed. Perhaps there are no words to explain what happened the night you came to meet me at the train station. How much I wish we could go back in time. What I wouldn't give to be the surprised, elated father you expected. But there is no going back in life. Mistakes can't be erased. And so I fell silent fearing that words would make things worse. As I write, I know the effort is futile. Yet, every time I ride the train after work, I try again to find the words to tell you how deeply sorry I am for being less the father, and the man, that you once believed me to be. Every night, I open the door to your room and watch you sleep. Part of me hopes you'll awaken so I might sit beside you and say something to ease your pain. The other part of me fears your eyes opening, as the words surely would not come.

The disdain you have for me, I have tenfold for myself. I am not good at explanations, Shamus. I hope you haven't inherited my trait of pulling in when those you love are suffering at your hand. I pray you will not need letters to tell your children how much you love them, to relieve pain you have caused. Tonight I will try again to slip this letter under your pillow, so you'll know how truly sorry I am. I love you, Shamus. I always will.
Dad

Shamus slowly returned the letter to its envelope and set it down. He looked into the mirror. He grasped both ends of the bureau, arms outstretched, and leaned forward as his head drooped. His body shuddered. He remained for a few moments as memories of squandered reconciliatory moments painfully flashed through his mind.

"Sorry, Dad," he whispered.

CHAPTER THIRTY-NINE

Shamus entered the kitchenette and took a soda from the refrigerator. He'd visited Rashid who was recovering well. Nida was by his side.

As he headed for the sofa, he noticed an envelope slide under the door. It was from Penelope. She was in her laundry office and wanted to see him.

He went out to the hall. As he reached for the elevators, a large arm encircled his neck and forcefully yanked him back. Another arm locked across his chest. Shamus stiffened and struggled to wrench free, but his attacker was extremely strong. He shoved Shamus into the stairwell, slammed him up against a wall and burrowed a gun into his back.

Turning his head, Shamus took in the mismatched eyes. "Reb," Shamus grunted between clenched teeth. "Or do I call you 'Erebus, god of darkness'?"

"Shut up, Doherty. We're going to take these stairs down to the basement. Move the wrong way and I'll open you up."

"How much are the Farnums paying you? The police have copped on to them, so you're probably next."

"Descend, asshole."

As they moved, a door opened on a landing below them. Reb yanked Shamus back against the wall. He jabbed the gun deeper. A man and a woman were laughing. They went down one flight and exited the stairwell.

"Go!" Reb ordered with fetid breath. He moved the gun nozzle to Shamus' skull.

They headed unimpeded down to the laundry level. As they entered, a few washers and dryers were running but no one was in sight.

"The exit," Reb said, pointing to the alley door Shamus and Penelope had taken after their first meeting.

Shamus' legs were two heavy blocks of wood.

"Move!" Reb growled, pushing Shamus violently from behind.

A dryer door slammed closed. Reb jerked back, Shamus in tow. There seemed to be no one there.

"Walk!" Reb ordered.

Another sound, this one closer.

Reb wedged the gun into the back of Shamus' head. "Show yourself!" he shouted.

Silence.

"I have a gun. This is no joke. I'll kill him."

"Over here." It was the voice of a frightened woman. "I just work here."

"Don't hurt her," Shamus snapped.

"Shut up!" Reb shot back. "Come out where I can see you. Now!"

Curly, black hair slowly emerged from behind a tall dryer.

As she appeared, Shamus' fears were confirmed. It was Penelope.

"What now, genius?" Shamus sputtered. "She's just a laundry worker. Are you going to kill her too?"

Reb eyed Penelope uncertainly.

Suddenly, Penelope dove behind the dryer. Reb fired twice in her direction. Shamus grabbed Reb's thick arm, yanked it upward and another shot rang out. The men fell. They rolled. Reb got his footing, but Shamus grabbed him around the waist and slammed him into the cement floor. A crack, and Reb grabbed his leg and writhed in pain.

"Penelope! Are you okay?" Shamus called.

He spotted the handgun on the floor, inches out of reach. Reb caught sight of it. They both lurched and grasped, spinning the gun across the floor.

Reb dove forward grabbing the gun. They struggled. It fired. Shamus slugged Rob in the gut, sending the gun once again sailing across the floor. It stopped at Penelope's feet. She was dazed, blood seeping across her blouse. Shamus froze.

Reb yanked a knife from his belt. Shamus snapped alert and grabbed his arm. Reb kneed him, raised an arm, blade flashing in the fluorescent light just above Shamus' chest.

The emergency exit door screeched open. Jeffries, Krawski and several officers rushed in, all diving behind machines.

Another shot rang out.

Shamus stood slowly. Penelope was holding Reb's gun with two hands, shaking, still aiming his way. She slowly looked down at her bloodied blouse, raised her head and met Shamus' horrified eyes. He was gently telling her to put the gun down. Jeffries was shouting for his officers to hold their fire. She held statue-like for a moment, closed her eyes and folded to the floor.

Jeffries rushed to her side, panic in his eyes.

"Penny," he said painfully. He held two fingers to the pulse in her neck.

Shamus hobbled over and knelt beside Penelope. He tore off his shirt and pressed hard against her gunshot wound.

"My God," Jeffries said. He looked up at Shamus.

They could hear the ambulance siren. Jeffries lifted her head. She was limp and unresponsive.

CHAPTER FORTY

Shamus awoke in a hospital bed. His eyes widened with recollections of what had transpired. He tried to sit up. Jeffries, looking disheveled and ten years older, nudged him back down.

"Is she...?"

"She's in surgery," Jeffries said, patting Shamus' shoulder.

"And?"

"She should be okay. No organs involved."

Shamus' eyes closed in relief.

"Damn good shot, isn't she?" Jeffries said with an inkling of paternal pride.

"Impressive for a journalist."

Jeffries looked at Shamus, one side of his mouth lifting.

"Ah. You taught her to shoot," Shamus said.

Jeffries nodded.

"Nice job."

"Before she went into surgery, I gave her hell for not waiting for me to take Reb down."

"I might not be here if she had."

"Her words exactly. 'Sometimes you only have one chance,' she said quoting me. Then she had the temerity to add, 'Besides, I'm a better shot.'"

Shamus smiled painfully.

"Your body will ache for a while. But you'll live. I'm of mixed feelings about that."

"I bet you are." Shamus tried to sit. "I've got to get out of this bed."

"No way."

"The Farnums have to be involved in this. Reb works for them."

"Worked," Jeffries said. "He's dead."

Shamus paused, then fell back onto the pillows.

"They want to keep you overnight again. You must be growing on them. You can relax that long. I've already spoken to the Farnums twice. They have iron-clad alibis for the times both murders took place. And the same for their bodyguards. So, sit back and recover while we do our job."

"Why would a guy like Reb take it upon himself to murder two professors unless doing it for the Farnums?"

"Or someone close to them," Jeffries added.

Shamus' eyes widened. "Wesley?"

"Two of my officers are talking with him right now."

"That son-of-a-bitch."

"Easy Rocky, we don't have anything on him yet. I've got to go check on Penny.

Shamus placed a hand on his head. "Damn that hurts."

"The Greek god of darkness slammed your head into the cement floor. Just rest. I'll be back when I know more."

Jeffries began to leave. He turned back. "I haven't been your biggest fan, but you did okay, Doherty."

Shamus' phone rang. It was Denise. She'd gotten to Los Angeles, had seen the patient who needed her, and had already made a plane reservation. She was coming back.

"No need for that," Shamus said. "I'm fine."

"That's not what I heard."

"Knocked around, but there's no need for you to fly back out here."

"I'll be there tomorrow."

Shamus smiled. I'll make you a deal," he said.

"No. I'm coming."

"Meg and I will go back to Connecticut tomorrow. I'm sure she'll do that, so her brother doesn't get into any more trouble. You and I can talk twice each day. How's that? You could come after Meg leaves."

"Are you sure?"

"Yes."

"And if you start feeling worse, you'll call me right away."

"Absolutely. The slightest sign of a problem and you're the first person I call."

"I'll talk with your doctor and if everything is as you say, I'll be in Ridgefield next week," Denise said.

"Good."

"When I didn't hear from you last night, I thought you might have had second thoughts," Denise said.

"Not a chance," Shamus said, tenderly. "I love you, Denise, today, tomorrow and always."

Police Interview: Wesley Farnum

"First my parents and now me. I'm not a murderer and neither are they. The guy Penelope shot worked for them. That's all. A lot of people have. They're elderly. Sometimes abrasive. They want the best for their son. That's not a crime."

Shamus had to see Penelope. It wasn't good enough to have Jeffries' assurance that she'd be fine. They had a bond. She'd saved his life. He needed to see for himself how she was doing.

He entered the corridor and noticed a wheelchair a few doors down. He gingerly worked his way to it and rolled along the corridor until he saw her name. He knocked. No answer. He slowly pushed the door open and moved quietly to her bedside. She was asleep. Gone was her pinkish complexion. She was pale. He drew close to the bed and took her hand in his.

"It's me," Shamus said softly.

He waited. Her eyelids fluttered slightly.

"She's improving," a nurse said as she entered the room full of purpose.

Shamus gently placed Penelope's hand down. The nurse smiled, then stepped to a white board, erased a name and wrote her own: Leanna.

"She's doing well. It won't be long before she wakes up."

Shamus breathed a deep sigh of relief.

"She must be quite brave," Leanna said.

"She's something else," Shamus replied, smiling warmly at Penelope. "She looks like she couldn't take on a fly right now. In fact, rather sweet. You should see her in action. She's unstoppable."

"That tenacious spirit saved her life and yours," Leanna said as she checked Penelope's blood pressure and the drip. "From what I hear, we'll have our hands full keeping her in bed once she awakens."

Shamus began to turn the wheelchair with a knowing smile on his face. He looked up at Leanna. "Better you than me."

Leanna had followed Shamus to his room. She finished helping him into bed and was leaving when Meg rushed in breathless.

"My God, Shamus!"

"Hey. I'm okay."

She hugged him and then somberly studied the bandage on his forehead.

"I'll be fine. Don't worry."

"What about Penelope?" Meg asked, afraid of the answer.

"It was close, but she's on the mend."

"Thank God. I misjudged her. If she hadn't been there, you might…"

"You just didn't want her bugging you for an interview," Shamus interrupted.

Meg looked contrite. "I seem to recall referring to her as 'Pulitzer Penelope'."

"That's a compliment in a way."

Meg looked at her brother appreciatively. "Do you have a concussion?"

"That's the rumor."

"Because those don't show up on CT scans," she said rapidly. "You need an MRI. And even then…"

"Easy Meg. I'm in good hands."

Meg pulled up a chair and sat, taking Shamus' left hand in both of hers. "I still can't believe the Farnums would have anything to do with this."

"Jeffries says they have iron-clad alibis, but naturally they would."

"They were out to lunch with friends when Stan died," Meg said. "I ran into Jeffries a few moments ago. They were both at a restaurant where people know them — L'Escale."

Shamus' eyes widened. He edged up on the pillows. "L'Escale," he repeated.

"What?" Meg asked, puzzled.

"I've got to get out of here," Shamus said as he pulled at the sheets. Help me."

"No. Absolutely not."

Meg tried to stop him from lowering the sidebars.

"Move, Meg. I'll explain later."

"You're supposed to stay the night."

"Not this night," he said as he struggled to pull on his jeans and shirt. "I'll need you to distract the nurses."

"I won't."

His determined eyes met hers. "You believe Wesley is innocent, right?"

She nodded.

"Then help me."

Police Interview: Bret Sax

"This is a free country. I can speak up at a conference meeting whenever I like. You had no right to arrest me. I was letting that bitch know that she needs to step down as editor. That wasn't a threat. It was just the opposite. If she stays an editor much longer, she'll turn up dead."

Madison put down her wine glass when she heard a knock at her hotel room door. She glanced through the security eye, then opened the door.

"Well if it isn't the superhero?" She stepped aside to let Shamus enter. "Shouldn't you be in the hospital?"

"The food didn't agree with me," he said, pushing the door closed behind him.

She smiled and gestured for him to take a seat.

"Nice digs," Shamus said as he sat down on the sofa.

"My publisher likes to splurge."

Shamus took notice of the long stem white roses in a crystal vase on the glass coffee table.

"Are those from your publisher?"

She grinned sheepishly. "Yes."

"Nothing's too good for the lead editor."

"I guess not."

"Especially if she's as lovely as you are," he smiled.

"You've certainly changed your tune," Madison said. "Last time we met you weren't at all friendly and chipper. You insisted that I find my own hotel room."

"Since then, I had an epiphany."

"Did it hurt?"

"Actually, it did."

"Cup of tea while you tell me all about it?"

"I'd like that, thanks."

Madison went into the kitchenette. Shamus got up and stood at the window. "Great view."

"It is gorgeous, especially at night," she called out.

Shamus noticed a slender box on a lamp table. Elegant wrapping paper and a ribbon lay beside it.

"I like my tea strong," Shamus called back, buying time as he reached for the box.

"Do you take sugar?"

"A teaspoon, thanks."

Shamus opened the box and separated the gray satin tissue paper to reveal a diamond-studded Cartier watch. He removed it and saw that a small turtle figure had been engraved on the back of the case. He heard a cabinet close and replaced the watch just as Madison entered the room carrying a tea tray. She glanced at the box and then at Shamus' face.

She smiled. "Do you like it?"

"Sorry for being nosey," Shamus said. It's lovely. Is that from your publisher too?"

"He's not that generous." She placed the tray on the coffee table and sat in a plush chair. "Actually, the watch is a treat from me to me."

Shamus returned to the sofa and sipped his tea. "After what you've been through, it's well deserved."

"Why are you really here?"

"Is my ulterior motive that obvious?"

She regarded him, unamused.

"Okay," Shamus said. "Did you first meet the Farnums at the dinner we all attended in Connecticut?"

"Yes," Madison replied stiffly. "Why?"

Shamus chuckled, placed his cup on the tray and looked into her eyes. "You didn't buy that watch. Mrs. Farnum gave it to you."

"Don't be ridiculous."

"You don't know about her love of turtles? There's one on the back of that watch."

Madison glanced at the box.

"They must be pleased about Wesley getting his paper in your journal."

"I see," Madison said gamely. "You think Mrs. Farnum paid me off. Well you're way off base. The watch was a gift after the fact. A thank-you for giving Wesley a shot at tenure."

"Then why did you say you'd bought it?"

"Wouldn't you have? It looks strange. I've never received a gift from anyone's parents. In fact, it's awkward. I should send it back."

"I would. It's, you know, unethical."

"You Dohertys. Always the high road."

"What road do you prefer?"

Madison tossed her head back in a disparaging laugh. "Why, you're investigating me like a mini-Jeffries! It's adorable in a way. You're so protective of your sister."

"Cut the crap, Madison." Shamus said, his eyes locked onto hers. "Do you honestly believe that the assistant professor group conspired to kill Stan and Blake, and then hired somebody to drown you?"

"What do *you* think?"

"No way. Not possible."

"Well then, who do you think did those things?"

"The Farnums come to mind," Shamus shot back.

"Spare me! You give them far too much credit."

"Maybe so, since it seems they have an iron-clad alibi. They were at your favorite restaurant, L'Escale, when Stan was killed; the one you can't afford on your own. I checked with the maître' d'. There was someone with them that night. He remembers her as a tall, lovely woman."

"I'm tired of playing this game with you, Shamus. So I received a thank-you gift from Wesley's mother, and you figured that out. Goodie for you. And yes, it isn't the height of professional ethics to accept papers for publication to protect my editorship and perhaps my life. But I did it. And to make sure there were no credible objections, I leaned on your sister to keep her mouth shut. Apparently, she is not above folding in the face of fear. End of story."

"Leaned on her hardly covers it. You blackmailed her."

"I see now your sister's disdain for me has rubbed off on you."

"Mostly I don't like the fact that when you might have helped Meg, you let her suffer alone."

Madison's eyes widened. "Is that what she told you?"

"You could have helped her the night Evans attacked her."

"She and I weren't close. My help would have been rebuffed."

"You could have tried."

"You're wrong about all of this. Meg wanted to keep what happened a secret. She felt not just violated, but stupid. Everything she'd believed was turned upside down. A man she couldn't conceive of distrusting had attacked, raped and nearly killed her. When she returned to the hotel, she hated herself as much as she hated him."

Shamus looked at Madison in silence for a moment, his brow furrowed.

"You seem pretty clear about how she felt. Almost as if you'd lived it."

"A woman knows." she replied, waving a dismissive hand. "It's time you left."

Shamus went to the door and opened it, then turned. "By the way, you should donate that watch to charity. If the Farnums find out you returned it...well, they like to exact revenge for the slightest offense, don't they?"

When she didn't answer, he said, "There is an alternate theory that came to me during my epiphany."

275

"Pray tell," Madison scoffed.

"You did it, didn't you?" He started back toward her.

"You mean that I killed Stan and Blake?" She smirked at him. "I've never killed anyone in my life. I may have helped things along…"

"What are you talking about?"

"I'm not going to jail. I suppose you might as well know a few things, since anything I tell you is my word against yours. And my sibling isn't a person of interest."

"Why don't you just spit it all out, then?"

"Blake's wife, Blythe, the supposedly grieving widow, had an affair with Stan," Madison said.

Shamus shrugged. "So?"

"Blake had no problem with Stan hurting other women," Madison went on. "But when the venom spread across his own threshold, things took a turn. The night before Stan was killed, I overheard Stan and Blake arguing. Blake threatened him. Stan laughed in Blake's face. He insulted Blake's masculinity, and then boasted about Blythe being 'enthusiastic in bed' because it had been so long since she'd had a real man. Blake was beside himself. All he needed was a little push."

"And you provided it?"

Madison rose, went over to the watch, and placed it on her wrist. "That scum tried to rape Emma, my graduate student, right here at this conference. For years, I've kept his secrets. All he had to do was keep his hands off my students. Emma was the final straw. Attacking her was an attack on me. He knew that. Sure, I would have killed him myself, but I didn't have to. That's the beauty of it."

"And the man at the pool?"

"I knew you'd come looking for me at the pool. You were so predictably protective. And the Farnums' goon was such a good actor. He exceeded my expectations in every way."

She chuckled, and went on, "You see, Blythe was literally Blake's whole world. I knew that. And where better to take revenge than here with hundreds of possible suspects? Anywhere else, and Blake might have come under suspicion. It was now or never. That's what I told him. I arranged to borrow two of Cole's bodyguards. He and Evelyn didn't ask why. Likely, they thought I was afraid of someone. They'd do anything to help Wesley publish. From there it was up to Blake. So, you see, I'm innocent."

"If Blake killed Stan, then who killed Blake?"

"Blake was a loose end, blubbering at me about his wife and how he would never be able to live with himself for what he'd done to Stan. I could see it was only a matter of time before he turned himself in. That might have jeopardized me. I couldn't take the chance. But, sorry to disappoint you, I didn't kill him."

"Then, who did?"

"The only person in the world who admired Stan. Loved him, in fact. As brutal as Stan was to him, he worshipped the ground that monster walked on."

Shamus searched his memory for someone fitting Madison's description. He came up empty.

"Maybe you aren't ready for the detective big leagues after all, Shamus."

"Enlighten me."

"He sat with you at Jeffries' meeting right after Stan's murder, nose running like a two-year-old, weeping inconsolably."

Shamus' eyes widened. "Rod?"

"That pathetic grad student's world came crashing down when Stan died," Madison said venomously. "The night Stan was killed, I went to Rod's room to comfort him, to sympathize with him, to offer a shoulder for him to cry on. At least that's how it looked, and it's what I'll tell any detective who wants to know. Then I told Rod about Stan's affair with Blythe, and how Blake killed Stan. By the time I left him, poor Rod was in a scorching rage. Have you ever noticed how weak people can become truly dangerous? You only need to push the right button at the right time, and all the anger and resentment they've been harboring comes raging through."

"You're an accomplice."

"So you say." Madison scoffed.

"You must know that I'm going to tell Jeffries about this."

"Go ahead. There were no witnesses. Well, except for the Franums' two ex-cons. One is dead, as you know, and the other has already flown the coop. Did I mention I have a great attorney? Even if the police come up with something to pin on me, I'll wind up with a few weeks at a five-star prison and maybe some community service."

"Jeffries will believe me," Shamus said.

"Oh, please," she snickered. "I'll deny whatever you say and hang it on your sister. She had the motive — the guilty secret and a need for revenge? Who found Stan's body? Who was with Blake when he was murdered?"

Shamus' fists were clenched, his heart pounding.

"Before you throw a clot in my suite, why don't you go and tell everything to your friend Jeffries? Frankly, I don't think he likes you."

Shamus stood. He further opened the door he'd left ajar. Rod was standing there, out of Madison's view, steaming. He'd heard them talking. Seeing him, Shamus turned back into the room.

"So, Madison, do you figure Rod will take the fall?"

"That simpering waste of space won't tell anyone about me. He's terrified of his own shadow and no doubt wracked with guilt. Besides, it's his word against mine and I'm very persuasive."

"I think you might be underestimating Rod."

Madison stretched her arms across the back of her chair and shook her head. "Not a problem. Rod is still pathetically clinging to a dead man who never gave him the time of day. By now he's probably curled up somewhere considering suicide."

"You have it all figured out," Shamus said, watching Rod now. There were no tears, only hatred emanating from every fiber of the graduate student's being. Shamus stifled his protective instinct. Madison, he told himself, didn't deserve it. She could fight her own battles.

With a sharp toss of his head, Rod signaled Shamus to leave. Shamus looked back at Madison. She'd picked up a photo book and was now idly paging through it. Shamus breathed deeply, stepped from the room and walked away.

CHAPTER FORTY-ONE

Shamus and Meg planned to catch an afternoon train out of the city. He had persuaded her to skip the last day of the conference and to stay with him in Connecticut for a few days.

First, he stopped by the hospital to see Penelope. She was improving, already working on a news story for the next day's paper.

"Are you going to see a psychologist?" he asked her. "Cops have to get counseling after a fatal shooting. Why not journalists?"

"Jeffries already talked to me about it. I told him the same thing I'm about to tell you. I'll be fine."

"Seriously," Shamus said with a short smile. "You're going to need it."

"Maybe," Penelope said. "We'll see."

"I'll be checking on you."

"You know where to find me."

A formidable looking nurse appeared at the door.

"I told you Mr. Doherty, five minutes only."

"I'd better go," Shamus said. He leaned over, kissed Penelope on her forehead and whispered, "Obey that woman."

"If she doesn't try to take my computer again, we'll be fine."

Shamus looked at Penelope with amused affection.

"Don't go mushy on me, Doherty. I'm not exactly dying here."

"I'll miss you," Shamus said.

"You see, that's exactly what I mean. I shouldn't have saved your life. Now I'm stuck with you. This happens every time I do something uncharacteristically nice."

"I suppose that might be it," Shamus replied with a stifled smile.

"What else could it be?"

Shamus thought for a moment. "That you grew on me kind of like a fungus."

"Now that's just rude," Penelope said playfully. "I'm going to call that nurse."

"No!" Shamus laughed. "I'm leaving."

"You better."

Shamus took her hand nearest him and squeezed it. "Do what they tell you or I'll be back sooner than you expect."

Penelope smiled. "In that case, I'll do my best."

At Grand Central Terminal, Shamus made a phone call. It took some convincing, but Loretta finally agreed to move into his nearly-finished Ridgefield bungalow, where she could be nearer to her daughter-in-law and granddaughter. He could tell by her voice that a weight had been lifted from her shoulders. Since he wouldn't be needing the house for at least two years, he told her that she could advise him on the rest of the work and finishing touches in lieu of rent. He had also wangled an interview for her at the local art museum.

During the train ride, he and Meg said very little. Shamus was preoccupied with what might have transpired between Rod and Madison. He had texted Jeffries after leaving Madison's room, but hadn't yet heard back.

They drove along quiet country roads impressed by the seemingly endless bucolic beauty.

"Tell me about this place," Meg said as they stopped to watch two horses, chestnut and white, scampering shoulder to shoulder across a white-fenced field.

"It used to be part of the town of Salem. A financier named John Lewis offered money to the town if they'd name it after him. So now it's Lewisboro."

"That's one way to leave a legacy."

"This part is still called South Salem."

"It's so beautiful," Meg said.

"How about a brief trip to Lake Rippowam? It's one of my favorite places."

"Sure. Why not?"

They arrived at the east end of the lake and pulled into a driveway next to an impressive white colonial.

"My crew restored this house. It's only used in the summer, and the owners let me sit out on the dock when they're away."

"If I owned it, I'd never be able to leave," Meg said.

"See that thick wood along the shore?" Shamus asked. "That's where I get my Thoreau fix. C'mon. I'll show you."

"Do you come here alone?" she asked as they walked toward the shore.

"Sure. This is God's country. Some things are best appreciated alone. I mean, that is unless your charming sister is with you." He smiled.

"But it's so romantic. Why not bring someone special?"

"Are you trying to marry off your brother again?"

"Just discouraging your hermit instincts."

They sat on an old stone wall.

"You know, there actually was a hermit living here at one time. A woman whose home was burned by British troops during the Revolutionary War took up residence not far from where we are. She'd been terribly mistreated by the soldiers. Traumatized and ashamed, she retreated to a cave that overlooks the north side of the lake. She lived there even in the cold of winter not wanting to talk with people about her ordeal."

He pointed off in the distance. "It's called Sarah Bishop's Cave. She lived largely off the land in solitude, except for showing up sometimes at church. Her brother tried to get her to leave the cave and live with him, but she resisted. One winter she froze to death."

Meg stared pensively in the direction of the cave. "If I'd found a hideout before having Johnny, I might have crawled into someplace like that. I suppose, in a way, I did."

Shamus picked up a small branch and tossed it into the water. "I wish we had been closer back then. You could have told me what happened."

She smiled reflexively. "Sarah Bishop did what she had to do and so did I. We all cope differently."

Shamus put an arm around her shoulders. "Let's go out on the dock."

As they walked, Shamus tried to avoid thinking about what was going on in the city. He felt that by letting his thoughts wander back there, he would be leaving his sister alone somehow. He brought blankets from the car and they sat huddled under them on the dock. Light danced among the trees, some with dry leaves left from the previous fall, others already starting to bud among the proud pines that had retained their tall splendor all winter. The day's last light glimmered in reflections across the trembling water. Dark gray slip clouds turned a rich gold before a sudden brightness seized the sky in the last embrace of day.

Shamus' phone buzzed in his pocket. He ignored it and turned to find Meg mesmerized by the lake's calm beauty. The real world could wait. This moment was one to savor deeply, to hold fast with no regard for what lay ahead.

ACKNOWLEDGMENTS

There are a number of people who helped bring *Damned If She Does* to publication. I wrote the first draft some time before #MeToo, but later edits benefitted from countless women who bravely shared their painful stories.

I want to thank Robin Stratton, Big Table publisher for her interest and editing. Having Parkinson's Disease has slowed my writing process. Robin told me that Big Table would wait. And she did.

Thanks to author and friend Michael Keith who brought us together and whose work is always an inspiration.

My husband, Chris Noblet, has been the editor of most of my books. Again, there he was on walks and drives making suggestions and editing early drafts. He put in many hours on the cover design, drawing on his expertise and learning new techniques. He is the love of my life.

What good fortune it was that Grant Abramson, superb photographer of the complexity beneath the surface of our landscapes, had taken the NYC photo that is the cover. Many thanks, Grant. Congratulations on two beautiful new publications of your work.

To my friend and superb artist Grace DeVito, thank you for introducing me to Michael Barrett whose knowledge of police procedure in New York City was invaluable. Thank you, Michael. And my thanks to Miriam Muscarolas for your warm friendship and introductions to people who shed light on the issue of sexual misconduct for this book and my academic work.

Karen Minihan of Schull, West Cork had the unenviable task of editing the earliest draft. She also narrated my first novel, *Shadow Campus,* for Audible.com. She is such a talent. And thank you to Katarina Runske for a wonderful launch at Anna B's bookshop in Schull, West Cork, Ireland.

My thanks to my book club whose enjoyment of *Shadow Campus* and enthusiastic interest in the characters and story urged me onward: Anne Marie Rogan, Aileen McGuire, Amanda Connell, Colette Newman, Fionnuala O'Meara, Lia Choice, Susan Hurley, and more recently Catherine Roycroft and Lorayne Duggan.

Many thanks to Roddy Doyle who encouraged the publishing of my first novel from which this one springs.

My nephew, Brian Reardon, was my guru for the helicopter scenes. He is a U.S. Navy Commander and helicopter pilot. It was great fun working with you, Brian. Hope we can do it again.

John Bowers, my senior colleague in communication, has always been encouraging of my writing. His willingness to talk with me about the story, read parts of the book, and give me his advice was both a pleasure and a gift.

Ellen Nichols, Andrea Hopkins, Marcy Pine and Emmeline dePillis gave me feedback on an early, rough draft. You are the best! My appreciation also to friends Hammond Journeaux, Ellen Bailey, and Jena Malone for your constant encouragement.

Thank you to my brother, Kevin, who always takes an interest in my writing and art and offers astute advice over the breakfast table whenever we're together.

Finally, to my children Devin, Ryan, Shannon and grandson, Brantlee, my enduring love.

Made in the USA
San Bernardino, CA
09 February 2020